VARIATION ON A THEME

Also by Barbara Delinsky

The Carpenter's Lady
Passion and Illusion

Barbara Delinsky

VARIATION ON A THEME

Published in Large Print by arrangement with
Harper Papberbacks, a division of Harper Collins Publishers
in the United States and Canada.

Wheeler Large Print Book Series.

This is a work of fiction. The characters, incidents, and dialogues are products of the author's imagination and are not to be construed as real. Any resemblance to actual events or persons, living or dead, is entirely coincidental.

Set in 16 pt. Plantin.

Library of Congress Cataloging-in-Publication Data

Delinsky, Barbara.
Variation on a theme / Barbara Delinsky.
p. cm.—(Wheeler large print book series)
ISBN 1-56895-316-X
1. Large type books. I. Title. II. Series.
[PS3554.E4427V37 1996]
813'.54—dc20 96-11050
CIP

one

His small overnight duffel swung from his shoulder to graze his hip as he took the stone steps two at a time. He'd hoped to arrive earlier, to catch the entire concert, but the plane had been late leaving Raleigh, even later landing in Chicago. Not that he should complain, he told himself. He'd been lucky enough to have gotten a last-minute seat.

The wooden doors of the hall stood open in invitation to the warm May breeze. Looking for all the world as though he'd been invited himself, he strode through the empty lobby and followed the sounds of animated applause to the main entrance of the auditorium. The house was packed. As he prepared to join the standing-room-only crowd just inside the door, an usher materialized by his side.

"Your ticket?"

He ignored the question. "How much have I missed?" His gaze passed over the throng of heads to the stage, there riveting on the one female member of Montage. Even if there had been other women in the ensemble, even if he had never seen her photograph, he would have been drawn to her. She was as breath-taking as he'd imagined, and Lord only knew he'd done his share of imagining since he'd first seen that picture atop Tom Busek's desk.

"We're about midway through the second half. Do you have a ticket?"

Never once looking at the usher, he launched a diversionary tactic. Diversionary tactics were his specialty. "Damn! I wanted to catch more of the show." Entranced, he broke into a smile that was broad in calculated pride. He jutted his chin forward. "That's my girl. Rachel Busek." In truth, the smile wasn't all for show. He couldn't take his eyes from her. "My plane just touched down from North Carolina. She doesn't know I'm here." His grin persisted, taking on a faintly mischievous slant.

The usher took a minute to look him over. He was certainly older than the average member of an audience filled to overflowing with students, late thirties, perhaps forty, clean, not bad looking. The voice was right, bearing just a hint of a twang. And the look of pleasure on his face could hardly be mistaken, any more than could the overnight bag he carried. The usher cast a glance toward the woman on stage, then refocused on the tall man beside him for a moment's speculation.

"Sorry I can't give you a seat. No one's budging. You'll have to stand back here with the rest."

"That's fine. Fine."

The crowd stilled as a soft piano struck the opening chords of an instantly recognizable tune. There was a murmur of appreciation, a scattering of applause, then strains of violin, cello and guitar as Rachel Busek raised the flute to her lips.

James P. Guthrie had never been a concert-goer; indeed, his background had held anything but culture. Yet he held his breath, feeling the anticipation of the audience, sharing it as she inhaled, and bowed into the song. "Greensleeves." Even he recognized it now, though the notes were more sweet and vibrant, the rendition more poignantly beautiful than any he'd heard before. He was mesmerized as much by the haunting sound of the silver flute as by the woman whose breath, whose lips, whose fingers orchestrated that soulful tone.

She was dressed in white, with gentle frills at her neck, wrists and ankles. Her long blond hair flowed gently over her shoulders, fanning as she moved with the feeling of the song, sorrowful, innocent and infinitely soft. Her skin was pale, her hands delicate. Though one of seven in the ensemble, she seemed apart, playing with them yet somehow rising above to the level of a true virtuoso.

His applause was as hearty as any around him when the song ended. Then she smiled, and his pulse quickened. His hands stopped midair, wavered, and dropped to his sides. In all his years, he'd never been as touched by a woman's smile. Direct and unfettered, it held warmth, gratitude, even a kind of shyness that he'd never have attributed to a seasoned performer. When, cheeks flushed, she turned her smile on her fellow musicians, Jim Guthrie felt sheer envy.

Propping his elbows on the wood railing before him, he stood, spellbound, through several classical pieces. They were utterly foreign to him yet familiar now in the richness of tone produced by that one gleaming instrument. When, after tumultuous applause, shouts from the audience brought another song he recognized, he grew more alert. "Duelin' Banjos." He'd seen the movie that had brought it fame, and the song itself, the spirit it embodied, was a hard one to forget. But "Duelin' Banjos" after Mozart, or Bach, or whatever the hell it was they'd played moments before?

Then, in a suddenly silent house alive with expectation, the guitarist began to slowly, skillfully strum the opening chords of the duel. His message was clear, a resonant dare that was picked up, after no more than several seconds' pause, by the coy vibrato of the flute. Jim leaned forward, one of many who held their breath. The guitarist plucked each note carefully, eyeing the flutist all the while; Rachel answered likewise, with the confidence, if not the laziness, of a purring kitten. When the guitar came again, tossing in agile slurs on the last two notes, the flute, undaunted, echoed smugly. Once more the guitarist boldly declared his terms; once more the flutist met them slyly, tone for tone. The next exchange was slightly faster, the next even more so, until at last, with a jumping into the fray of the violin, cello, and finally piano, the heart of the duel was on.

Jim's eyes were glued to the blond-headed figure perched on the high stool, her white slippered foot tapping gaily against its supporting wooden rung. It seemed that her tap echoed through the house; indeed, the exuberant audience had picked up the beat. She was a study in animation, her flute held securely to her lips as she moved merrily with the clip of the song. It was a musical battle . . . and more. The gazes of the guitarist and flutist were interlocked; it was a battle of the sexes. Jim could have sworn that he saw the gleam in Rachel's eye that spoke of her thorough enjoyment of the contest, and he dared surmise that for all her softness and innocence she held a spark of fire deep within. For an instant he wondered what it would be like to hold her in his arms, to spar with her, man to woman, on a raw physical plane, and he felt his body leap to the challenge. But the music and the enthusiasm of the audience snapped him back to reality, and he was once more swept up in the onstage rivalry, waiting to see what she'd do next, whether she'd trip, more likely whether she'd show up the more limited range of the guitar with her own astounding dexterity on the flute. To his dismay, man's man that he was, he found himself rooting her on with the others, until, all too soon, the music ended and the house shook to the uncontrolled appreciation of the audience.

To unanimous shouts of "Encore!" the

ensemble picked up in the middle of the song and gave it another go-around, until finally, breathless and beaming, the players took their bows and left the stage, only to be drawn back for several more songs before the curtain fell and the house lights came up.

Jim Guthrie, man of the street, die-hard fan of professional hockey, Coors beer and chewing tobacco, stood perfectly still as the reluctant crowd filed past. Recovering slowly, he hitched his bag back to his shoulder. Then, more anxious than ever to meet Tom Busek's daughter, he made his way backstage.

He wasn't the only one with that intent. There seemed to be dozens of people swarming in the same direction. Standing taller and more broad-shouldered than the rest, he wound his way confidently toward the stage door, where he was stopped by a pale young man wearing a college blazer and horn-rimmed glasses.

"I'm sorry, but do you have a pass?"

Jim reached into the inner breast pocket of his cropped jacket and withdrew a worn notebook and pen. Then he straightened his shoulders and stood to his full height, making his interrogator look all the more fragile by comparison. "I'm with the press. I'm here to interview Miss Busek."

"The reception is by invitation only," the younger man advised. Then he caught himself and helplessly blurted, "What press?" Though he tried to sound sure of himself, his tone wavered, revealing that he was beginning to feel intimidated.

Jim didn't have it in his heart to prolong this play for power. Rather, he said simply, "The *Times*." Without so much as mention of a city, it worked every time. It was all in the tone of voice.

The young man's eyes widened behind his glasses. "The *Times*?"

"That's right. May I?" He cocked his head toward the door. "I've just flown in on assignment and I'm beat. I'm supposed to get to Miss Busek as soon as possible."

The young man cast a glance at the low-slung duffel. It amazed Jim that neither the usher who'd stopped him when he'd first arrived nor this meek-looking fellow now before him suspected something sinister in it. But then, perhaps it was his own brand of cynicism. Too many pocket searches going to and from heavily guarded courtrooms. Too many nights spent staking out sting operations with nothing but his Remington for company. Too many days badgering potential stoolies who'd as soon stab him in the belly as spill their guts to him.

Here, though, things were different. This concert was different. Rachel Busek was different. And the naivete of this spindly young university student was different. Not that Jim minded. It was actually refreshing. And it certainly made his mission that much easier.

"Go on in." The young man scowled, opening

the door behind him to let Jim pass through, closing it with relish to regain his dignity before the next person in line.

Tucking his notebook and pen back into his pocket, Jim found himself in a dim hallway at the end of which was a stream of light. As he neared, the growing murmur of voices discouraged him. He'd hoped to meet Rachel Busek in the privacy of some sort of dressing room. It seemed that he'd have to wait a bit for that.

Stepping into the doorway, he paused to quickly scan the room. It was already half-filled with a motley assortment of university representatives. He moved aside to let others behind him enter, then leaned back against the doorjamb, casual but quite attentive.

It took him a minute to find her, sheltered as she was by a tight-knit group of admirers. Her blond crown gave her away, gleaming like a beacon beneath the overhead lights. When one of the circle moved away, he saw her face. It was small and oval, its features as delicately defined as the notes she'd so magically drawn from her flute. Once again he was touched by her softness, then by something else as her eye caught his and held it. An unbidden surge of sensual awareness coursed through him much as it had when he'd watched her on stage. Then, though, his thoughts of holding her, of caressing her, of making passionate love to her had been the thoughts, he was sure, of many in her audience. Now she was looking directly at *him*. His pulse sped; his hormones skittered. His easy stance became a studied thing.

Someone within her group spoke to her, and as though startled, she turned her head sharply. Jim reached for a glass of wine from a passing tray, never once taking his eyes from her face. She smiled and talked slowly, first with one then another of the group. He sensed the same shyness that her onstage smile had hinted at. Once again it surprised him.

Newcomers joined the circle, replacing those who excused themselves to seek out other members of the ensemble. Wine flowed freely. For the most part Rachel held her glass in both hands, as though grateful to have something to do with fingers that would have been far happier playing over silver keys than rented crystal. Smiling his agreement, Jim raised his glass to his lips as, coincidentally, she did the same. In that instant their eyes met once more, locking with an unfathomable intensity that was broken only when her attention was again sidetracked by a follower.

He slowly released a deep-held breath and then took a huge swallow of wine. He was playing with fire. He'd known it from the moment he'd made the decision to seek Rachel out. True, he'd been guided in part by the altruistic motive of alerting her to Tom Busek's condition. At the moment, though, he was more concerned with his other motives for coming after Rachel.

He'd been fascinated by her picture, by the

exquisitely gentle expression that crossed her father's face each time he spoke of her. Father and daughter, Jim mused, so very different. Where one was dark, the other was light. Where one was tall, the other was petite. Where one was rough-hewn, the other was highly polished. Was she like her mother? Tom Busek had never spoken of his wife, and Jim had been hesitant to ask. He assumed that she'd died when Rachel had been very young. He also assumed that Tom had loved her very much. He seemed that kind of man, one who gave his all to something, as he did to his research. Tom Busek was a brilliant scientist. His daughter was a brilliant musician. Brilliance . . . one thing they shared.

And Jim Guthrie? He'd never thought of himself as being brilliant—streetwise, without a doubt, and dedicated to his work. Possessing an uncanny instinct for solving mysteries, reputedly so. But was he right on this one?

Talk swirled around Rachel as, across the room, she slowly sipped her wine. Though she answered questions as politely as possible, she was happier simply to smile and listen. Playing the flute was her greatest joy. Receptions . . . ah, receptions were another matter. They were a necessary evil in the world in which she moved.

She was tired. It had been a long eight months on the road, with visits home too few and far between. She missed her father and Pine Manor, the beautiful antebellum home he'd bought fifteen years before. She missed the towering pines cording the drive, the aged white oak on the front lawn, the peach orchard that would now be in bloom beyond the manicured lawn that sloped down behind the house. She missed the attic solarium where she'd spent such precious hours playing her flute with no one in attendance but the birds and God.

Three more weeks and she'd be back. She was looking forward to the summer's rest, to relaxation and recuperation and a shoring-up of her energies before the cycle resumed in the fall.

"Your rendition of Dvorak was breathtaking," a young woman dressed in peasant garb commented, tugging Rachel's attention reluctantly back to the present. "Have you ever played with a symphony?"

Rachel smiled and laughed. "Oh, no. I've been with Montage for the past five years. It's about all I can handle."

The woman's partner, tall and skinny, with wiry hair and the semblance of a beard, prodded. "Would you like to . . . do symphony work, that is? You're certainly qualified."

"I don't know about that. Symphonic playing is in many ways more rigorous, more structured and disciplined. It's sometimes more fun to be able to pick and choose your movements, such as Dvorak's second, without being committed to his first, third and fourth."

"But what about dreams? Aspirations?"

another member of the group interjected. "Where do you go from here?"

"From here?" Rachel sighed facetiously. "From here I go to Indianapolis, St. Louis, Des Moines, Omaha and Oklahoma City . . . then home." It was never far from her mind. "We'll be cutting another album at the end of the summer, then the tour will begin again. I can't think further than that. . . . How about you? Are you studying music here?"

And so she was off the hook for a few minutes at least. Again she smiled and nodded, letting the talker indulge himself while her own thoughts floated above the conversation. She lifted her wineglass to her lips and sipped, shifting her gaze momentarily to the tall, dark-haired man by the door. She'd become aware of him the instant he'd entered the room, yet she couldn't quite understand why. Yes, he was different. Taller. More sturdy-looking. There was a weathered look to him, a healthy tan that skimmed his mature features and contrasted sharply against the paler, more academic mark of the other men in the room. Of the other men in her life, period. Except her father. That was it. The man propped tall against the doorjamb reminded her of home. Lowering her gaze to the drab carpeting, she realized that on this night *anything* would remind her of home. Resigned, she reentered the conversation.

Fifteen minutes passed. The group around Rachel was now a new one, asking many of the same questions she'd already answered twice. A quick glance told her that the tall man was still at the door, watching her closely but not at all disconcertingly. She fancied that he was her protector and hazarded a guess that he was as bored as she was. He hadn't mixed to speak of, had barely even finished his first glass of wine. She doubted that he'd eaten any of the hors d'oeuvres that had been passed around, hoped for his sake that he hadn't gone near the something parading as goose liver pâté. Mmmmm, but a hamburger sounded good about now . . .

After another twenty minutes, her smile felt shopworn. Her own voice came to her like a broken record. "Why, thank you. I'm glad you enjoyed the concert. . . . Yes, the crowd was wonderful. . . . Thank you for coming." The group shifted again, and she darted another glance toward the man by the door. Was that a smile playing at the corner of his lips. Could he know what she was thinking? Her eyes lingered on his lips, and she noted the strength of their thoroughly masculine line. He was attractive. Very attractive.

Frightened by these newer thoughts, she averted her gaze and made a concerted effort to throw herself into the ongoing talk. Five minutes later, though, she found herself admiring the way his jeans hugged his slim hips without clinging, the way the button-down collar of his cotton shirt lay open over a dark haze of hair, the way the swell of his shoulder easily held the weight of his duffel. Was he too just passing through?

"Rachel?"

Her head swiveled sideways, her eyes locking quickly with those of Montage's road manager, Ron Lynch. An auburn-haired man in his mid-thirties, Ron was, in Rachel's book, average of height, build and personality. Where he excelled was in his work; he was the grease that kept the wheel turning.

"Hi, Ron." She smiled gently.

"You okay, babe?" he asked softly, slipping an arm around her shoulders. She couldn't miss the glance he shot toward the figure by the door. "You seemed distracted for a minute there."

"I'm fine," she whispered back. "Just tired."

"We'll be done here soon," he murmured, then raised his voice and spoke to the people around her. "If you'll excuse us for a minute, I'd like Rachel to meet Dr. Iber." As they headed for another corner's conclave his voice, low and close by her ear, filled her in. "Dr. Iber is Dean of Engineering. Knows next to nothing about music. Did enjoy the concert, though." He raised his head as they arrived at their destination and released her to make the introductions. "Ah, Dr. Iber. This is Rachel Busek, the prettiest member of Montage."

Rachel's becoming blush was a perfect foil for her annoyance. Ron did it all the time . . . the "little lady," the "femme fatale," the "dearest one of the lot." She felt the reference to be demeaning, somehow detracting from the professionalism of her performance. She was first a flutist, then a woman. It had never been otherwise.

For the sake of public relations, she let his comment pass, as she did much of the ensuing conversation. There was talk of acoustics, of the mechanics of cutting a record, of the role of electronic synthesizers in modern music. Rachel's head bobbed from one man to the other and back, growing more leaden by the minute. With her back to the rest of the room, furtive glances in search of escape would have been obvious, if not rude. It occurred to her that the escape she wanted—fresh air and quiet—was as yet out of reach. She'd just about given up hope when a tall figure suddenly materialized by her side, slid an arm around her waist and kissed the top of her head.

"Almost ready, darlin'?" its deep voice drawled in a tone that couldn't be mistaken for anything but that of the boy back home. Even before she looked up, Rachel placed the vibrant body flush by her side as the one that had spent the past hour propped patiently against the doorjamb. She should have been alarmed, but she wasn't. She felt as though he were an old friend. Accordingly, she did something she'd never before done in her life. Throwing caution to the winds, she played to the hilt the role of the courted woman.

"Almost," she whispered with a shy blush, darting her gaze from Ron to the dean in alluring apology. Her flush deepened as she smiled up at her savior; if she'd found him attractive from afar, he was that much more striking close by, and close by he was. His arm crossed her back in a diagonal sweep, comfortably fitting her shoulder in its crook. In response to the unexpected embrace, her own hand found itself at his waist and now clutched it with a fierceness that belied her outer ease.

Sensing her equivocation, Jim gave her a rakish grin before turning his attention to Ron. He extended his right hand, holding Rachel with his left. "Jim Guthrie, here. I don't believe we've met."

Ron returned the larger man's clasp. "Ron Lynch," was his terse reply before he shifted his skeptical gaze to Rachel. "Mr. Guthrie's a friend of yours?"

She didn't know what to say. She'd never seen the man before, much less ever heard his name. Tongue-tied and in dire need of direction, she looked up at Jim, who, taking his cue, graced her with a melting smile and an affectionate squeeze. He kept his eyes on her as he spoke, fueling the implication of intimacy in a way his words did not.

"We're both from North Carolina. I work for Rachel's father."

Rachel took the words in, utterly unable to break from his gaze until one strong forefinger nudged her ribs in subtle prompting. Tearing her eyes away and back to Ron, she grinned. "I didn't know he was coming. It's a surprise." Then, recalling the original purpose for Jim's arrival, she set out to make good on it. "If you'll excuse us, Ron . . . Dr. Iber. As you can see, Jim just got in." His bag still hung by his right hip. She hoped that she'd made the correct assumption. "I'd like to have some time to talk with him before he falls asleep on his feet."

The Dean of Engineering simply nodded as Jim dropped his arm from her waist and caught her hand in his own, turning her away and starting through the crowd. Ron was by her other arm instantly.

"You really should linger, babe."

She smiled in passing at several faces that turned her way, and spoke very softly. "I'm exhausted, Ron. Besides, you handle things so beautifully." She squeezed his hand with her free one. "I'll see you in the morning. Okay?"

They'd reached the door, where Ron stopped. "For brunch?"

Rachel shook her head, calling over her shoulder as Jim led her on. "At the airport. Twelve-thirty is it?"

"That's right." Her manager's tone was guarded, his eyes studying Jim warily. "Twelve-thirty."

"Hey, Rachel!" A new voice came from just behind Ron, a lanky figure pushing around him and loping forward. This time Rachel forced Jim to stop. Peter Mahoney was the guitarist of the group and their relationship, far beyond the musical, was a special one. "You're taking off now?" he asked. She nodded. "Don't want to join us for something to eat?" The guitarist was nearly as tall as Jim, though nowhere near as solid or dark. Fair and good-looking, he wore his hair long and sported a well-trimmed mustache.

"Thanks, Pete, but I think I'll skip it tonight." When Pete glanced questioningly at the man to whom she seemed umbilically bound, she followed his gaze and blushed once more. "Oh, I'm sorry, Pete. I'd like you to meet Jim Guthrie. Jim is . . . a friend. Jim, this is Pete Mahoney, our guitarist."

"Pleased to meet you," Pete ventured. Though his handshake was easily offered, Jim sensed the same guardedness that Ron had displayed. It seemed that Rachel Busek had more than one caretaker. Or beau? Could either man be her lover?

"The pleasure's mine," he countered in a voice that was deep and confident in denial of the thoughts he harbored. "I heard 'Duelin' Banjos.' That was unbelievable."

"I only did half. We've got Rachel to thank for the rest."

"That's just what I intend to do," Jim said with a grin, "if I can ever get a minute alone with her." He tugged on Rachel's hand and started to move on. "Nice meeting you."

Pete looked suddenly forlorn, thinking how unlike Rachel it was to run off by herself. But then, she wasn't by herself, was she? "Rachel? . . ."

"It's all right, Pete," she called louder as the distance between them increased. "I'll see you in the morning. Give my apologies to the others!"

And then she and Jim were through a side door and in the dark, silent solitude of an alley. Sagging against the cool brick wall, Rachel let her head fall back and breathed a deep sigh of relief. "Aaaaaah, that's better." There were only echoes of sounds, dim reminders of the party behind and the city beyond. It was a momentary respite.

"Are you all right?" he asked. She seemed suddenly small and utterly fatigued, a fragile wind-up doll whose wind-up had wound down.

Righting her head, she gazed up at the shadowed face of the man named Jim Guthrie. The fact that his twang had mysteriously disappeared was secondary to the abundant warmth in his voice. "I am now." She inhaled again, deeply and with relish, then went on. "I sometimes feel that I'll lose my mind, subjecting myself to that endlessly inane chatter."

"Why do you do it?"

"It's my job."

"I thought your job was to play the flute."

"If only it were that simple," she chided, pushing away from the wall and starting slowly down the alley. When Jim materialized by her side, she paused. "But thank you anyway."

"For what?"

"For saving me. Back in there. I didn't know how to get away."

He chuckled. "I'm not sure whether *you* were

more uncomfortable there . . . or *me*. But when you started shifting from one foot to the other, I decided to make my move."

His words sobered her, bringing with them the realization that she knew neither this man nor his motive for seeking her out. Facing forward, she headed again for the street, then quickened her pace when she felt him beside her. She'd never been so reckless as to leave a concert with a stranger. Why had she? Had it been the patient indulgence she'd seen on his face as he'd stood propped against the door? Or the way his lips had twitched in understanding of her plight? Or the twang? Or her need for home? Or his reference to her father?

"Whoa!" Jim caught her lightly by the arm and slowed her pace. Unknowingly, she'd practically begun to run. "Where are you off to?"

"Do you really work for my father?" she asked, her voice breathless in sudden fright.

"Yes. I wouldn't lie about that. . . . You don't believe me. I've frightened you." He could see it in her eyes, round again, more doelike and alert. Damn, but she was lovely! But real? Was she? Mesmerized by the pale glow on her cheeks, he lifted his hand to touch it, but she flinched and ducked away.

"I've got to run," she gasped.

"No, no, Rachel." He was beside her in an instant. "Please. I won't hurt you." Emerging from the alley, he could see the shine of her eyes. When she lowered her head and ran along the sidewalk, he stood stock still for a moment. He should have been thinking of Tom Busek and the more legitimate reason he'd flown to Chicago. But he wasn't. "Rachel!" He thought of nothing but that the woman he'd waited so long to meet was slipping away from him. "Rachel!"

She was a vision in white, delicate, ephemeral, her blond hair streaming behind as she ran. The city, which threatened to swallow her up, was, by contrast, drab, concrete, aged—and dangerous. Suddenly, Jim saw her as a lone, unprotected figure and he bolted after her.

Once his long legs were in motion, it took him no time to close the distance between them. "Rachel, please. I've got to talk to you."

She held up a hand and, refusing to look at him, simply shook her head and continued forward.

Unable to believe his own ineptness, Jim thrust a hand through his hair and muttered a quiet oath. With a determined step he caught up with her once more. This time, he took her hand and held tightly to it to preclude her escape as he matched his stride to hers.

"Who are you?" she asked, her emotions in turmoil. Had rape been on his mind, he could have done it back in the alley . . . or dragged her down any one of those they'd passed since. Had he been a violent creature, he could have taken a swipe at her the instant she'd turned from him and begun to run. But he hadn't. He'd simply followed her, calling her name not in anger but . . . pleading.

"Jim Guthrie. Just as I said. And I *have* just arrived from Raleigh."

The reminder brought her to a dead halt. "You really work for my father?"

"For the past two months." Reaching into his back pocket, he extracted his wallet and sought the simplest form of proof, two IDs. One was his driver's license. Rachel scanned it carefully, James P. Guthrie, and indeed, a Raleigh address. Then a pass to SCT, which was equally as familiar to her, evoking a more visceral reaction. Southern Computer Technology was her father's company. The picture was clear and verified Jim's claim.

"I'm sorry." She smiled sheepishly. "I shouldn't have been so mistrusting." She wondered why she had been, more than half-suspecting that the fault, if it could be called a fault, lay in this large man's good looks.

"To the contrary." His voice was as gentle as the palpitations in her chest—in his own chest—as he responded to her smile. "I shouldn't even have expected that you'd have played along with my game and left that reception with me. It wasn't the safest thing to do." He arched a brow. "And that alley . . . well, let's just say that many an alley has seen mayhem in its day." How well he knew.

Remembering her fear of personal danger that had sent her running from the alley, she shivered.

"Cold?" Before she could open her mouth to explain, he had his jacket off his shoulders and draped around hers. Its warmth was an instant sedative, erasing all thought of mayhem. His voice was as soothing with its sudden concern. "You didn't leave a coat or purse back at the concert hall, did you?"

"No. It was so warm when we left the hotel earlier that a coat seemed silly. And I hate to be bothered with a purse." Wiggling the toes of her left foot, she felt the reassuring crinkle of the ten dollar bill she'd stuffed in her shoe before leaving the hotel, just in case. "It's only another something that Ron has to keep track of while we're on stage. As it is, he'll take care of my flute."

"Ron is? . . ."

"Our road manager. He makes all the arrangements, keeps track of the equipment, does his share of PR through it all."

"And you trust him with your flute?" Given the way the smaller man had all but glared at Jim, he doubted that he'd have trusted him with much.

"Implicitly." Though she didn't always agree with Ron, she did trust him.

With a light hand at her back, Jim turned her and slowly began to walk. "That's strange. I would have imagined that a musician hated to be parted from his instrument. I had this picture of your refusing to let anyone else handle it, of your polishing it each night, of your lovingly tucking it into its velvet case and kissing it goodnight."

Rachel eyed him in mild reproach, as much

for the seductive drawl of his voice as for his words. "You're making fun of me."

"It's true then?"

"No, it's not true. Not with me, at least. I mean, I'm sure there are those who have a . . . a *thing* for their instruments. . . ."

"But you're not one."

"No. Don't mistake me. I love playing the flute. It's always been my"—her voice took on a poignant note—"my salvation. . . . But I'm one of those who takes a practical attitude toward the whole thing."

"Oh?" he coaxed her on, delighted to hear her speak. Her voice was as musical as the rest of her. "And what *is* this practical attitude?"

Again she looked up at him, silently calculating. "Have you ever used a camera, Jim?"

He grinned, liking the way she said his name. "Sure."

"A Nikon?"

He chuckled. "Sorry, but that's a little rich for my veins." And for those of most of his clients. A simpler, less expensive camera more often suited everyone.

"But wouldn't your pictures be better with a better camera?"

He thought of the dark of night and infrared film, the resolution of which was dubious regardless of what camera was used. "Not really. Either you've got the subject matter, or you haven't. Either you know how to use a camera . . . or you don't. I've taken super pictures with an

Instamatic." Which could be whipped from his pocket to catch an unsuspecting pair of collaborators in the act, he said silently to himself.

A satisfied smile curved her lips, adding a flash of white in echo of her dress. "So . . . the key is in the subject and the photographer. The camera is only a tool, and so is my flute. Actually, flutes. I have several. None is custom-made or superordinary. Any one will do for a particular concert. The key is in the music . . . and me." Then she blushed. "I'm sorry if that sounds arrogant. What I mean is that it's up to me—or Pete, or Stefan or Bill or Tony—to produce the kind of sound, to interpret the music in such a way that justifies the money people spend to hear Montage."

"No need to apologize," Jim ventured gently. Her reasoning was sound, her manner of explanation charming. "Your point is well taken." Wasn't it the same with a gun? The cheapest of the lot could kill a man dead when aimed properly. "But a flute is small enough to carry several with you on the road. What about a guitar? Or a cello? Or a piano, for that matter?"

She chuckled. "The pianist excepted, each of the others does have more than one instrument. And, in all fairness, I have to admit that I take a more cavalier attitude than some on the issue." She thought about that attitude and grew more distant. "You could say that I've learned the hard way to keep things in perspective."

Jim stared at her for a minute. "Is that bitterness I detect?"

Stunned not only that he'd heard it, but that she'd let it escape in the first place, Rachel looked quickly up. "Oh . . . no . . . it's just that . . . well, when I was first with Montage, I *did* have a favorite flute. It was stolen our second month on the road."

"It *was* more valuable than the others?"

She crinkled up her nose. "Only sentimentally. My dad gave it to me for my sixteenth birthday." There was more to the story, but she stopped there. Jim Guthrie, eminently hardy man that he seemed, would hardly be interested in tales of endless practices, auditions, contests played out on an instrument that had been given to her with a card that read, "From your Dad, with love and every bit of the pride your mother would have shared had she been with us." Even now, at the thought, Rachel's eyes misted. Then, she'd been deeply touched at the memory of the mother she'd assumed had died at her birth. Now, though, there was a world of doubt. What if her new suspicions proved to be right? What if she did have a mother out there somewhere? What if there was indeed a woman who, for some frightening reason, had chosen to deny completely the existence of her daughter, of Rachel?"

She hadn't realized that she'd stopped walking until strong fingers cupped her chin to turn up her face. Jim stood looking down at her, his eyes seeming to delve far deeper than any man's had ever done.

"It must have hurt badly . . . losing something that meant so much to you," he murmured.

Losing a cherished memory? Could he have known? But no, she was sure her father had confided in no one. Lord, he hadn't even known he'd confided in *her*! "It did," she whispered. But, suddenly distracted, she wasn't thinking about that loss. Rather she was thinking about the tall man before her, about the smooth, strong line of his cheekbone and the faint shadow of a beard on his jaw. There was a physical magnetism about him. He was alive, aware and vibrant, his life's blood throbbing in the vein at his neck. Had it begun with a "P", virility might have been his middle name.

Uncomfortable with the course of her thoughts, Rachel backed away and lowered her head. Jim allowed it, needing the distance himself to regain control of his senses. He couldn't remember having been as instantly attracted to a woman. Given his way, he'd have kissed her to oblivion, led her straight to her hotel room and spent the night buried deep inside her. Instant attraction? Oh, yes, there were any number of women who could stir his blood. But this was different. He'd seen her eyes, had felt the warm flow of her gaze crossing his face. He'd seen the way her lips had parted so helplessly. He'd also seen the flicker of unease that, with its moment's pain, had broken the spell for her.

"Well," she croaked, clearing her throat and looking straight ahead as she started to walk once more, "you haven't told me what's brought you to Chicago."

Reluctant to upset her, he briefly thought about lying. Looking down at her now, so fair-skinned and delicate and soft-spoken, he understood why Tom hadn't wanted to call her. Her shoulders seemed too frail to be burdened. That, though, he realized, was the male chauvinist in him speaking. The more practical side of him knew that Tom needed her and that she had a right to know. Further, the more whimsical side of him guessed that any woman who'd met the challenge of "Duelin' Banjos" as she had was no shrinking violet.

"I came to see you."

She blushed, feeling all the more awkward, still refusing to look at him. "You're great for my ego, but something tells me there's another reason you're here. My father's never before sent anyone on a trip just to see me."

"Other people come?"

"In the line of business." She smiled then, in affection for her father. "Dad keeps a detailed itinerary smack out on his desk. It tells where I'm going to be on a given date, where we're playing, where we're staying. When any of the men pass through, he tips them off about a super concert they shouldn't miss for the world. They usually don't. And I love seeing them. Any word from home is welcome." Her eyes climbed the distance to his, and she took a steadying breath. "So, James P. Guthrie of Raleigh, North Carolina, what brings you to Chicago, Illinois?" The question was no sooner out than another followed suit. "What do you do for SCT, anyway? I don't recall having heard your name before."

"I doubt you have." If Tom Busek hadn't told Rachel about his darkest suspicions, it was certain that he hadn't told her of his hiring Jim. "Here we are. Your hotel."

She shot a surprised glance ahead, then grinned. "So my father *did* tell you."

"Actually," Jim mused, guiding her toward the revolving door, then waiting until they were reunited in the hotel lobby to speak again, "I read upside down."

"You do what?" Tipping her head back to look up at him, she noted that his eyes were amber, dancing now with gold flecks of amusement.

"Read upside down. It's a skill I picked up a long time ago. Purely to spite my first grade teacher, mind you. Her attempts to teach me to read right side up nearly drove her into early retirement." Upside-down reading was a handy trick in his trade. He couldn't count the number of times he'd gleaned pertinent information that way. But . . . Rachel didn't need to know that.

They'd come to a standstill in the middle of the lobby, neither sure of where they were going. Rachel knew that she should thank him for walking her back from the concert hall, excuse herself and call it a night. Jim knew that, without further delay, he should quietly explain to Rachel why he'd come.

When their eyes locked, clear thought grew more difficult. He cleared his throat. "You must be tired. Playing and all."

She spoke quickly. "No, I'm fine. But what about you? Traveling and all."

"I'm okay. Hey, I really shouldn't keep you. . . ."

"You're not. Unless . . . unless you have to get going. . . ."

"I don't. . . . Listen," he studied her face, as though searching for the key to a deep, dark mystery, "I'm . . . I'm really starved. They served something on that flight that rivaled dog food." He glanced quickly around. "How about if we get something to eat? There must be a coffee shop, nothing fancy, someplace we can get a burger."

Recalling her wish in the face of a mildly rancid goose liver pâté, she grinned. "Great minds think alike. I know just the place." Suddenly buoyant, she reached out and took his hand, leading him down a winding staircase to the hotel's sandwich shop. It was only after they'd been seated, after the waitress had taken orders for baconburgers, steak fries and beer, after they'd spent several moments' dumb silence grinning at one another, that Rachel took an uneven breath.

"So . . . now . . . you were going to tell me what you do at SCT."

"I was," he teased, prolonging the moment. She looked so carefree, so happy and . . . beautiful . . . that he hated to throw a wrench in the works. But the longer he waited, the worse it would be. "I am," he vowed, his lips thinning in resignation.

Sensing his hesitation, Rachel felt her own smile fade. "Yes?"

"I work more for your father than I do for SCT."

"I always thought of them as one and the same."

"Not in this case. Your father hired me to handle something particularly sensitive."

Her eyes brightened. "The irrigation project? You're working on it? Funny, I wouldn't have pegged you for microelectronics."

He paused, welcoming the reprieve. She was so fine, so schooled, so much a lady. He felt distinctly outclassed, and for the first time in his life, it bothered him. "How *would* you have pegged me?"

A shy smile tugged at her lips and she shrugged. "I don't know." She thought of the skill with which he'd extricated her from the party. "Corporate management . . . Development." Then her eyes fell to his hands, to the fingers that were long, strong and sunglazed. "Or farming. Are you with the farming cooperative Dad's worked with?"

"Would that bother you?"

"Bother me? Why ever would it bother me?"

"A farmer is more often a man of the flesh, while a scientist, like a musician, is cerebral. If tonight was any example, you seem to be surrounded by the latter. Is it the cerebral type you prefer?"

The question within the question was obvious. Rachel heard it in the velvet of his words, saw it in the warmth of his gaze, felt it in the fluttering of her own pulse. "I don't know," she admitted slowly, softly. "The other, the man of the flesh, as you call him, is a mystery to me. I've . . . never known one."

Awkward once more, she averted her gaze. She didn't know what it was about this man that affected her so, only knew that the excitement he brought came hand in hand with a certain silent warning. Though twenty-nine and outwardly a woman of the world, she felt disconcertingly inexperienced and . . . sexually overwhelmed. That was it. Jim Guthrie was tall and muscular and filled to the brim with sex appeal. A man of the flesh? Oh, yes, he was that. And she was a musician, nothing more.

"What *do* you do for my father?" she blurted out, desperately needing an escape from her thoughts.

Jim tried to think of something evasive, something witty, something gentle. But as her now trusting brown eyes held his, he could think of nothing to blunt the truth.

Once more he dug into the pocket of his jeans for his wallet, this time ferreting out a dog-eared card, passing it silently across to Rachel. She studied it, uncomprehending at first, then gradually grew pale before her eyes shot to his in alarm.

two

"A private investigator?" She whispered. "Why does my father need a private investigator?" Did it have something to do with those dreams . . . with the shocking things he'd been saying in his sleep? Did it have something to do with a supposedly dead mother who was not dead at all but was haunting Tom Busek? Rachel felt as though something were choking her and forced herself to swallow.

Instinctively, Jim reached out and took her hand, surrounding her small fingers with his larger, warmer ones. "It's all right, Rachel," he reassured her, touched by her concern for her father. "Nothing life-threatening." Only indirectly so, but he'd work into that more slowly.

When the waitress arrived with two large mugs of beer, he pushed hers forward in silent urging and watched while she took a drink.

"What is it?" she asked more strongly then, knowing that nothing could be worse than her imaginings. "I want to know."

He hesitated for only a minute longer. "You were right, actually. It's the irrigation project."

The relief Rachel felt upon hearing that the problem was, indeed, work-related, was short-lived. The irrigation project had been her father's dream, the one project into which he'd poured so much more of himself than the others. "What about it?"

"Over the past few months, your father has come to suspect strange goings-on—unexpected setbacks, unnecessary delays."

Her eyes widened. "Sabotage?"

"Not exactly. It looks more like a case of industrial espionage. Someone may be attempting to buy time, to copy the blueprint for that microchip and get it into production and on the market a step ahead of SCT."

"But that's ridiculous! My father has been the force behind that project from the word 'go'! He conceived the plans for it when no one else was interested. If he'd the financial backing for it, he might have had the chip developed years ago. But the idea of using a tiny silicon chip to regulate water and other nutrients to plants was thought to be nothing more than an exotic vision of the future." Eyes flashing, she paused only to catch her breath. "Now that it's nearing reality, now that we can almost *taste* the plants raised on land once given up as too dry for farming, do you mean to say that someone else is going to jump on the bandwagon?"

He held her hand tighter in an attempt to calm her down. She was obviously furious. "It looks that way," he said quietly. "At least, that's what your father hired me to find out."

"And have you?"

"I'm getting there. But it's slow."

"What do you mean 'slow'?" She withdrew her hand from his and clenched it in her lap. Her expression held a raw form of the same frustration he'd long since learned to control. "Either there's something going on, or there isn't."

"Oh, there's something going on, all right," he explained patiently. "It's just that to prove it, and prove it conclusively, we've got to collect the evidence very carefully. The whole point is to be able to bring our case to the authorities and know that it will stick."

He was right. As reason edged out emotion, Rachel had to agree with him. "The authorities," she snorted softly, looking more sadly at Jim. "Poor Daddy. He's always been so mistrustful of the . . . authorities."

"It's understandable," Jim answered quietly. "Anyone who grew up as he did, who lived through the political terror of a country like Czechoslovakia at the close of the war, is bound to be mistrustful."

"He told you about that?" she asked, surprised. Her father rarely discussed his past, and his foreign roots were far from obvious with his accent as negligible as it was. He'd worked hard on that, too, determined to be as American as possible.

"He had to. I insist on knowing my client well, if I'm to take on his case. One of the first questions I asked was why he hadn't sought the government's help. After all, SCT does have federal funding for the irrigation project. In that sense, the government has a personal stake in it. It was then that your father told me the story of his escape from Czechoslovakia."

"He doesn't suspect *our* government on this, does he?"

Jim gave a quick headshake. "It's only natural for someone like him to be constantly looking over his shoulder. After all, the Czechoslovakia he fled would have had no qualms about seizing SCT and every blueprint it owned." He glanced up with the arrival of the waitress and leaned back to allow room for the platters she set before them. When he was alone with Rachel once more, he popped a pickle round into his mouth. "Anyway, we've ruled out that possibility."

"What have you ruled in?" she asked, shook her head when he offered her the ketchup bottle, then watched as he removed the top bun and doused his baconburger first with ketchup, then relish. "Got anything left under there?" she mocked lightly, leaning closer to peer at the fluid mess.

"You bet!" With a broad grin, he deftly lifted the sandwich and took a huge bite.

Rachel sat back, brushed her hair behind her shoulders and watched him eat. The strong line of his jaw made short work of the mouthful, the muscles of his throat carried it down as nicely. She'd never seen a man built quite as well. Or perhaps, she told herself, it was that she'd never noticed one . . . or been thrust into such close company with one. That was it. Surely Jim

Guthrie had no monopoly on virility. The world had to be full of brawny men. *Her* world . . . well, that was another story. Indeed, her father was tall and strapping; but he was her *father*.

"Eat, Rachel." Jim's voice broke into her wanderings. For a split second, she was stunned by the familiarity of the order.

With an uneasy laugh, she picked up her fork and poked at a large steak fry. "You sound like my father. 'Eat, Rachel. Sleep, Rachel. Go on out and take a walk, Rachel.' "

"Does he stifle you?"

Her head shot up. "Oh, no! Well, not really. It's genuine concern." Her voice dropped to a heartful murmur. "And love. How could I possibly resent that, particularly when I'm gone so much of the year. It's actually . . . kind of nice. I think everyone needs to be pampered sometimes."

Jim had seen the love in her eyes and, for the second time that night, felt a surge of envy. Then he thought of his own life, and his gaze hardened. To his dismay, Rachel instantly sensed the change.

"Don't you?" she asked, using the moment to satisfy a suddenly urgent need. "There must be a wife back home in Raleigh? And children?" Unknowingly, she held her breath.

He searched her features for a soulful moment before answering. "No. No wife. No children. My line of work . . . precludes that type of thing." In response to her frown, he offered a rueful grin.

"It's not like it is on television, all fancy cars and glamor. Hell, if I ever drove a red Ferrari . . ." He chuckled and shook his head. An errant lock of dark brown hair dabbed his brow. "Suffice it to say that successful surveillance requires far more subtlety than that."

"What kind of car *do* you drive?" she asked on impulse.

He shrugged. "It depends. I get a new car every six months or so. Not new, actually. Used. Something a year or two old, with a nondescript body and a color that blends into the scenery. The whole point is *not* to be noticed. What's under the hood . . . well, that's a different story."

Leaving Rachel in suspense, he took another bite of his burger. Again she was fascinated, this time by his hands. In contrast to the paler, more finely shaped hands to which she was accustomed—those which stroked piano keys, or manipulated minuscule computer parts, or sloped around the delicate stems of fine wineglasses—Jim Guthrie's hands were larger and stronger. They were tanned, as were the forearms revealed by the rolled cuff of his shirt, and bore the finest mat of silky brown hair. Rather than being rough or beefy, as might have been the case with a man of his size, his fingers were lean and well-formed, beautiful in a thoroughly masculine kind of way.

Shaking her head to free herself of the urge to reach out and touch him, she lowered her eyes to her own slender ivory-hued hand. It seemed to have taken a stranglehold on her fork.

"What's wrong?" Jim asked softly.

She swallowed once, then shook her head again, this time in self-reproach. "Here I am, asking about your car," her eyes shot back up, half in accusation that he'd let her be so easily diverted, "when I should be asking more about the troubles at SCT. You must think I'm callous." She worried about the *other* things he'd think of her, if he could have read the direction of her other wayward thoughts.

"You're not callous." His amber gaze, if anything, heightened the flush on her cheeks. "I know that you're concerned about your father. I also know that diversions are sometimes necessary for easing tension, for keeping things in perspective." He paused then to study her lips and his voice grew deeper. "But I'd like to think that it wasn't simply a matter of necessary diversion."

"What do you mean?" she whispered, trying desperately to keep her breathing steady.

When his arm easily spanned the table to tuck a strand of hair behind her ear, she couldn't move. When his fingers curved about her neck and his thumb settled on the outer corner of her mouth, she couldn't breathe. When the pad of that thumb, rough with a delightfully male kind of friction, began to lightly trace the outline of her lips, she thought that her heart would drum her hollow.

"You're a beautiful woman, Rachel," he murmured. Huskiness gave his voice a sandy-smooth quality. His hand trembled lightly. "I must be like so many of the men who see you perform and fall half in love with you there and then." He gave a slash of a grin that was strangely poignant. "It would be poetic justice if the tables were turned."

So he'd known her thoughts, after all! Her cheeks grew pinker, though whether the color was caused by that discovery . . . or by the hand that caressed her neck so faintly, she couldn't tell. She only knew that there *was* something to the concept of instant biological attraction. Either that, or someone at the reception earlier had slipped something into her wine!

"And if I were?" She heard herself playing along with his game once more, her voice sounding odd, as though coming from a person she'd never had a chance to know. It was the same stranger who quite helplessly raised a hand to join his at her neck. Though her fingers were small over his, they held him to still the torment . . . or were they merely pressing him closer?

Sucking in his breath, Jim sat back. His hand broke from her neck, turned to catch her fingers and circle them as he lowered them to the tablecloth. "If you were," he said with profound sadness, "I'd say we were both crazy. My life is no more conducive to lasting relationships than yours is. I spend three-quarters of my time in my car, you in ever-changing hotels and concert halls. . . . Crazy . . ." The last word was whispered on a hoarse, somehow angry note.

It was enough to bring Rachel to her senses. Dragging her hand from beneath his, she buried it in her lap. "I'm sorry," she said. "You're right." Breathing deeply, she tipped up her chin and met his gaze. "It must be beer on top of wine."

She was ignorant of the double entendre, the image her innocently offered words spawned in Jim's man's mind. "Then eat," he growled, eyeing the burger she hadn't touched, waiting with brows drawn low until she'd lifted it and taken a bite, which she did, first one, then another, until indeed she felt better.

The physical renewal brought a clearing of her thoughts. "Tell me more about what you're doing for my father. He must be very upset about all this." She frowned. "I only wish he'd told me."

"He knows that you're under pressure yourself," Jim reasoned. "But, yes, he's upset. Angry, just like you were a minute ago. It helps now that we feel so close to a breakthrough."

"Are you? Tell me." Of her own accord, she ate more of her sandwich.

Chasing down the last of his own with a huge swallow of beer, he explained. He knew that he was waffling, knew he was simply avoiding the inevitable. But he couldn't help himself. Protectiveness, when it came to this woman, was second nature.

"I've boiled it down to two men—"

"Do I know them?"

"You may. Connors and Renko. Both need money—Connors for the double alimony he's paying and for the sweet young thing he's recently picked up, Renko for the second mortgage, the kids' college expenses, his father's nursing-home bill." At Rachel's look of sympathy he added, "And for a gambling debt that's drained his other resources."

"Oh . . . It's always financial, then?"

"Not always. There can be emotional reasons behind industrial espionage. The need for power or glory. Revenge."

"Revenge? Revenge against what? My father's never hurt a living soul!"

"I'm not saying that revenge is involved here, Rachel," Jim stressed gently. "Simply that it was one of several possible motives. It might have been conceivable that, at an early stage of the game, your father inadvertently hurt someone."

"My father is the epitome of kindness. He wouldn't—"

"I know." Again his voice was soothing. "But a man doesn't build a corporation like SCT without hiring and firing, without accepting one bid and rejecting others, without competing for sales against other companies. There was always the possibility that way back there someone or other was offended. Perhaps jealous. And sitting pretty until just the right moment arrived to get even."

A chill passed through Rachel. *Way back there*, Jim had said. Then her father's voice, sleep-blurred but discernible. *Don't leave, Ruth. It'll work out. . . . He's wrong about that. You're wrong. . . . But what we have . . . and the baby . . .*

"Rachel?"

Her eyes shot up. "Hmmm?"

"Where were you?" Jim's voice was indescribably soft and filled with concern. "Just now, out of nowhere, you blanched and . . . were gone."

"I'm back," she said shakily. ". . . It was nothing."

"You're sure?"

She nodded, slowly regaining her poise. "Then it's Connors or Renko?"

Momentarily, if reluctantly, he accepted her evasion. "Connors or Renko. I'm ninety-five percent sure."

"Only ninety-five?" she asked on a pretense of lightness. "When do you find out about the other five?"

"When the case is finally solved."

"And when will that be?"

He shrugged. "I hope within the next month or two. The irrigation chip was to have debuted in November. Your dad's moved that date up to September."

Her eyes widened. "How can he do that? As it is, he's been working himself ragged."

Jim cleared his throat and arched a brow, prepared to agree and proceed to the matter of Tom Busek's health. But Rachel rushed on before he could make good his vow.

"And what will the next month or two tell you? What are you looking for?"

"What I need is that concrete evidence I spoke of before. Assuming one of these two men is selling the blueprints to a competing enterprise, I need photographs of meetings between them and proof of money being transferred."

"You've got to catch them in the act?"

"If possible, yes. But it's unlikely that two thiefs would stand in the middle of a public street handing money over for the camera to record." Anticipating her follow-up, he went on. "What I'm doing is keeping tabs on both men, watching their comings and goings, checking their bank balances, sitting for hours outside their homes to follow them when they go out at night."

She frowned on a matter of logistics. "How can you follow both?"

"I have an associate."

"I see. And your . . . associate is working closely with my father, too?"

"No. I work at SCT alone. To anyone who asks, I'm a government coordinator, working in a consulting capacity to help speed up the release of the chip. What we're hoping to do is to make the culprit nervous. To rush him. To force his hand. To make him make a mistake."

Watching Jim closely, Rachel was fascinated by his animation. Red Ferraris notwithstanding, she'd somehow assumed private eyes to be drab, even-toned and dispassionate creatures, lurking in shadows, smelling of stale cigarette smoke, wearing scars and disfigurations like a badge of honor. Jim Guthrie was nothing like this.

"You enjoy your work, don't you?"

He smiled his guilt. "I'd have to, to spend the hours I do at it." When Rachel laughed, he tipped his head to the side. "And what's so funny about that?"

"Nothing. It's just that you've just recited verbatim one of my pet lines." She lowered her voice in mock gravity and proceeded in sober imitation. " 'You must enjoy playing the flute, Ms. Busek.' " She returned her voice to its normal pitch, though sweetened it with the sugar of experience. " 'I'd have to, to spend the hours I do at it.' " A glint of understanding passed between them. "Are you good at what you do?" she asked.

"I hope so. The clients have been coming for over fifteen years now."

"And they've all left satisfied?"

"Well," he drawled, "I can't quite bat a thousand. There's the man who pays me to find out if his wife is playing around, then is incensed when I give him proof that she is. There's the defendant in a murder trial whose lawyer hires me to come up with evidence to help his case and then finds that the evidence is all against his man."

"What happens then?" Rachel asked, intrigued.

"Nothing, really. The lawyer simply knows more of the truth and can plan his case more effectively."

"To get a guilty man off?"

He shook his head. "To see that his client's rights are fully protected. If the guy's guilty, more than likely he'll get his due."

She thought for a minute. "You sound confident, then, that your work serves a purpose."

"I am. Even when the results go against you, there's a purpose. Take missing persons. There's the one who simply disappears from the face of the earth . . . and the one who turns up dead. It can be heartbreaking. But isn't it better to know . . . than to always wonder?"

Rachel shuddered at the aptness of the question. It was the same one she'd been asking herself for months now. *Was* her mother alive?

"I suppose it is," she murmured distantly. "But you're right, it can be heartbreaking."

The play of emotions across her face held Jim's rapt attention. It was as if she put herself into that mythical client's place and felt the pain as her own. Strange . . . people usually felt more sympathy than empathy.

"Does it ever bother you?" she asked in the smallest of voices.

He stared at her for a minute before focusing on the froth that had left its ring at the top of his mug. "I ought to say no. That's the image, isn't it?" He wasn't bitter, simply direct. When he went on, though, he sounded vaguely reluctant, surprisingly vulnerable. "But, yes. It bothers me. There's a hell of a lot of grief in the world. I sometimes think I see too much of it. Some"—

he made a gesture of dismissal—"slides off my back. Other things stick. Such as dead kids. Wasted lives. *Real* heartache."

Real heartache. Rachel heard him and pondered his words. Perhaps she'd been feeling sorry for herself. Perhaps it would have been that much worse to have had a mother all these years, to have relied on one and loved one, only to have her die now . . . or next week, or next year. *That* would be heartache . . . just as it would be if anything happened to the father she'd known and loved.

"Not to change the subject," she began softly, "but, after all this, I'm still not sure why you've come to Chicago. Dad knew I'd be home in three weeks. And he hasn't mentioned any of this on the phone." Her brow puckered. "It's not like him to send someone on an errand."

Jim tread on shaky ground. "He didn't. I came on my own."

It took her a full minute to react. "You mean, he doesn't know you're here?" That *didn't* sound like her father.

"I think he suspected I'd come, after I spent so long trying to convince him to tell you himself. He may not know that I'm here right now, but he did nothing to stop me when I . . . when I started to read upside down."

His attempt at humor fell flat. Rachel was more disturbed than ever. "But why? Why wouldn't he tell me?"

"He didn't want you worried."

"But you felt I should know. Why?"

"Because I'm worried, Rachel."

"About the project?" she asked, but her concern lay elsewhere. There was something more. She knew it.

"About your father."

"What's . . . what's wrong with him? . . . Jim?"

Her hands lay flat on the table. Jim covered them with his own. "He's been working too hard," he said as gently as he could. "He's not well."

Rachel's eyes widened. "What is it?"

"His heart. The doctors want to operate."

"Operate? How . . . operate?"

He'd come too far to pull back. She was a grown woman who deserved to know the truth. "They're recommending triple by-pass surgery."

Her gaze focused unseeing on him before dropping blindly to the table. Without realizing it, she turned her hands palm up and sought his touch. "A triple by-pass?" she breathed. "My God!" When she shook her head in disbelief, golden hair slid over her shoulders. Jim reached up to push it back, but she was too stunned to notice. "I had no idea! . . . He seemed fine."

"When was the last time you saw him?"

"Six weeks ago. But we talk every week. I spoke with him just last Sunday." She raised her eyes in protest. "He was enthusiastic about the project. He went on and on talking about it."

"He'd collapsed at work the Friday before. He was talking from his hospital bed."

"But . . . that couldn't be. You see, *I* call *him*. . . ." Her words trailed off with the recollection that last week it had been different.

"He called you?" Jim probed softly.

Only after a pause did she nod her head in dismay. "I didn't think anything of it when he said that he wanted to catch me early. He seemed so eager. I assumed he was just in a good mood." Releasing a shaky sigh, she withdrew her hands from his and put her fingertips to her temples. "I can't believe it. . . . He was always so strong."

"He *is* strong, Rachel. Mentally, at least. But that's part of the problem. That's why I've come here to speak to you. He's refusing to have the surgery. Now, at least. He says that it's too critical a time for SCT. Someone's got to talk some sense into him. I've tried my best but . . . I'm just someone who's grown fond of him in the past two months. Your argument, on the other hand, might be more effective."

"If he didn't want me to know in the first place, I doubt that." Then she shook her head in disbelief. "His heart! . . ."

"His heart. He had chest pains for a week before he finally collapsed. According to the doctors, there's no way he can wait four or five months for the operation. You've got to convince him of that."

"And you think he'd listen to me?"

Jim eyed her gravely. "You're his daughter. You're all he's got."

His words struck with stunning impact,

shaping Rachel's face into a mask of misery. She looked from Jim's earnest expression to the table, then across toward the strangers on the far side of the room. She didn't know them . . . any of them . . . any more than she'd known the people she'd dined with yesterday or the day before or the week before that. Strangers . . . who'd never know if she died in her sleep one night in her hotel room. Tom Busek would know.

Feeling alone and particularly mortal, she whispered a hoarse, "I've got to leave." Before Jim could begin to follow, she'd slid from her seat and run toward the door. When the hostess regarded her questioningly, she murmured, "Room 3205. Please charge it." Then she rushed past, knowing only that there were things to be done.

Once in the privacy of her room, she lifted the phone and dialed direct to Chapel Hill. It was nearly one in the morning. As she reasoned it, she would happily bear the brunt of her father's annoyance if he were to answer the phone and deny Jim's story.

The phone rang three, then four times before it was finally answered by a soft voice stolen from sleep. "Busek residence."

"Mrs. Francis? It's Rachel."

"Rachel?" The voice grew louder. ". . . Is everything all right?"

"That's what I wanted to ask you. My father . . . Is he there?"

There was a pause, an answer in itself before the housekeeper spoke. "No. He's . . ."

Rachel understood that Gertrude Francis would have been sworn to secrecy. ". . . In the hospital?" So it was true. Her hopes fell the thirty-two flights and more. "How is he tonight?"

Audibly relieved that the secret was out, Mrs. Francis grew bolder. "Still tired and weak. They've been running tests that he doesn't much care for. But he sounded better when he called earlier. Rachel . . . how did you find out?"

"I had a visitor."

"Mr. Guthrie?" She sighed. "Thank goodness he finally took things into his own hands. I'm telling you, your father's been giving that man quite a time."

"Jim's been at the house?"

"Several nights a week. He and your father closet themselves in the study to hash over whatever it is they hash over. Mr. Guthrie's been after him to relax, to take it slower, to let *him* do the worrying. But your father's a stubborn man."

Having learned what she'd called to learn and then some, Rachel found herself tuning out and managed, with some grace, to wind up the conversation and hang up the phone. Her mind in a whirl, she lifted the receiver again and dialed Ron's room. He'd have to be told of her plans.

"Ron?"

"Rachel! I tried you a little while ago. Is everything all right?"

"Not really. Listen, Ron, I've got to go home for a couple of days."

There was silence, then a low cough. Rachel could picture Ron tugging at the knot of his tie. In a standard uniform of slacks, blazer and tie, he was usually more dressed than the musicians. She half suspected that he needed that tie to tighten, to loosen, to whip from around his neck when the mood suited him. It seemed his one outlet.

"What's wrong, Rachel?" Ron Lynch had two major worries—his players and their schedule. While some of the members of Montage played second fiddle to the latter, Rachel did not. Ron, like the rest, adored her.

"My father. He's sick."

"Oh, babe. I'm sorry. Is it anything serious?"

"His heart." She felt stunned. The words sounded like cardboard, flat and gray. "I just found out a little while ago. I'll be taking the first plane out tomorrow morning."

"He's had a heart attack?"

"I . . . don't think so. But the doctors want to do surgery."

"Now?"

Again she hesitated. "I think so. I don't . . . know all the details." She knew so little that it bothered her.

"And . . . Indianapolis?"

"I'll be there. I'll fly directly back in time for the concert. Explain to the others for me, will you, Ron? I'll call and let you know what's happening."

"You do that, babe. Hey . . . do you need any help? Have you got reservations and all?"

She hadn't thought that far. "No. But I'll make them."

"Want me to?"

Her sad smile held all the appreciation she could muster. "Thanks, Ron, but I can do it. I need something to keep me busy. Otherwise I'm apt to break down, and God only knows I can't do that!"

"God only knows you could, though I've never seen you do it!" That, to him, was the mystique of Rachel Busek—a delicate, almost fragile woman with a magic flute and a sense of self-command and discipline to rival the greatest of stoics. He exhaled in resignation. "If you change your mind and want me to do something, you know where I'll be." It was wishful thinking. Then he thought again and grew quieter. "Was it that Guthrie fellow?"

"Excuse me?"

"Tim Guthrie."

"Jim." If there was one thing Ron never did, it was to mistake names, unless he intended to.

"Did *he* bring the news?"

"Yes."

"Hmph. He seemed happy enough at the party."

"That wasn't the time or place to tell me."

A long distance phone call wouldn't have

served as well? Ron thought to himself. But hell, he couldn't really blame the guy. Hadn't he been the one to offer a shoulder a minute ago? "It's that bad, then?"

Rachel's voice rose in frustration. It was the first hint of true emotion he'd heard. "I don't know. That's why I've got to go home. I just don't know. And I won't be able to breathe freely until I see things for myself."

"Okay, babe. You go on home, and take it easy. If there's any problem, you let me know."

Her breath slipped from her lips as she regained her composure. "Thanks, Ron. I will." Her slender forefinger cut the connection, then pushed 'O'.

"Operator. May I help you?"

"Uh . . . yes. I'd like the number of . . ." What hospital *was* her father in? "Of . . ." And his doctor?

"Yes?"

"I'm sorry," she mumbled. "Never mind." Dismayed, she let the receiver fall to its cradle.

As though in echo came a faint knock on her door. Her eyes flew to the broad wooden expanse with its familiar fire information and check-out listing. How tired she was of hotel rooms; more than anything at that moment, she wanted to be home.

Then the knock came again, a tentative tapping, and was accompanied by a low intoned, "Rachel?"

It seemed inevitable that Jim Guthrie should

evoke thoughts of home. He had from the first, when she'd spied him across the room, not knowing who he was, simply knowing that she found him attractive.

"Rachel?"

Without further thought, she crossed to the door and opened it. Drawn magnetically, her eyes rose to his and were held by a tender concern that, quite against her wishes, began to melt her numbness. He was the reality she'd have to believe. He was here, had come all the way from home with the sole purpose of breaking the news of her father to her.

Her hand on the knob trembled, reflecting the twist her insides had taken. Her eyes misted. Turning her back on the rush of emotion, she walked slowly to the far window and struggled to salvage her poise. She heard the door shut quietly, heard the whisper of denim as he walked to the coffee table and set down the paper bag he'd been carrying. Looking over her shoulder, she saw him extract two take-out cups, remove their lids and approach her with the lighter-colored one of the two.

"Tea," he said simply. "It might help."

The lump in her throat kept her from speaking. Nodding, she took the cup from him and turned back to the speckled void that was Chicago at night. It was dark and impersonal and held little solace for a woman who felt her roots suddenly shaken. Lowering her eyes, she sipped her tea. Its liberal lacing of sugar was settling. At length she turned back to Jim, who had stretched comfortably in a chair and was drinking his coffee as he watched her.

"I'm sorry," she murmured, finding her voice at last. "It was very rude of me downstairs . . . walking out like that. It wasn't your fault. . . ."

"No apologies necessary. You were upset. You needed time." He took a sip of his coffee. ". . . You called home?"

"Yes. But . . . how did you know?"

"If I were you and a total stranger showed up with news the likes of mine tonight, I'd have called home too. . . . How is he?"

"Mrs. Francis thought he sounded better this afternoon. I would have called the hospital, but . . ."

"He's at Duke. A doctor, a heart specialist, named Raymond Balkan is heading the case. He's a good man."

Rachel nodded, then spoke more forcefully. "Why didn't you tell me sooner? I feel horrible . . . the way we meandered back from the concert hall, then sat over dinner as though nothing in the world was wrong. You should have told me!"

"Where?" he asked calmly. "At the reception? Or in that dark alley afterward? Besides, there's nothing that can be done until morning."

His gentle reasoning took from her sails any wind that might have remained after her brief outburst. Putting two fingers to her forehead, she pressed at a point of pain. "No," she whispered, "I suppose not. . . . Damn . . ." Her hand hovered aimlessly in the air before falling to her side. "I'm sorry again. It's not your fault that my father is sick." She looked at Jim in time to see him lean forward and pat the chair kitty-corner from his. Feeling drained, she accepted his silent offer and sank down into the soft cushions. "Thanks for the tea."

"My pleasure."

"How did you know I like it over coffee?"

He smiled crookedly. "Just a hunch." She seemed far too delicate for the stronger stuff, though he didn't dare say so aloud for fear she'd come down on him for the sexist that he was.

"And my room . . . how did you know the number?" She knew the hotel would never give the information freely.

"I wanted to pay for dinner. When the waitress returned the check to me, I saw your room number neatly written in."

"Clever," she murmured but shied from his amber gold gaze. It was too warm, too intense, too . . . distracting. Bowing her head, she shifted gears. "*He* should have let me know. I should be with him."

"You've got your own life. Tom is proud of what you do."

"But there are priorities." To an extent she felt hurt that her father hadn't wanted her with him. "Family is a precious thing. He should know that. What he's done is . . . is selfish."

"Don't be too hard on him, Rachel. He acted out of love for you. Be grateful he's that way.

You know, he's really pretty generous, giving you up for such long periods of time."

"Generous?" she echoed sadly, then forced a feeble laugh and buried her gaze in the thickness of the carpet. "There are times I wish he weren't that 'generous.' It'd be nice to be home more."

"You mean . . . you don't enjoy playing with Montage?"

Only then did she realize what she'd said. Her head shot up. "Oh, I enjoy it. I love it. When I'm playing the flute, I'm in seventh heaven. It's just . . . the other times." She took a deep breath, then let it out in defeat. "It's lonely."

Draining the last of his coffee, Jim stretched to put the cup on the low table. He stayed forward, his elbows on his knees in a pose of studied nonchalance. There was nothing nonchalant, however, in the gaze that caught hers. "There's no one special here?"

"On the road? How could there be?"

"I mean . . . even in the group. Six musical men plus Ron. No companionship?"

"Oh, sure. There's companionship. And they're wonderful. All of them." Even Pete had come through as a true friend, in some ways closer and more doting than the rest. "But . . . they're still my colleagues. It's different."

"Different . . ."—his voice flowed smoothly—"as in closing the door at night and finding yourself all alone?"

She wondered if he knew, if he understood. "Yes," she whispered softly, unable to move when he reached to stroke her cheek. He was suddenly much closer, large and reassuring. Where a minute ago she'd felt cold, the touch of his skin warmed her. Where a minute ago she'd felt alone in the world, his nearness gave her comfort.

"I know the feeling," he murmured as his fingers curved around her ear to trace its intricate shell shape. Lambent eyes followed the exercise, then stole off on their own to savor the softness of her cheek, the small upward tilt of her nose, the gentle pink curve of her lips. But it was her eyes that fascinated him, for they seemed to hold a hint of all that was in her. Beyond sadness and loneliness, there was such potential for happiness, and love.

He took a deep, shuddering breath, unaware that Rachel was barely breathing herself. "Rachel . . . Rachel . . ." He half moaned. "This isn't the time, is it?"

Captured by the magic of the moment, she numbly shook her head. While one part of her ached for a rapturous oblivion, the other part knew that this *wasn't* the time or place. Closing her eyes and lowering her head, she put her hand over Jim's for a minute, breathed deeply of the man-scent of his skin, then lowered both their hands to her lap. "I'd like to fly back home first thing tomorrow. I've already told Ron. I'd better call the airport."

"Let me do that. You finish your tea."

Feeling distinctly debilitated in the region of

her knees, she didn't protest. Rather, she watched Jim push himself from his seat, cross to the phone by the bed and punch out first the operator's number, then that of the airport. Studying his tall frame, the dark bend of his head, the solid span of his back, she realized that he no longer had his duffel bag and wondered where he'd be staying. Of its own accord, her eye skipped to the bed. It was big enough. If only she was woman enough!

"There's a seven-twenty flight," he called, the receiver tucked under his chin. "Is that all right?" Snapped from preoccupation, she nodded. He murmured something else into the phone, then hung up and turned back to her. "We're all set."

"You'll be with me?"

"If you don't mind."

How could she mind, when, for some inexplicable reason, this man seemed the brightest spot on her horizon? "Of course not," she murmured as she recalled how he eased her sense of aloneness. She'd need that tomorrow. . . . Today. It was well after one-thirty in the morning.

As though hearing her thoughts, Jim glanced down at his watch, a wide band of leather and gold cutting across the lean cord of his wrist. "We should leave here by six. How about if I give you a wake-up call at five-fifteen?"

She had her own alarm clock, but she didn't say so. She also knew that the hotel could as easily give her a call. "That's fine," she murmured, hoping that the longing she felt inside wasn't as visible on the surface. For better than four years, she'd held that longing at bay. Why had it returned now?

After what seemed endless minutes looking at one another, Jim drew her gently from her chair and, wrapping his arm around her waist much as he'd done at their introduction that evening, walked with her to the door. There he turned, put both hands on her shoulders and gazed into eyes that were, to his wonderment, rich as chocolate and brimming with soul.

"Our day will come, Rachel," he whispered raggedly. Both hands rose to frame her face. Leaning slowly forward, he put his lips to her brow.

Rachel closed her eyes to savor his touch. Its tenderness was exquisite, its underlying strength enticing. Standing before her, his sinewed body barely touching hers, Jim seemed able to evoke a warmth in her, a special heat that could radiate from the most feminine center of her being. Hearing the faint unevenness of his breath, sensing the ghost of a tremor in his hands, she felt precious and . . . wanted. It was almost enough to make her wonder whether this time it would work.

"Five-fifteen, then?" he asked, pulling a hair's breadth back to look into her face again.

Reluctantly, she opened her eyes. The dream had been so lovely. "Five-fifteen."

"Sleep well," he whispered, reaching for the knob and opening the door.

"Wait!" Her voice startled them both. "Where are you going? I mean, where are you staying? You've got a room? . . ."

His knowing grin sent tingles bouncing through her nervous system. "I'm on the . . ."—he paused to pull a key from his pocket and read its tag—"twenty-second floor." His thumb and forefinger gently kissed the soft lobe of her ear. "Get some sleep. I'll be fine."

She assumed that he would be fine, though she doubted that she'd get any sleep. Her mind seemed to be a three-ring circus, her thoughts jumping from act to act within a large arena of unrest. A warm bath helped some, as did listening to her favorite James Galway tape. But her greatest respite came when she removed her recorder from her bag, sat back against the headboard of the bed, closed her eyes and began, ever so softly, to play. At times like this, alone and pensive, she never knew what would come from her pipe. From time to time, she'd recognize a tune. More often, as now, the notes would simply flow freely, expressing her emotions of the moment.

Had Jim remained in the hall beyond her door, he might have heard her voice once removed, speaking of worry and longing. He might have been touched, as he'd been earlier that evening, by the depth of her expression. He might have been pushed beyond the limits of his all-too-finite control.

But he hadn't remained in the hall beyond her

door. He was on the twenty-second floor, seeking salvation in one hundred pushups and a cold shower.

three

Less than three hours after Rachel had finally fallen asleep, the phone by her bedside rang. Groggy and blissfully ignorant, she reached for it. She had to hear the deep voice at the other end repeat itself several times before reality surfaced.

"Rachel . . . are you up?" Silence. "Rachel? It's Jim. Wake up, darlin'." The endearment slipped out as the extension of a dream Jim had been having when his watch had buzzed him awake. "It's quarter past five. . . . Rachel?"

It all came back with the lurch of her stomach. "Um-hmm."

"Are you up?"

"Um-hmm."

"I'll be by for you at six. . . . Okay?"

"Um-hmm."

"See you then."

After replacing the receiver, she groped for the light. Its harshness only illuminated the facts of the day, so she switched it off again and lay back down for a moment's gathering of her wits. There was Jim . . . warm, comforting, exciting. And . . . her father.

He was ill. She was flying home to see him.

Dragging her feet from the warmth of the bed, she pushed herself to a sitting position, swept her hair back from her face with both hands and stared into the darkness. Then, with the conviction of one disciplined to face both the good and the bad, she disappeared into the bathroom.

It was six on the dot when Jim knocked at her door. A final look in the mirror told Rachel that she'd not disgrace herself in either his eyes, nor those of her father's, with her appearance. She wore a chic linen suit, whose dirndl skirt and short, puffed shoulder jacket softened the slenderness of her lines just as its pale pink hue eased the pallor of her face. Makeup had helped there, a calculated dab beneath each eye, a fine layer over all, graduated shades of blusher to emphasize her cheekbones, and lavender shadow and darker liner and mascara to play up her eyes. Her blond hair was swept back from her face, caught up from the sides and top in an enamel clasp at the crown, with the rest falling freely past her shoulders.

It was some comfort to know that she didn't look as disconcerted as she felt.

Her hand hovered over the doorknob for an instant before grasping it firmly, turning it and pulling it back. Her stomach fluttered. Her teeth sank into the softness of her lower lip as she slowly looked up. He was as handsome as he'd been in her thoughts during the brief time since she'd seen him last. Newly shaved, his skin glowed with a healthy tan. Newly shampooed, his hair glistened a vibrant mahogany. Newly showered, he smelled clean and male. And his presence gave her instant comfort.

"All set?" he asked, looking beyond to the two large suitcases by her bed.

She followed his gaze. "Ron will take those on to Indianapolis with the group." Then she crossed the room to a smaller carry-on bag that stood on the dresser and finished zipping it. "I'll take this one with me." No sooner had she slipped its strap onto her shoulder than Jim slipped it off and lifted it to his own. "But you've got yours—" she began, eyeing his now familiar duffel.

"And a broad enough shoulder for both." Sure enough, he had one strap overlapping the other, both bags hanging at his left side. "I mean," he drawled in self-mockery, "there's got to be *some* practical purpose for it."

A tremulous smile made its way to her lips. "With the way I feel right now, I may need *both* of your broad shoulders before the day is out."

"They'll be here," he said softly, holding her gaze for a briefly intense moment before forcing a scan of the room. "Have you got everything?"

Catching her breath, Rachel reached for her purse. "Uh-huh. I've checked. After so many hotel rooms, I think I can do it in my sleep."

He enveloped her small, cool hand in his far larger, warmer one and led her out the door and into the hall. "Did you? Sleep, that is?"

"Some."

"But not well." He could see her fatigue more within than without. Her eyes told so much.

"No."

At the end of the hall, he pressed the elevator button. The door slid open instantly; the elevator hadn't moved since it had carried him up. If only his trip had been one way . . .

As they began the downward glide, he glanced at Rachel. Her apprehension was obvious. "Cheer up," he said, gently massaging her shoulder. "You'll feel better after you see Tom. It's always worse imagining."

A faint frown marred the ivory perfection of her skin as she gazed up at him questioningly. Then, knowing he was right, she nodded.

They arrived at the airport in time to stop for a fast breakfast before boarding. "Is that all you'll have?" Jim asked with a dubious eye on the tea and toast that seemed paltry fare opposite his scrambled eggs, sausages and muffins.

She smiled apologetically. "I don't think I can eat. This may be pushing it."

"Flying doesn't bother you, does it?" he asked in a tone of measured nonchalance.

"I'd be in trouble if it did. We're constantly in the air flying from one concert to another. . . . No. It's not that." They both knew what it was. She scrunched up her nose and lifted a piece of toast as though it were medicine, then dropped it with the blunt reminder of her mission. ". . . Did he actually have a heart attack?"

"No. And that's good. A full-fledged attack

would have weakened him and made the surgery more risky."

"It's risky anyway."

"So is flying in an airplane. . . . Drink your tea."

Conversation was sporadic, though by no means uncomfortably so. With departure imminent, they ate quickly. At least, Jim did. Rachel spent more time with her tea than her toast, seemingly preoccupied with its pale amber hue. Content simply to look at her, he respected her need for silence. She struck him as being decidedly self-contained, and recalling the shyness that curbed her smile from time to time, he wondered whether it was the artist in her or simply the product of a childhood spent in a large house with only a father and a housekeeper. So different from his own background, so very different.

At Jim's direction, after he'd subtly located and analyzed every free pair of seats, they settled midway back in the plane, just over its wing. Eyes closed, head back against the seat, Rachel was barely aware of the takeoff, which was mercifully smooth and on time. Her thoughts were hardly as smooth, and she quickly opened her eyes to seek the reassurance of Jim's presence. Catching him off guard, she saw an unexpected tension in him.

"What's wrong?" she asked in a whisper, only then realizing how much she sought his strength.

He bounced back in the instant, gracing her with a sheepish smile and a slow-drawled, "Aw

. . . it's nothing. Nothing. I was . . . just thinking about a case I've got to tackle when I get back. It's a toughie."

"I thought you were working for Dad."

"I am."

"Then . . . you handle several cases at once?"

"Have to. It's an economic fact of life."

"Doesn't it get complicated?"

"Not really. Unless I'm on nonstop surveillance, or out of town on a case. Then, sure, it gets complicated. But most of the surveillance work is at night. And traveling doesn't account for that much of my time. So . . . there are still plenty of days to fill. Actually, it's pretty hard to work exclusively on one case. I mean, there are delays and there are delays. I can wait days for one phone call that will make or break a case. Or, I may get information on something that isn't going down for three weeks. In between, I've got to keep busy." He chuckled. "I've never been one to handle free time well."

"No?" she asked, enjoying hearing him speak. It was a diversion. His voice had the soothing quality of deep blue velvet. "What *do* you do in your free time?"

A hint of laughter remained in his eyes. "It used to be that I looked for trouble. I wasn't exactly the model child of the neighborhood."

"Where did you grow up?"

"Brooklyn."

"*Brooklyn*! But . . . I thought you were a southerner! You haven't got a Brooklyn accent."

He produced it with flair. "An accent is an accent, the frosting on the cake. New York may be in my blood, but I can easily slip it off my tongue." He did so. "It's not all that hard, actually. I'm one of those people who pick up on the subtle differences in speech. Put me with a Londoner," he clipped Britishly, "and I'll be talking the Queen's English within the hour. Put me with a Wisconsin farmer," he altered his vowels accordingly, "and I've got a midwestern twang. And you southerners," he drawled, then paused for effect, "well, you folks talk prettiest of all. Slow and lazy. Kinda romantic."

Entranced, Rachel took a breath and smiled. "Bravo. Quite a show."

"So's that."

"What?"

"Your smile. It's lovely."

It had been a long time in coming that morning. Simultaneously, both realized why. Very slowly, her natural flush began to fade. With a tired sigh, she lay her head back and turned a dulled gaze to the window.

"Ach . . . Rachel . . ."

She heard a note of sympathy in his voice, felt his hand close over hers. With her eyes glued to the distant landscape, she spoke her thoughts aloud. "You do make me forget. It's amazing, that power . . ."

"I'm glad, darlin'," he murmured in her ear. "That's as it should be." He drank in the faint floral smell on her skin as he put a gentle kiss on her cheek, then sat back to let her ponder his words.

They were far from settling. Strangely, he *did* hold a power over her, a power that could make her forget everything but him. Yes, it was unsettling. It was also, in its moment, phenomenally exciting.

As though attuned to her thoughts, Jim tightened his hand on hers. She found the touch of his flesh to be a searing balm, disturbing, comforting, ever reminding her of his presence. Even with her eyes closed now, he remained, his fingers forming a fixed net around hers, ensnaring them as he could her entire being when he looked at her just so, talked to her just so, smiled at her just so.

Hitting mild turbulence, the plane took a dip, prompting him to squeeze her hand reassuringly. Sighing, Rachel tried to make herself more comfortable in her seat. It was still early in the morning. She felt as though she'd missed an entire night somewhere along the line.

Suddenly she grew aware of an increase of the pressure on her hand, as though that reassuring squeeze had never let up. Her eyes flew open to focus on the taut lines of Jim's fingers. Puzzled, she shifted her gaze to his face, only to find that his eyes were closed, his lips tight-set and his other hand was tightly gripping the arm of his seat. About to speak, she paused. He seemed to be deep in concentration.

Momentarily forgetting his near painful grasp,

she studied his face at will. Everything about him was strong, yet there was an odd warring among his features. On the one hand there was the rigid line of his jaw, the determined set of his chin, the tiny scar on his neck just below his earlobe, on the other there was the leather-smooth softness of his skin, the lushness of his hair as it fell across his brow and the thickness of the lashes lying just above his cheekbone. He was hard and soft, and she knew instinctively that he was hard in work, and soft in loving. A wave of warmth flooded her veins at the thought.

Even now, he was a contradiction, still as though sleeping yet somehow alert. Rachel knew that, even before he opened his eyes and stared at her.

"You're . . . tense again," she whispered with a gentle smile, then grimaced. "I think that you're . . . about to crush my hand."

He looked down in surprise, then instantly eased his grip. "My God, I'm sorry. I hadn't realized." He stroked her fingers with both hands, coaxing the circulation back into them. "Better?"

"Better." She tipped her head to eye him speculatively. "More villainous thoughts?"

His grin was decidedly lopsided. "That's one word for them."

"And others?"

"Aw . . . it's not important. . . . Tell me. How long have you played the flute?"

"Since I was eight."

"You always knew you wanted to be a flutist?"

"Not really. I always loved music," she reminisced. "My father would put on the record player at night when he was working in his study. I used to sit in a corner and just listen."

He could almost picture it, a small, tow-headed child with the face of an angel, tucked quietly in a corner listening, enrapt, to the masters. "Sounds very peaceful."

"It was. To this day, music is one of the only things that can relax me when I'm tense." Sighing, she turned her head toward the window again. "Last night, even *it* didn't help all that much."

Through a broken layer of clouds, the land far below stretched for miles and miles. She glanced down at her watch.

"We're getting there," Jim said, following her thoughts. "What would you have done today, Rachel? If you weren't winging back with me? On days when there's no concert scheduled, what do you do?"

She shrugged. "Oh, relax. Sleep late. Practice. Take in a movie . . . or another concert. More likely than not"—her lips thinned in resignation—"spend a good part of the day traveling to the next stop."

"There are many who'd call it a glamorous life," Jim challenged when he sensed her hint of disenchantment.

"Rewarding, yes. Glamorous, no. When one loves music the way I do—the way all of us in the ensemble do—it's a thrilling thing to be able to play to enthusiastic crowds. As for the glamor, there's nothing glamorous about a wayfarer's existence. Not to me, at least." Her eyes shot up when the steward arrived with a breakfast tray for each of them. Though her appetite remained negligible, she knew that she needed something to combat her underlying fatigue. Orange juice was good for starters. She shook the cup and peeled back its seal. "This looks lovely," she drawled, eyeing something that vaguely resembled scrambled eggs and sausage. "Not dog food after all."

Jim, too, recalled his comment of the night before, but barely spared a glance at his tray. "Will you eat?" he challenged, half expecting a repeat of her earlier refusal.

"I think I'd better have something," she mused grimly. "Lord only knows I'll need energy."

The silence that ensued was a potent one, broken at last by his gentle inquiry. "Was your manager upset at your leaving?"

She took one sip of the juice, then another. It felt cool and refreshing. "He was worried for me, if that's what you mean. But," she amended with a knowing smirk, "that wasn't what you meant, was it?" She'd sensed Ron's jealousy of this man; she half hoped that the reverse was true as well. "No, he wasn't upset that I'd have to temporarily desert the group. Well . . . maybe a little, underneath it all. Not that I can really blame him. It's his job to see that things run smoothly. A small detour like this can jar him." Opening the plastic utensil bag, she extracted a fork. "You're not eating?"

Her tall companion cast a distasteful glance at his untouched tray. "I . . . don't think so. This is a poor imitation of my first breakfast. I think I'll pass."

"You have no idea what you're missing," she teased, taking a bite of the egg. "Mmmmmm, this is better than what I make."

"I can't believe that."

"You've never tried mine."

"True," he agreed. "But homemade *has* to have an edge on this."

"You've never tried mine."

He feigned a grimace. "That bad?"

"That bad."

"Well . . . it's not your fault."

Her gentle laugh lingered in the air. "That's a new one. How could it not be my fault, when I'm the one wielding the spatula?"

"You're a musician," he said with conviction. "And you don't exactly have a kitchen to practice in when you're on tour."

"I have my summers."

"And? . . ."

"And Mrs. Francis gave up on me the day I tried to make meatloaf. She figured that anyone who could ruin *meatloaf* should be barred from the kitchen. I'm only allowed in there on her days off. She swears she'll give those up one of these days, to save herself the heartache of wondering what she'll find when she returns. . . . I do try, mind you. And I can make some things. It's just pot luck as to whether it's edible." She paused for another bite of egg, another sip of juice. "This really isn't bad, Jim."

"Thanks. I'll pass," was his quick reply. "Mrs. Francis. She's been with you for years, hasn't she?"

"Since I was a child." A thread of sadness crept into her voice. "She's as close to a mother as I've had . . . and I still call her 'Mrs. Francis.'" It was a statement in itself.

"Your mother died when you were young?"

"I never knew her." Evasive answer that it was, she could do no better without feeling that she was perpetrating a lie. But her thoughts continued along that tangent, and she finished her breakfast in silence.

Jim watched and wondered. He sensed, from things she'd said—and perhaps wishful thinking of his own—that there was something missing from her life, and knew that, at her age, it was hardly a mother. Earlier though, she must have missed one. It puzzled him that Tom had never remarried. He seemed such a vital man, startlingly dynamic . . . for a scientist. But then, Jim saw himself as a vital man, and he'd never married at all, attributing his bachelor status to his work, to his penchant for solitude, which, in turn, he attributed to the constant human congestion of his early years. Now, though, he looked at Rachel and wondered what it might be like. . . .

His pulse skittered, then shot onward when the

bell of the overhead monitor rang. His eyes shot up in alarm to find that the seatbelt light had gone on. He touched his seatbelt buckle to reassure himself that he'd never taken it off. When the plane seemed to lose altitude momentarily before finding itself, the pilot's voice came over the speaker to place the blame soundly on turbulence. Jim muttered a quiet oath.

"I'm sorry?" Rachel asked, thinking he'd been talking to her.

He shook his head and managed to manufacture the semblance of a smile. Returning it, she put her head back against the seat. Food had helped, but she still felt drained. She glanced at her watch, then lay her head back again. She turned to look out the window, then straightened and shut her eyes.

Finally, she looked at Jim. He'd beat her to it. For that matter, he'd been watching her twisting and turning, guessing the course of her thoughts, trying to decide how best to comfort her. He knew what he *wanted* to do. . . .

"This operation," she began timidly. "Will it guarantee results?"

The steward's abrupt arrival intruded on their discussion. "You've had enough?" he asked Rachel. She nodded. "And you, sir. Not hungry?" Jim shook his head. As soon as the trays were gone, he answered Rachel's question as best he could.

"There's never a guarantee on something like that. Doctors deal with odds. You know, chances are nine out of ten that it will work, or whatever. When you speak to them, they'll explain it all to you." The plane bobbed several times before settling. Jim fell silent.

Rachel grew more melancholy by the minute. Life was strange—roses one minute, thorns the next. There *were* no guarantees, were there? Take Jim Guthrie. She'd somehow accepted him fully, yet it struck her that she knew practically nothing about him. On the surface he was a hale, hearty individual. But . . . he did look vaguely pale, now that she studied him closely. Was *he* sick? For all she knew, his strapping frame notwithstanding, he had some chronic illness himself. For all she knew, given his proven ability to mold his speech at will, he was a con man extraordinaire. For all she knew, despite his seeming dedication to her father and his cause, he had ulterior motives for his involvement with SCT. For all she knew, his conviction that her father needed an immediate operation related to his *own* wish to stall the irrigation project.

"What are you thinking?" he asked as he pondered her troubled expression.

Her gaze shot to his and she prayed it wasn't so. "I was . . ."

"Come on. The truth."

Since he asked for it, he'd get it. She desperately wanted to hear him deny it. "I was just wondering about your feelings for my father. You haven't known him very long, yet you seem to have become his confidant. Mrs. Francis said that the two of you were often holed up in the study at home. That's surprising. Dad always tried to separate work from home." She took a breath, purposely ignoring Jim's utter stillness for fear she'd lose her nerve. "It's strange that, given your closeness, Dad never mentioned you to me. It's also strange that *you* should be the one to come fetch me." Her voice wavered. "When you stop and think of it, you're in a position to get your hands on that blueprint yourself."

She regretted her forthrightness instantly. Jim's face grew dark, his eyes hard. "Is that what you think?"

"I don't know what to think."

"Well, you're wrong, darlin'," he declared, his voice rising forcefully. "Your father hired me to find out who *is* trying to get those plans. The hours we spend in that study are devoted to weeding through records and personnel files, work that can't very well be done at the SCT center, with employees all over the place." He paused only to perfect his glower. "Even if I hadn't taken an instant liking to your father, I'd have to be crazy to mess with something that could mean the end of my career, much less my freedom." His jaw was as straight and hard as she'd ever seen it. "I may be able to con a crook when its necessary, but I do have a sense of decency. Hell, if my intentions weren't upright, I can assure you that I'd never have subjected myself to this plane ride!" As though to make his point, the plane dipped again and he looked sharply forward.

Rachel saw his hurt . . . and something else. For an instant, there in his eyes before he'd looked away, she'd seen . . . fear? Suddenly things fell into place, the uneaten breakfast, and the hands white-knuckled on hers and on the armrest . . . even now it seemed he was gripping it for dear life.

She lay a comforting hand on his arm. "You're not a flier?" she asked gently.

He looked back at her, hesitated, then let out a long hiss of a breath. "Not quite."

"Oh, Jim." She couldn't help but smile as a wave of affection washed over her. "I'm sorry. I had no idea. And I didn't mean that I *believed* you were the bad guy." Her hand caressed his arm in a gesture of encouragement. "You asked me what I was thinking, so I told you. So much has happened to me in less than twelve hours. You have to admit that any rational person would have doubts."

"I suppose," he granted in a begrudging tone of voice, one that was thoroughly endearing for the sensitivity it marked.

Her heart beat quickly. "I do believe in you. You know that, don't you?"

When the plane bounced again, she felt his forearm tense. She worked her fingers over the taut muscle and then, driven by an impulse she couldn't control, she leaned up and placed a soft kiss on his cheek. "I'm sorry. For doubting you. For putting you through all this."

Their faces were close, mere inches from one another. Struck suddenly helpless, Rachel stared at him, devouring the rugged texture of his skin, the strength of his jaw, the enticing firmness of his lips. Unable to move away, she sucked in her breath. Her eyes widened, then closed when his lips touched hers.

His kiss was light, a feather-touch at first, as he sampled the sweetness that had tempted him from the start. And she couldn't resist. It was what she wanted too. When he pulled back for an instant, she met his gaze, feeling deep within herself the hunger reflected there. He brought his hand to her cheek and threaded his fingers past her ear when he lowered his head once more.

His lips were bolder this time, moving over hers in a slow, steady exploration. Rather than demanding penance for her sin of doubting him, they were warm and persuasive, speaking of the dissolution of any anger or hurt her words had caused, speaking of desire.

"This is what I've needed," he rasped, his breath sizzling her skin. Then, to her delight, he unleashed his tongue to a moist probing of every curve and corner of her mouth.

Rachel felt as though she were floating high in the clouds without benefit of a craft. The headiness of his kiss blocked all other thought from her mind. Everything was gone . . . but Jim Guthrie. Her being seemed suddenly an extension of his, its meaning defined solely by the arena of pleasure he'd created. Never before had she felt so inextricably bound to another human being; never before had her senses soared on notes of such passionate harmony.

A small cry of pleasure slipped from her throat, only to be swallowed in his as his lips took hers once more. This time his tongue delved further, circling the soft insides of her mouth, tasting the cleanness of her teeth, then slipping beyond to suck an exquisite nectar from her depths. It was from this intoxicating point that he finally dragged himself, as breathless and trembling as she.

"Oh, God," he whispered, closing his eyes and resting his cheek against her temple. "I can't believe it. . . ."

She didn't need to ask what he meant. She was as disbelieving as he. Drawing back, she raised unsteady fingers to his lips. They were beautiful, she thought, as was every one of his features. He was virile to the core, evoking her femininity in ways that made her ache for more.

"Jim . . . I . . . I . . ." She felt stunned by the force of what had happened and by the fact that, regardless of saner choices, she hadn't wanted him to stop.

"Don't speak," he whispered, then turned himself as far as his seatbelt would allow and took her into his arms. He held her tightly, her head pressed to his chest, and felt an intense satisfaction when her arms slid around him. "That's right." He hugged her all the more forcefully, running his fingers the length of her spine and back. "Oh, Rachel," he groaned, and she felt his fierce need merge with hers.

After several minutes, he loosened his grip, taking his arms from around her, touching her face and her shoulders, finally curving his fingers loosely on the sides of her neck. It was as if, with that kiss, the barrier of self-restraint had been waved aside. His only care now was dictated by his sense of propriety. They were on a crowded airplane, rather than the more private bed he wanted.

Rachel's mind raced along a similar track. As they sat facing one another, leaning sideways against their seats, she couldn't resist touching him either. One hand ran the length of his arm, the other slipped beneath to rest against his chest. She felt his heart, its galloping beat keeping time with the pulsepoint of her thumb. She savored his corded strength, his muscles flexing at her touch. And like tempting tongues of fire, she welcomed his thumbs circling ever lower, following the downward direction of the open collar of her blouse.

"Women have all the fun," he whispered, leaning closer, his expression soft to counter his hoarseness.

"How so?"

"Your hand. Look where it is." She did. Her fingertips had blindly provoked a small nub on the right side of his chest. "If I were to touch *you* there now, I'd be called a lecher by half of the passengers on this plane."

"Only half?" she gasped, tingling just where he wanted to touch.

"The women."

"And the men?"

"The men would be jealous as hell. And nearly as horny as I am."

A becoming blush crept up from her neck and she gave a soft chuckle. "You are impossible."

"Not impossible. Horny."

"So you've said." Suddenly intimidated, she lowered her gaze. She'd never been with a man as decidedly frank, as thoroughly physical, as apparently aroused as Jim Guthrie at that moment.

"Oh, darlin'." He caught her chin up tenderly. "Don't go shy on me now. There's as much passion deep down in you as there is in me. Maybe it's the one thing we have in common."

She thought of what else they had in common and grew grave. "We have my father." She shook her head in dismay. "How can I forget everything and feel so . . . carefree in your arms?"

"You're a woman, Rachel. A grown woman. With her *own* needs. Hell, you should be able to accept that. I mean, maybe the men you've known before haven't been convincing enough, but I intend to be." He thrust a hand through his hair and swore softly. "Damn, I'm not good at this." But he tried again.

"I came to Chicago looking for Tom Busek's

daughter and found a woman who happens to have him for a father. Sure, I know that you're worried about him. And I respect—and agree with—your feelings. But I won't stand back and let you suffer like the martyr *he* wants to be. Tom's a brilliant man, but he was wrong in lying there alone without telling you of his problems. He thought he was sparing you, but he didn't stop to think about how you'd feel to learn everything afterward." Hearing himself, he let the breath hiss through his teeth. He might be a fool for being so blunt, but he didn't know how else to say what was on his mind. Rachel Busek was the first person, the only person in the world, he never wanted to con.

His eyes shone with twenty-four carat richness. "If kissing me feels good, I want you to kiss me. If holding me gives you strength, you can have all you want. And if making love is the most natural thing in the world for the two of us, Tom Busek would be the last one to object." When she bit her lip and eyed him sadly, he softened his tone and lowered it to a near whisper. His hands framed her face, his eyes adored all within their bounds. "Because, sure as this plane's going to get us home, we'll be together."

Nearly as stunned by his outpouring as she'd been by his kiss, Rachel could barely breathe. It was only after long moments of silence that she was able to muster sound, speaking the first words that came to mind, using teasing as an escape from the tenterhooks on which she dangled. "Then you *are* sure this plane will get us home?"

For a minute, she wondered if Jim had heard her. His eyes were ablaze with the passion of the moment. Then, as she waited, she saw the flame flicker and shift direction, blown by the winds of gentle understanding. His smile was slow and infinitely tender.

"It'll get us home, darlin' . . . if I have to hold it up all the way."

As it happened, that wasn't necessary. By some miracle they seemed to have left the turbulence behind, though it was more than likely that neither of them noticed much of anything after that kiss. They were in a kind of pleasurable vacuum. Jim held her hand. They sat close. At one point, Rachel let her head fall to his shoulder. It seemed a perfect place to be.

Mirroring her thoughts, he put his lips to her ear. "You're good for me," he whispered.

"Oh?"

"Uh-huh." He breathed in deeply, enjoying the fragrance of her hair. "I'm relaxed. Well . . . almost."

She slid her hand up over the swell of his chest to his shoulder. "You feel . . . fine."

"Minx."

Tipping her head back, she met his lips with an ardor that frightened her. She'd never been this way with a man, not even . . . then. But Jim was a different sort, inspiring all sorts of different feelings.

"Rachel, Rachel." He dragged his mouth from hers and spoke thickly. "What am I going to do with you?"

"What's wrong?" she asked in alarm, wondering if she'd gone too far. She'd just . . . kissed him. . . .

"You've no sense of prudence, my girl." He settled her into the crook of his shoulder. "Thank God for this armrest. If it weren't there, you'd be on my lap, and *then* where would we be?"

Her tension ebbed. "Where?" she whispered.

"In big trouble," he drawled and left it at that. As it was, by the time the plane had begun its descent, he was in big trouble anyway. The frustration of being so close to Rachel without being able to salve the incredible hunger he felt for her was causing him considerable discomfort. For the first time in his life, he almost welcomed the ordeal of landing. When he sensed Rachel's corresponding anxiety, however, he realized that her ordeal would begin only after his had ended.

"Relax, darlin'," he crooned, his own fears suddenly secondary to hers. "It'll be fine."

She cast him a worried look. "I hope so. Will we . . . can I go directly to the hospital?"

"We'll do that."

"You'll come?"

"Sure." He watched as her eyes filled with tears and felt his own throat constrict. Unable to speak, he simply pulled her close and held her tightly until the plane had rolled to the terminal. When he finally released her, she'd regained her composure. Again he marveled at her self-command.

To Rachel, the deplaning seemed to take forever. Since she and Jim had carried their bags on with them, though, they were spared further wait. "My car is in the garage," Jim said. "I thought it would be easier than having to bother with a cab."

She nodded, a strange numbness setting in. She was home. Home under conditions she'd never dreamed she'd be. On shaking legs she walked beside Jim, his warm hand on her elbow reassuring her. He looked down at her from time to time, shortening his stride to accommodate hers.

"There it is." He jutted his chin toward a row of cars, then, when they had passed half of them, stopped at a silver blue Camaro. He released her hand to unlock the trunk and stow their bags. Then, slamming it shut again, he faced her. One large hand slid beneath her hair to cup her neck. "Are you all right?"

She gave a jerky nod and whispered, "I think so," but even the darkness of the garage couldn't hide her worry, and his heart ached for her.

Wordlessly he drew her to him and wrapped his arms around her. It was the closest their bodies had ever been and, even in her distracted state, Rachel couldn't deny the pleasure of their fit. She felt safe and secure, comforted as she'd never been in another person's arms. She was home. Now it was true.

Burying his face in her hair, Jim pressed her closer. He liked the way her ear fit snug against his heart, the way her arms curled tightly around his middle, the way her hips melted into his. He held her in testimony to his presence, wanting her to be assured that he'd be there when she needed him.

Intuitively he knew that there'd be no dating games, no "playing it cool," no strategic courtship between the two of them. With his fortieth birthday not far down the road, he was too old to feint and parry. And . . . he needed her too badly for that. Oh, how he needed her. With a growl of desperation, he gave her one last hug, then set her gently back.

"Come on, darlin'. Let's go." Turning, he unlocked the car, opened the door and tucked her inside, leaving his hand to linger on her shoulder for an instant before he circled to his own side. Rachel watched him slide behind the steering wheel, thinking how wonderfully understanding he'd been.

"Jim?" she asked, laying a hand on his arm when he would have turned the key in the ignition. Eyebrows lifting, he looked at her. "Thanks," she said, her voice as soft as thistledown.

"For what?"

"For . . . being here."

Unable to help himself, he leaned forward and kissed her tenderly. "I wouldn't have it any other way." He took a deep breath. "Rachel—"

When no words followed her name, she raised her own brows. "Yes?"

"I . . . uh, I have a confession to make."

His utter solemnity sent a whisper of apprehension through her. *Was* he too good to be true? "A confession?"

He nodded his head slowly, and steadily held her gaze. "My decision to fly up to Chicago . . . it wasn't entirely for your father's sake."

"No?" Her wide eyes held her uncertainty.

"No. It was for my sake as well." He wanted to touch her but kept his hands to himself. It was more important that she know everything, that he say it all before she could think it. And once he touched her . . . well, he was lost. "I saw that photograph of you on Tom's desk the very first night I met him. I've never been able to put it out of my mind. So it was in part that fascination that motivated me to come after you. But now . . ." —he turned his gaze to the blank concrete wall beyond his hood—". . . now I'm almost sorry."

"Sorry?" she gasped, and he looked quickly back to explain.

"Sorry . . . because you're so much more than your picture. Because you're so different from me, so educated and refined, so dignified. Because you're facing a hard time . . . and, damn it, I'll be taking advantage of that!" The last was muttered through gritted teeth, the next with as much vehemence, though an added touch of softness. "I'll be here, Rachel. Whenever you need me. And I'll be here sometimes when you don't.

But I can't help that, any more than I could help showing up at the concert last night and squirreling off with you afterward." He took a shuddering breath. "I just want you to know that I wish to hell we'd met under different circumstances, but that even then I'd have felt the same. So if you want to think me a louse for preying on you when you're down, I won't argue."

Rachel listened to his self-effacing monologue with astonishment, unable to believe his utter honesty. Had she indeed met Jim under different circumstances, his message might have spooked her. Now, though, her life seemed shaken, as though the realization of her father's mortality had somehow pinpointed her own. Suddenly she felt that she had little to lose by yielding to instinct and the warmth that stole through her veins. "If you're trying to scare me off, Jim Guthrie, it won't work," she said softly. "Don't forget. It's a two-way street. For all *you* know, I'll be taking advantage of your sympathies. Will you mind being used?"

A rogue of a smile heralded his answer. "Darlin', you can use me any time you want." He stuck out his hand. "Deal?"

She met it without hesitancy. "Deal." Then, sucking in a breath of his confidence, she murmured a determined, "We'd better be going."

"Sure thing." His eyes held respect and a touch of awe in that last moment looking at her before he started the car. As they left the airport behind and headed for the medical center, his thoughts gravitated toward her words. *Would* he mind being used? Contrary to the pat answer that had rolled from his tongue, he wasn't sure. Oh, he'd happily be there for her as he'd promised; nothing could change that. But . . . in the long run . . . he wanted something more from Rachel Busek. She had it in her; he knew she did. Whether it could be channeled in his direction was another story.

four

Her heart thudded as she stood at the window of the intensive care unit and stared at her father. He lay quietly in bed. His eyes were closed, his silver-thatched head turned slightly away. Large machines stood by the head of the bed, their thin wires stretching like feelers to his chest.

A soft moan came from nowhere. Rachel didn't realize that it was from her own throat until Jim put a comforting arm around her shoulder.

"He's resting, Rachel. They've kept him mildly sedated."

She didn't have to ask why. Her father had never been one to lie idle for long. "He looks so . . . out of place," she managed tightly. "Like a wounded lion." The image wasn't inapt. With the head of hair that hadn't thinned with age, the broad shoulders and imposing frame that, even in repose, spoke of subtle strength, Tom Busek maintained a certain stature.

"Why don't you go on in."

She wavered, suddenly skittish. "Oh, I don't know . . . maybe I shouldn't . . . disturb him if he's resting."

Jim disagreed firmly but gently, understanding that her fear went beyond worrying about disturbing her father. "Nonsense. He's awakened constantly by the nurses and doctors, and you're a damn sight prettier than they are," he teased. Then he grew even softer. "The sight of you would be an instant pick-me-up. Go on, darlin'. You'll make him feel better."

Still doubtful, Rachel looked up at him. His wink was accompanied by a quick dip of his head, a go-get-'em gesture that reminded her she had every right to be in that room with her father. Then, with a softer smile and a squeeze of her shoulder, he gave her a gentle nudge toward the door. "I'll be down the hall making some calls. I won't be far." Her weak smile was the only thanks she could muster. Her insides felt like jelly. "Go on, hon," Jim whispered. "It'll do him good, knowing you're here."

The door stood ajar. She slipped through without touching it. Everything was heartrendingly quiet, broken only by the faint and mercifully steady blip of the heart monitor by his side. Even her high heels made no sound on the linoleum as she approached the bed.

"Dad?" she whispered tentatively, then a hair louder. "Dad?"

Slowly, as though waking from a dream, Tom Busek turned his head on the pillow and opened his eyes. Rachel's own were wide with apprehension, and she waited uncertainly while recognition dawned in the pale face before her.

"So he did it, did he?" Tom asked, a twitch of humor at the corner of his mouth. His voice might have been quieter than usual and somewhat slowed by his medication, but his spirit had lost nothing of its fire. "Son of a gun, I could see it in his eyes. And you, young lady, look as though you're at someone's deathbed. How about a smile for your father."

She did better than that. Leaning forward, she gave him a hug. When she straightened, her smile was firmly in place, held there by a flood of relief. She hadn't been sure what she'd find, yet here was the father she'd adored all her life, patting the edge of the bed for her to sit. His present indisposition was only temporary; she knew it was. "I was so worried. When you're that far away and imagining all kinds of things . . ."

"Which is why I didn't call you myself."

"But you should have!" she chided, scolding him softly. "I mean, it only took a few hours' travel for me to get here and see for myself that you're okay. . . . How do you feel?"

"Not bad. How was the concert last night?"

Rachel knew that he was purposely changing the subject and indulged him momentarily.

Though he was calm on the surface, the faintest thickening of his accent told that he'd been shaken by something. "It was great. A very enthusiastic crowd." Her grin had a mischievous slant. "And an interesting reception . . . the most interesting part of which was the good-looking guy who rescued me just when I was about to fall asleep on my feet!"

"Jimbo. Good man."

"Jimbo?" She eyed him askance.

"That's what they call him in the trade. Jimbo." He nodded, satisfied with the very native sound of the nickname. "He's a good man, Rachel."

"So you've said. . . . But," enough pussyfooting around, "how *do* you feel?"

"About Jim?"

She frowned in frustration. If her father was trying to give her a message, it was unnecessary. She'd gotten it on her own. "About *you*. You're not lying here for the fun of it. Are you . . . in pain?"

His lips curved down. "Nah. A twinge every once in a while." He pointed to his head. His eyes seemed heavy. "The pain is up here. I gotta get back to work."

"Not until the doctors say so. And don't tell me about the project. I know it's on the homestretch." She arched a brow in backhanded accusation. ". . . I also know about the problem you're having."

Tom scowled. "Jimbo squealed."

"I'm glad *somebody* did. You've got to share your problems," she argued softly, then sharpened her gaze in pointed accusation. "Otherwise you're apt to wind up in a hospital bed with a score of wires tied into you."

"Share my problems, should I?"

"Yes," she declared.

He looked suddenly contrite. "Then . . . I got a problem."

She arched a brow. "You've got several. Which one would you like to discuss first?"

"You."

That was one she hadn't counted on. "Me? I'm no problem."

"You're twenty-nine years old and single."

"So? . . ."

"So," he mimicked her, "I think it's about time you were settled."

Somehow she knew just what he meant, but she skirted the issue with as much confidence as she could. "I *am* settled. I've got a lovely home and a wonderful career."

"What about a husband?"

"And I thought you were sedated," she muttered under her breath, then gave a good-natured scowl. "No beating around the bush for you!"

"I can't afford it," he stated unequivocally.

His words got to her. She took a minute to recompose herself. "You can afford to, Dad. You'll be around for a long time to come."

He groped for her hand and held it loosely.

"I'd like to believe that, sweetheart, but I've got to face the facts. This heart may give out on me yet. And it would make me feel better to know that you've got someone to watch over you."

Her heart ached at the lines of tension that seemed to emphasize the ashen hue of his skin. "I'm fine, Dad. I'm self-sufficient. And I've got seven terrific fellows keeping watch over me."

"It's not the same, and you know it. You should have a man who adores you. You should have his children to adore. . . . I, for one, don't know what I'd have done all these years without you."

"You might have married again."

He shook his head sadly. "No. I loved your mother too much to think of ever living with another woman." His expression grew urgent, and she wanted to tell him that he shouldn't upset himself, only she sensed it was futile. "I want *you* to know that kind of love, Rachel. And I want you to hang on to it!"

The last was said with a vehemence that terrified her. She knew that it went beyond the simple tale of the man whose true love had died giving birth to his child. There were those dreams, the alarming things he'd cried out in his sleep. She wondered for a minute if he'd sensed this day coming, if, as his body had begun to silently betray him, he'd spent more time dwelling on the past and what might have been.

"If you don't relax, Dad," she said shakily, "those machines will blow the whistle on you."

With uncharacteristic docility, he quieted instantly. "Not yet," he said. "I'm not going yet." Then his expression softened and he smiled, as though seeing her for the first time. Though his voice was weak, it was warm and loving. "It's good to see you, Rachel. It seems so long since you were home. You look wonderful. The tour's going well?"

Hearing his fatigue and, in truth needing the respite herself, she bade him lie still while she told him of the concerts Montage had played that week. His enthusiasm was as strong as ever, pleasuring her in turn. For those few minutes, they might have been back home sitting in the sunlit breakfast room on the morning after she'd returned from a leg of the tour. It was only the arrival of a nurse to check on her patient that reminded Rachel of her mission. Now that she'd seen her father and satisfied herself that he had more than a bit of life left in him, she wanted to see his doctors.

Rising from the bed, she leaned down and kissed his warm, familiar cheek. "I'm going to run now and let you rest. I'll be back soon, okay? Is there anything you need, anything I can bring from the house?"

"You can bring me a good cigar."

"Afraid not . . . Anything else?"

"Just yourself." He paused. "You're gonna talk with Balkan?"

"Uh-huh."

"And Jim. Where's he?"

She tossed her head toward the hall. "Out there making some calls. Don't worry," she quipped. "He's already informed me that he intends to cling."

"Good man, Jim Guthrie," he said for the third time.

With a good-humored "Hmmph," Rachel turned and left, waving from the hall, then heading for the bank of phones. It was down a long corridor and around a corner. En route she passed the nurses' station, with its complex row of monitors and its eagle-eyed attendant. Suppressing a chill, she addressed herself to one of the other nurses.

"I'm Rachel Busek. I've just flown in from Chicago to visit my father. I understand that Dr. Balkan is heading his case. I'd like to speak with him if I may."

The nurse, a spare woman with tired eyes, cast a passing glance at a paper Rachel couldn't see. "He's in surgery. He probably won't be free until later this afternoon."

She'd hoped for something sooner. "Will he be coming around then?"

"Certainly."

"And I might catch him?"

"If you're here." Reading the anxiety on the face before her, the nurse relented. "If not, he can give you a call. We've been hoping that a relative of Mr. Busek's would be by. There's the matter of surgery that the doctor will want to discuss with you. Is there somewhere he can reach you?"

"I'll . . . I'll be around here, I guess. I'd like to see him as soon as possible."

"Fine. I'll make a note of it."

Not knowing what else to say, Rachel thanked her and moved off toward the phones. A kind of hollowness had taken root in her stomach, and it had nothing to do with hunger. Her pace quickened as she approached the telephone bank. She desperately needed the reassurance of seeing Jim's face.

She looked expectantly into booths bearing, in order, an overweight woman, an elderly gentleman and a uniformed hospital employee before she finally found Jim in the fourth from the end. With the phone clamped between his jaw and shoulder, he was busy scribbling in a small worn notebook.

The sight of him was instantly calming . . . and exciting. Unaware of her presence, he was deep in concentration. She noted the way his dark hair fell to brush the back collar of his shirt, the way the muscles of his forearm flexed as he wrote, the way his denim-sheathed legs extended through the half-opened door, as though they'd simply refused to be folded and boxed. Then, suddenly, as though he'd physically felt her presence, he looked up at her, and she could only think of the tethered power of him.

In that instant, she was struck by the fact that a day before she hadn't known that this man existed. It astonished her that she'd been so quick to lean on him. She wasn't a leaner. Yes, she'd always been fortunate enough to have caring people around her—first her father, then Allen Cheswyk at the university, Dyson Friedrich at the conservatory, and Ron Lynch and the members of Montage. But she'd been far from helpless in those years. It had been *her* decision to seek a music degree at Duke, *her* decision to accept the New York offer to study further, *her* decision to audition for and finally join Montage. Just as, indeed, it had been *her* decision to fly home today.

Facing Jim now, though, she marveled at the way every one of her senses responded to him as though he held the key to her most private self. None of the other men in her life had done that. She felt suddenly shy.

Yet, when he kicked the door open all the way, stood and held out an arm in a silent offer of shelter, her shyness vanished. All she could think of was how wonderfully warm he made her feel.

Sensing a homecoming in it, she moved to his side. His arm circled her back and held her close, and her body molded easily to his. All the while his eyes examined her, trying to decipher her emotional state, while he listened to the voice on the other end of the phone.

"Yeah, Pat. Go on."

She couldn't hear that other voice, could only hear the rapid beat of the heart by her ear with its message that Jim was as affected by her nearness as she was by his.

"Yup . . . No. What about the license number? . . . Damn. What in the hell's Maxell waiting for?"

Though she had no idea what he was talking about, she found his vehemence exciting, his tone as pleasantly authoritative as the hand on her shoulder was supportive. The length of his body was firm and well tapered, its warmth exuding the special scent that she had quickly come to identify as his and his alone. Closing her eyes, Rachel drank it in with a long, savoring breath. Unknowingly she wrapped an arm around his lean, hard waist.

"Nah, hold on that," he instructed the faceless recipient of his call. "And Byson . . . any action?"

Tipping her head back, she met his gaze. It was golden and glowing, tickling her insides. Or was the sensation caused by his fingers tightening on her ribcage, so close below the swell of her breast.

"Okay," he went on, his voice mildly strained. His eyes never left Rachel's. "Keep on top of it. He'll make his move sooner or later. And give Henry another call. I want that ID." He paused, listening, then added a reluctant, "Yeah, I'll be in later," before he finally nodded and hung up the phone.

"Is everything all right?" Rachel asked, wondering at the agitation in his expression.

Jim still couldn't believe she was here. Without

releasing his arm, he drew her around until she was fully in his embrace. Then he lowered his head and ghost-whispered a kiss on her lips. "I'm the one who should be asking the questions," he growled, his hands lightly caressing her back as he looked down at her. Then his voice was suddenly as tender as his touch. "How did it go?"

"All right," she sighed, wishing he'd kiss her and make her forget it all. But he didn't. "You were right. The imagining was worse. But I haven't spoken with the doctor yet. He's in surgery and won't be around until later this afternoon."

"That's par for the course. Since he's the best, he's in demand. Later this afternoon? Can I take you home for a little while?" His hands continued their soothing, but it was his thighs of which she'd grown vividly aware, sinewed and strong against her own.

"Home?" She cleared her throat. "Uh . . . no. Maybe I'd better stay here. I'd like to spend some more time with Dad . . . in case he needs anything or if by chance the doctor finishes sooner. . . ."

"They'd call you at home, you know," he remarked with compassion, unknowingly echoing the nurse's offer. Somehow, though, he knew that she wouldn't budge. "Listen," he proposed in a velvet-soft voice, "Why don't we go back to see Tom for a minute. I'd like to say hello. Then we can take a walk around outside, maybe get something to eat. We won't be gone from the floor for more than a few minutes at a time. Fair?"

She smiled in appreciation. "Fair. But . . . don't you have to work?" She shot a glance at the phone. "What was that all about?" She took a breath. "It wasn't anything to do with SCT, was it?"

Jim shook his head. "Don't I wish it. Nothing seems to be happening. Nothing at all."

"But it will? . . ."

"In time."

"And this phone call?"

"Just checking up on things," he said, shifting her to his side once more and slowly starting back down the hall. "I'll have to do some work later, but I'm okay for now."

"I really feel guilty keeping you here."

"Don't be silly," he breathed against her hair. "If I didn't want to stay, I'd leave. I'm sure you're more than able to handle things on your own." He slanted her a wry grin. "Maybe that's why I want to stay."

"Why?"

"To make sure you don't *remember* how well you handle things on your own. It's nice to feel needed every once in a while."

"But you're needed every day in your work."

"It's not the same. You should know that."

She did. She understood exactly what he was saying. She also recalled almost identical words spoken by her father just a few minutes before and wondered if *she* were the one marching to the beat of a different drummer. Perhaps she had been wrong to assume that Montage could be all-fulfilling. Perhaps she had been short-sighted to suppose that a home with her father could be enough. Perhaps she, too, needed more.

"Well," she mused quietly, "I am glad you're here. And as long as you promise to tell me when you do have to work, I'll let you keep me company."

Jim's lips twitched. "You will, will you?"

"I will." She smiled, doubting whether he would have left if she'd asked, knowing that she would never have asked. It felt so good to be with him like this. She felt strangely . . . full.

Jim was wonderful with her father. She could see it from the start, from the good-humored banter they exchanged on the topic of Rachel's untimely return to the more serious discussion about the latest word on Jim's investigation. Despite Jim's disclaimer to her, Renko was indeed showing signs of tension. Something was bound to happen. Jim knew it, as did Tom.

That the two men admired one another was obvious; that Jim was as concerned about the older man's health as Rachel was, was similarly so. He kept the tone of the talk quiet, careful to make sure that nothing upset Tom. And at the moment when the patient seemed the slightest bit tired, he excused himself and Rachel, with promises to be back.

"You're very good with him," Rachel commented moments later when she and Jim stepped out into the early afternoon sunshine. The air was warm and fresh, its springtime bouquet light and welcoming. Her elbow was linked with his in a most natural way as they idly began to amble along the walkways of the university.

"It's easy to be with him. I like him."

"Is he like your folks?" she asked impulsively.

"My folks?" Jim stared pensively at the ground. "I'm not really sure. I never knew either of them as an adult. My mother died when I was sixteen, and my father . . ."

Rachel looked up at him in anticipation. He seemed very far away, very sad.

". . . My father followed her a month before I was to return from Vietnam. I had never gotten along with him when I was a kid. I was always in trouble; he was always on my back. It was only . . . only after I'd seen the suffering over there, only after I'd learned the importance of self-discipline, only after I'd won a slew of medals that I felt I could come home and seek him out." As though snapping from a trance, he inhaled sharply and met her gaze. "It was too late."

"I'm so sorry, Jim," she said and meant it. Having seen how gently he'd handled her father, she sensed how much Jim must have grown over the years. To have come home too late . . . must have been devastating for him. In some ways, it helped her understand why he'd felt she should know about her father. It also made her realize that, as a family man, Jim would hold special potential. "Do you have any brothers or sisters?"

"Oh, yes," he drawled, shifting to happier thoughts. "Five sisters and three brothers."

"You're kidding!"

"No, ma'am."

"Nine of you?" She couldn't begin to imagine it, having grown up an only child. "That's phenomenal! . . . Tell me what it was like," she pleaded, her face alive with curiosity.

Jim couldn't resist her spontaneous animation. She looked so pretty with her eyes alight and her cheeks the palest of pink. "It was . . ."—he feigned deliberation—"busy. Something going on all the time. . . . And noisy. No flutes or anything, just . . ."—his tone adopted a grandiose slur—". . . a symphony of voices. Out of tune."

She chuckled. "You're terrible."

"No. Just honest." He grew more serious, swept up once more on a current of memory. "I suppose I could rationalize and say that it was a wonderful experience in loving and sharing. But . . . it wasn't. At least, I never thought so then. I felt insignificant in the midst of such a large family, and that made me angry."

"Where were you in the nine?"

"Next to last. The youngest boy. My oldest brother was nearly sixteen when I was born, my oldest sister was fourteen. They raised me much more than my parents did. And I was too young to realize that my father was holding down two jobs simply to feed us." He shook his head in regret. "When I think of the anguish I caused my parents, I'm ashamed."

Once before he'd alluded to getting in trouble as a kid, but she'd more or less chalked it off as prank-playing. Now he'd repeated it, though, and she wondered. "What, exactly, did you do?"

"You name it. Play hooky. Steal things from the local five and dime. Hang around on the street corner harassing little old ladies who dared walk by." There was nothing boastful in his tone. Rather, he spoke with a fair margin of self-disdain. "I was suspended from school more times than I can remember. I resented any and all authority, and did anything I could to get back at my parents for ignoring me. It was a miracle that I ever graduated from high school." Sarcasm gave his mouth a hard twist. "To this day, I'm convinced that it only happened because the principal wanted me flat out. A suspension or expulsion could have led the way to my return. By graduating me, he got rid of me for good."

They'd reached a low bench banked by shrubs. Jim nodded toward it and let Rachel take a seat before he lowered himself to her side.

"Then what did you do—after graduation?"

"There wasn't much I could do . . . other than be slightly shocked when reality set in. My father informed me that I'd have to begin supporting myself. I went looking for jobs. Let me tell you, there wasn't a hell of a lot for a near high-school dropout. At least, not much I cared to do. That was when I enlisted. It was the best thing I could have done."

"The army settled you down?"

"The Marine Corps, and, yes, you could say it settled me down," he offered in understatement, with more than a hint of sarcasm in his tone. "But"—he waved it aside—"you don't really want to hear about that. Everyone's got his war stories. One's as gruesome as the next. Suffice it to say that I grew up real fast."

"And when you got out?"

"I took advantage of the GI Bill and went to college." A moment's sadness returned to his amber-eyed gaze. "It would have pleased my father."

"But that's not why you did it," she stated softly.

"No. I did it because I wanted to make something out of myself. Because I didn't want to go through life saying, 'Yes, sah!' to someone I could barely respect. Because, I guess, for all my resistance, my parents' values had seeped in. Neither of them was terribly educated. They had wanted more for their children."

"The others—your brothers and sisters—how have they done?"

"Not bad. We've got one banker, one lawyer, one veterinarian, two nurses, two full-time mothers . . ." He seemed to hesitate.

Rachel had counted to seven. "And? . . ."

". . . And a convict."

"A *convict?*"

"Sadly, yes. I guess I got all that stuff out of my system before I could do any real harm to anyone. My next-up brother wasn't so lucky."

"What did he do?" Rachel asked breathlessly.

"He attempted to bribe a public official."

"Oh, no."

"Oh, yes. He was working in Utah as an insurance salesman and was one of four agents making competing proposals for state workers' coverage. When he got worried that the contract was going to go to one of the other agents, he made the mistake of suggesting to the official he'd been working with that a kickback might easily be arranged . . . and, well, that was when the dam burst. Not only did the official turn him in, but it was discovered that he'd been skimming from policies for several years."

"But *why*?" In her mind, it took either dire need, real stupidity or a warped sense of ethics to commit such a premeditated act.

"In part he wanted the money. He wanted to send the kids to private school and take them on vacations and buy a second home in the mountains."

"And the other part?"

"The other part, I guess, had to do with his own sense of insecurity. With roots such as ours, there's a tendency to constantly struggle against that lower-class self-image. Drake took the struggle to the extreme in his need to be successful. Unfortunately, he blew everything."

"My God, Jim. It must have been awful."

"For his wife and three kids, it still is. We've all been chipping in to help them out, but there's the disgrace that those kids have to live with. My heart goes out for them."

He grew silent then, and Rachel watched him withdraw into himself. Recalling an earlier discussion when he'd anxiously sought her opinion of the physical as opposed to the cerebral man, she imagined that he might somehow identify with his brother's struggle.

"Did it bother you to tell me that?" she asked softly.

Startled by her bluntness, he swung his head sharply her way. It took him a split second to remember that this was Rachel Busek by his side, Rachel Busek, a fine blend of sophistication and innocence. Softening his gaze, he forced himself to relax.

"Some," he admitted truthfully. "I'd rather have been able to tell you that my brother was a Rhodes scholar on his way to a Nobel Prize in physics."

"Did you think I'd care either way?"

He shrugged. "Some women would. I mean, it's not as if I'm a Rhodes scholar either, and they sure as hell don't give Nobel Prizes in my field."

"Rhodes scholars can be very boring, and, take my word for it, Sweden is overrated. But . . . you've really gotten off track. I haven't figured out how you finally became an investigator."

Jim eyed her with something akin to wonder. It really *hadn't* bothered her, what he'd told her about his brother. He rarely told anyone that story. Even now it surprised him that he'd let it spill here, though there was something about her that definitely inspired confidence. He suspected that it had to do with the aura of innocence that surrounded her . . . or the cloak of honesty she wore.

She was a gem, a gem with eyes the color of mahogany, hair of a flaxen hue, the features of an angel and a heart of gold. Momentarily mesmerized, he reached out to touch her lips. She held her breath, letting the delight of the moment have its way. It was only the chime of the nearby cathedral bells that broke their spell of silence.

"Hey, we'd better be heading back," he said as he took her hand in his and drew her to her feet. Talk of his career could easily wait. "Let's go check at the nurse's station, then if Balkan's still in surgery, we can go down for something to eat. If you'd like, I can bring something up from the cafeteria. That way you can spend more time with Tom."

They started walking slowly. "No," she mused, "I'll come down with you. Dad's a trooper and he'll do his best to let me think he's feeling great by carrying on a steady stream of conversation while I'm in the room. But he needs to rest. As long as he knows I'm here, I feel better," she reasoned.

Jim drew her hand through his elbow and

threaded his fingers through hers. "He loves you very much. I can see why."

Swallowing hard, Rachel looked up to meet his fathomless gaze. She wondered whether Jim had ever been in love himself, whether it was what he wanted in life. Oh, he'd spoken of a loneliness, a need for companionship, for something more than he'd had in the past. But love was something else, something far more dangerous. Her father had spent years and years pining over a love that, for whatever the reasons, had gone awry. Rachel half suspected this to be the very pain she'd avoided all these years by burying herself in her music. Or was it simply that she'd never before found a man she truly wanted to love?

Stunned by the direction of her thoughts, she tore her gaze from Jim's and sought comfort in the sights and sounds of the university. It was all so familiar, so reassuring with its sun-kissed walkways corded by shrubs and spring green trees, its birds flitting from branch to rooftop, its students walking from class to class. She recalled the time when she'd been enrolled here herself, and felt a strange melancholia descend on her. Was it a simpler time? A more carefree time? Or was it just that now she was older, with an abrupt focus on life's fragility?

One of the worst things, Rachel was later to discover, about holding vigil in a hospital was the near impossibility of escaping such thoughts. By eight o'clock that evening, when she found herself in the main lobby waiting for Jim to pick her up, she'd about had it. Sitting quietly, as it seemed she'd been doing for most of the afternoon, she thought back on those later visits with her father and that eventual meeting with the doctor.

Raymond Balkan, a tall, thin man with a sparse head of hair and wire-rimmed glasses, had assured her that while the good news was that her father was responding well to bedrest, the bad news was that bedrest wouldn't eliminate the problem. He wanted to give her father another four or five days of rest to gain his strength, then operate. It was up to her to convince Tom Busek of its importance.

She hadn't the strength to argue with her father then. It had suddenly seemed an eternity since she'd been awakened by a phone call in her Chicago hotel room. She was exhausted. When Jim had left, albeit reluctantly and only at her urging, to spend several hours attending to work, she had simply sat quietly with her father, watching the news with him but hearing nothing, responding to his conversation with a makeshift enthusiasm.

Now, with Tom resting quietly in anticipation of a good night's sleep, she wondered whether things would ever be the same.

"Heeey, darlin'!"

The familiar deep voice snapped her from her anguished daze. Raising tired eyes, she saw Jim fast approaching. The sight of him was like a shot of adrenalin.

"Uh-oh." His smile drooped. "Bad time?"

Reaching down to grasp her arms, he lifted her to her feet. His hands lingered to massage the tension out of her shoulders.

"I guess you could call it that," she murmured. "I mean, he's fine. It's just . . . this waiting. . . ." She closed her eyes as Jim drew her into the comforting circle of his arms.

"And you're beat. Damn, I knew you should have gone home sooner."

"I didn't want to go home sooner," she breathed against the smooth fabric of his shirt. His chest was a wall of living warmth beneath, its strength slowly beginning to penetrate her inner chill. "And you had things of your own to do. No, I would have stayed here anyway. But"—her voice dropped—"I'm so tired."

The soothing band around her back tightened. "Oh, darlin'. I'm sorry. Let's get you home."

He did just that, holding her hand all the way but otherwise letting her rest undisturbed, with her eyes shut and her head fallen against the back of the seat. Concerned, he glanced at her frequently. When she didn't move, he realized that she'd fallen asleep. Reluctant to disturb her, he would have driven around longer. But all night? What she needed was the quiet of her home and the comfort of her own bed.

Arriving at Pine Manor, he brought the car to a smooth stop before the front door. He slid from behind the wheel and circled to her side, opened the door as quietly as he could and gently slipped his arms, one beneath her knees, one around her back, into a cradle that easily conformed to her slender shape. Then, he strode up the front steps and pushed the doorbell.

Mrs. Francis was there instantly, nearly calling out in fright at the sight of Rachel and restrained only by Jim's soft, whispered "Shhhh. She's sleeping. It's been a long day." He strode into the spacious front hall and eyed the winding staircase. "Which room is hers?"

Mrs. Francis motioned without a word and led the way up the stairs and down a short corridor to the room she always kept with special care. The door was already open. She stood back to let Jim pass with his limp burden, then scurried ahead to pull back the pale blue and green bedspread. She watched as he lowered Rachel to a sitting position, propping her up with one strong arm while he went to work on the jacket of her suit with the other.

"Would you like me to do that, Mr. Guthrie?" she asked in a hesitant whisper, in truth taken aback by the man's lack of inhibition.

Jim was not about to let another person touch Rachel. "No, thanks, Mrs. Francis. You could warm some milk and bring it up just in case she wakes up." He raised his eyes then to scan the room, closing in on a long white dresser set that hugged the far wall. "Is there a nightgown in there?" He'd left her bag in the trunk of his car but guessed, from the paltry size of it, that she kept a full wardrobe at home.

Again without a word, Mrs. Francis went

straight to one of the drawers and extracted a soft piece of pale green silk. With its high neck and cap sleeves, it was as modest as any in the drawer. Nervously she handed it to Jim, who promptly set it behind him on the bed and returned to his task of undressing Rachel. Oddly embarrassed, Mrs. Francis disappeared.

The suit jacket landed squarely on the chair. Jim had barely begun on the buttons of her blouse when she stirred in his arms.

". . . Jim?" she whispered. Though she was still more than half asleep, his name was the only one on her mind.

"Right here, darlin'," he said, his hand shaking slightly on the bottommost button. When it was done, he carefully pushed the blouse open and off her shoulders. His voice was noticeably strained. "Just putting you to bed," he managed, then swallowed hard against the urge to touch her. Her breasts were small and high, delicately rounded and exquisite through the gossamer cloud of her bra.

She turned her face in to burrow against his neck. "I'm sorry to conk out on you like this," she whispered. Her eyes never opened.

Jim's mouth had gone positively dry. For an instant he indulged himself and slid his arms around her bare back, closing his eyes to savor the satin of her flesh. Then, feeling the tell-tale pulsing of his body, he groped for the nightgown behind and struggled one-handedly to open its neck button.

"No problem, darlin'," he rasped as he spread the opening and gently held her back to slip it over her head. With a flick of his wrist, he scooped the weight of blond hair from her neck and freed it from the bonds of the gown. Then, cradling her head beneath his chin and looking straight ahead, he released the catch of her bra and slipped it off. It was only when he knew the gown was safely lowered to her waist that he dared lay her down. Her head fell quickly to the side. She was asleep again.

Acting on an instinct of pure self-preservation, he narrowed his gaze on her feet, slipping her shoes off and dropping them to the floor before turning his attention to her skirt. Its catch was easily released, its full-cut linen easily slid over her hips. Her slip and stockings were miraculously removed and then, lowering her gown over the triangular silk of her panties, he pulled the sheet up to her waist.

Heart thudding so loudly in his chest that he feared the racket alone would wake her, he was nonetheless helpless to move. Even had his muscles not been quaking under the burden of passion's restraint, he would have stayed to study her.

She was exquisite—as airy and ephemeral as she'd seemed that first night on the stage in Chicago. That first night . . . Was it only last night? It seemed that he'd known her for years and years. He knew he wanted to.

A soft knock on the door brought a flush to

his cheeks. Mrs. Francis stood there with a timid look on her face and a glass of milk on a plate of crackers in her hand. At any other time he would have been on his feet and at the door to retrieve the snack without a second thought. This time, though, he had more than second thoughts. The woman had been unsettled enough by his determination to undress Rachel. *He* had been . . . unsettled undressing Rachel. It simply wouldn't do to shock Mrs. Francis further.

Soundlessly the older woman crossed the carpet and set the plate on the night table. Avoiding Jim's speculative gaze, she gathered up Rachel's things, hung the suit and blouse in the closet and deposited the underthings in a hamper in the bathroom. Then, addressing an ever so quiet, "Good-night," to the floor, she made her exit.

Jim watched her shut the door behind, heard the soft click of the catch when it was finally closed. And he sat still, puzzled, on the edge of the bed. He could have sworn that Mrs. Francis had been bothered when he'd undressed Rachel, yet now the housekeeper had more or less issued him an invitation to share Rachel's bed. From beneath a visor of dark brown brows, he studied the sleeping figure on the bed. Had she shared this bed with others? Was it simply *his* presence that had taken Mrs. Francis off guard?

No. Everything about Rachel spoke of a kind of innocence. She had, herself, denied the presence of a someone special in her life. And Jim somehow couldn't believe that beneath her father's roof she carried on a stream of one-night stands. That there had been men in her life in the past he had no doubt; he'd tasted the depth of passion in the one kiss they'd shared. She was nearly thirty. If only he'd found her sooner, *he* might have been the one to teach her the secrets of love. It was a beautiful thought . . . and an uncomfortable one, given the instant effect it had on his body.

But Mrs. Francis's presence moments before had served as a poignant reminder of the differences between Rachel and himself. She was a wealthy young woman, one who'd had the very best of everything along the way. He, on the other hand, had only recently reached the point of economic comfort. Did he have a right to pursue Rachel, knowing that what he had to offer would be that much more modest than what she had on her own? As many times as he could ask himself that question, what really worried him was whether he could possibly *keep* from pursuing her.

Watching her now, her golden lashes resting atop her cheekbones, her blond hair fanning the pillow, her arms so pale and graceful even in repose, he felt the same inexplicable attraction he'd felt when she'd been on that Chicago stage. There was the urge to love and protect her, an urge he'd never before felt for any woman. Where did he go from here?

As though thoughts of Chicago reminded him

of his own fatigue, he reached to switch off the light. Sliding his loafers off one at a time, he let them fall silently to the carpet. Then he rolled his shirtsleeves higher, released another button of his shirt and stretched out beside Rachel.

She wouldn't mind, he reasoned. Her double bed was certainly big enough, though he doubted she'd move an inch, so exhausted was she. He, on the other hand, would simply close his eyes and rest. Later, when he was convinced that she would sleep undisturbed through the night, he'd leave.

That was his noble plan. If only he'd been able to see it through.

five

The pale light of dawn tripped through the branches of the large oak, waking Rachel with its gentle kiss. Opening one eye in a cautious squint, she studied the sea-washed hue of the Austrian shades, trying to recall what concert she'd played last night, what city she'd awakened in today. Her groggy gaze slid to the matching silk loveseat beneath the window and she frowned. Which hotel had such elegant decor, which such divine silence?

Home . . . she was home! In a rush, it all came back to her. Chicago. Her father. Jim. Sitting bolt upright, she put her hand to her forehead. Last night . . . she could barely remember. She'd been in Jim's car, then . . . nothing.

With a bewildered twist of her head, she caught sight of the sprawled male form beside her and, startled, cried out. It was after she'd bit down on her lip that she realized Jim Guthrie was dead to the world. Or had been. Sprawled on his stomach with his face turned away, he took a long, loud drag of air, began to stretch, then stopped.

Rachel held her breath, imagining that his thoughts weren't all that different from those she'd harbored when first *she'd* opened her eyes. The muscles of his back flexed. Her eye skipped beyond to the thickness of his sleep-mussed hair, then returned to skim his entire tapering length. Neither his prone position nor his semisomnolent state could hide the latent power of his shoulders, his torso, the legs that seemed to stretch forever.

She raised a hand to her chest in an effort to still the heart that raced now not in fear, but in sheer appreciation of the six-plus feet of raw virility that had evidently spent the night on her bed beside her.

As though Jim suddenly felt the God-awful thudding she struggled to subdue, he whipped his head around and stared at her. She couldn't pinpoint his expression; before her apprehensive gaze it went from blank to disbelieving to confused, all in a matter of seconds. Then he raised one large hand to his eyes and rubbed them, before looking back up at her.

"Rachel!" he whispered at last, pushing himself up to face her. "My God, I'd only planned to close my eyes for a little while!" The light of day, growing brighter by the minute, told the story that his wristwatch confirmed. "It's nearly seven. I can't believe I slept here all night!" His eyes held hers in astonishment, then, drawn helplessly, fell to the bodice of her gown.

It was only then that Rachel realized what she was wearing . . . and what she wasn't. "When did I . . . uh, my clothes . . ." A deep flush worked its way upward from her neck. "I don't remember anything!"

But Jim did. He remembered the way she'd leaned into him when he'd slipped off her jacket and blouse, the way his hand had brushed the swell of her breast when, beneath the cover of her nightgown, he'd eased off her bra. He remembered the slimness of the hips over which he'd peeled her pantyhose and the soft silk of the legs that had been subsequently unveiled. He remembered all these things, though he didn't have to. For Rachel was before him now, even more beautiful with her hair disheveled and her eyes sandy with sleep, her lips soft and parted and her body's warm, sweet scent filling his senses.

Her question went unanswered, though Rachel had quickly surmised the facts. She must have fallen asleep in the car and been carried upstairs and put to bed by Jim. How could she be angry, when he'd been so concerned with her care? How could she be embarrassed, when one part of her wanted him to see her, to know her? She couldn't even find it in herself to feel frightened now, as, abandoning all vestige of grogginess, his eyes began to shimmer.

Rolling up on his haunches, he captured her face in his hands. "You're lovely," he murmured against her lips instants before he rediscovered them. "A vision that I keep expecting to . . . just . . . vanish." His mouth brushed hers with slow, reverent strokes. "You won't vanish on me, will you?"

His voice was nothing more than a husky ache, yet it sounded positively resonant to Rachel. "How could I possibly do that?" she whispered back, feeling the chords of something new and wonderful beginning to swell within her. She was vividly aware of the open front of his shirt, the deep vee that revealed a fine mat of soft, dark chest hair. Her fingers itched to touch him there, but she was overwhelmed by the utter intimacy of it. Rather, reaching up, she touched the sandy roughness of his jaw, timidly at first, then, liking its very masculine texture, with more confidence. "You're the detective," she teased breathlessly. "You could always find me."

He leaned sideways to plant a row of kisses from her jaw to her chin, then nourished them with the warm moisture of his tongue. Rachel shivered at the earthiness of so gentle an act. "But would you try?" Jim pursued on a note of urgency. "If I touched you and held you and made the kind of love I want to make to you, would you . . . run?"

Run? How could she run, with the languor that seemed to have struck her limbs. Her innards were another matter. She felt as though something new and wonderful was about to burst. It seemed to simmer in the depths of her being, then bubble up through her veins to every nerve end, before finally seeking outlet in the shift of her hands from his jaw to his shoulders. She shaped her palms to those sinewed swells, then ran her arms up around his neck. The movement took her forward onto her knees and brought her body flush with his.

Never in her life had she felt as high. Even the moments spent on stage with her flute seemed to pale against the sheer force of the emotion that held her now. For, while her music never failed to carry her to heights, they were heights attained only through years of study, of discipline, of self-control. What she felt now with Jim, on the other hand, was spontaneous and inherent. It was uncontrolled, unschooled and utterly instinctive. Most exciting, it was wildly primitive in nature. Run? Could she run from the sun, from the ebb and flow of the tide, from the inevitable cycle of life and death?

She shook her head, her brow against his cheek. "No, Jim. I wouldn't run from you." Then she waited, praying that he'd meant all that he'd said, that the force of his desire would guide her, would be strong enough to overcome any failings she might have. She'd sworn that she'd never try again, that nothing could induce her to tempt that awful fate again. But with Jim, she was helpless. It felt so good, so right. If she didn't try, she'd always wonder. . . .

She felt a tremor shake his body as his arms closed around her, and for a moment she knew the fright of being trapped in something that, for all her protestations, she might *not* be able to complete. Then his hands began a slow roving of her back and, as she'd known she would, she forgot all else but the glory of the moment.

Her shoulders, her spine, her hips and bottom, all came under his touch. His hands, like large sensual conductors, slid from one spot to the next, swirling her silken gown over her skin with soft deliberation.

With a tiny sigh of delight, she arched closer. Eyes closed, she gave herself fully to the sensations that this giant with the golden touch had invoked. Of their own accord, her lips sought his neck, tasting its heady morning tang in slow sips, while her hands flexed against the Oxford cloth of his shirt to gather in the firm flesh of his waist.

"Ahhhh, Rachel," he moaned. "Do you have any idea what you do to me?"

She reveled in his words, in the obvious sexual tension that coiled within his body. With Pete there had been *nothing* like this. Had she been more experienced then, she might have recognized a problem early on, before things had gotten to the point of embarrassing clumsiness. But, having spent her growing years devoted to her studies and the flute, she'd been new to the game Pete had suggested when she'd joined Montage. He'd been so good to her, taking her under his wing during those early weeks and months on tour, when everything had seemed strange and more than a little intimidating to her. His kisses had been warm and quiet, much as her life had always been before. She thought she was in love. . . . Then they tried it. And failed.

With Jim, things had been different from the start. There had been that first spark, which she'd never felt with Pete, the slow smoldering that he'd never inspired, and now this sizzling, this sense of imminent explosion, this undercurrent of suspense that seemed to surge from her body to Jim's and back. Ah, yes, she sighed, it was different. Different as Pete from Jim, cerebral from physical, night from day. And she liked it.

With a startling spurt of hunger, she sought Jim's mouth. He accommodated her lips eagerly, striving to devour her with a similarly fierce need. His mouth slanted ravenously, parting hers and consuming all that was within. Once there had been time for a slow, leisurely kiss; that time would indeed come again. For now, though, there was only a passionate tempo that raced across the bars of a stirring rhapsody. No amount of baton-rapping could have possibly slowed its momentum.

Suddenly Rachel felt the heat within her soar, and she realized that the flame emanated from the large hand that had stolen to her breast. A soft cry escaped her throat. Her head lolled back, and Jim's mouth slid down her neck. Then they were falling backward to the rumpled nest of sheets on which they'd so innocently spent the night. There was nothing innocent, though, in the hands that explored her breasts now, or in the fingers that found twin turgid buds and taunted them to even greater peaks.

She cried his name in agony as her fingers dug into the muscles of his upper arms. But he continued the torment, now with lips that nipped at her through the delicate fabric of her gown, with a tongue that rolled across her nipples and sent bolts of white-hot awareness to her deepest heart. The fire was ignited; she writhed against its heat.

Then it seemed that he was everywhere. His body, still clothed from yesterday, lay half-atop her. His mouth wolfed down her impassioned moans. His hands ran down the length of her body, then slid up under her gown to her thighs and higher. Driven by instinct alone, she arched against the hand that found her, the fingers that probed her warmest secrets while she softly moaned her pleasure.

Blind to everything but her overwhelmingly stimulated senses, she closed convulsive fingers on fistfuls of his shirt and hung on as though it were a lifeline. Moving beneath him to an instinctive rhythm, she felt his hardness against her thigh and, twisting closer, sought satisfaction from it.

Suddenly and mindlessly impatient, she knew she needed more. As though there were no time to lose, her hands found their true purpose. Emptying themselves of their burden, they worked their way between bodies to attack the remaining few buttons of his shirt. They spared only a minute to skitter over the warmth of the newly revealed flesh before lowering to his belt and fumbling with its buckle.

But her frenzy was contagious. Having worked her gown to her waist, Jim all but tore it upward, over her arms and shoulders, then off. His eyes never left hers as, propped above her on one arm whose muscles trembled in anticipation, he used his free hand to dispense with the buckle of his belt, unsnap and unzip his jeans, hook his fingers under his waistband and begin to shove. Then . . . he halted. His chest labored with each ragged breath he took.

"My God!" he whispered in wonder as, only then swerving from her gaze, his eyes took in every inch of Rachel's flesh. They grew warm on her bare shoulders, began to simmer on her breasts and her belly, then smoldered on the flaxen triangle of downy hair that marked the quintessence of her womanhood. Rachel burned beneath his gaze, aching for his possession as she had for no other man.

"Please, Jim," she whimpered. "Please . . . I need you so badly."

She knew that she wasn't the only one in need, could feel it in the tension that raged about him.

But he held off, continuing to stare at her. To her dismay, his gasps began to slacken. She gripped his arms and watched in horror as his mouth grew tight.

"Damn, I can't do this!" he growled, and she felt as though history were repeating itself. "I thought I could, but I can't."

"Jim? . . ." she cried, but he'd already sat back on his heels and reached for the nightgown he'd stripped her of in such a wonderful burst of passion moments before. "What is it?" she gasped, but her voice was muffled beneath the silken fabric. When she finally emerged and caught her breath, Jim was at work on the zipper of his jeans. It took him a minute; even her panic-stricken eyes could see that it hadn't been for want of physical capacity that he'd withdrawn. Bewildered, she watched him slip off the bed and jam his feet angrily into his loafers. Then he headed for the door, turning only when his hand was firmly on its knob.

"I'm sorry, Rachel. You do strange things to me. I . . . I don't understand it myself." Then he thrust taut fingers through the disarray of his hair. "Damn," he swore softly. "I should have known!" Turning on his heel, he left.

Frozen in place, Rachel stared dumbly at the door long after it had closed behind him. Her limbs, which moments before had been shaken by passion, now trembled for far different reasons. She drew her knees to her chest and secured them with the band of her arms, but even that defensive gesture couldn't salve the gaping void within. That, too, had been present before, but then as an ache for fulfillment. Now it was something deeper, more intense. She felt alone. For the first time since she'd first set eyes on Jim Guthrie, she felt truly alone.

It wasn't a totally new feeling, she knew, yet somehow, after having had Jim for the past day and a half, it was all the more glaring. Thirty-six hours . . . it seemed impossible that that was all it had been. Thinking back over those hours, she realized that Jim had slipped into her life with the ease of a soft leather glove. He had fit her well, had protected her from the elements. She might have actually thought he'd been custom-made for her.

What had happened, then? She didn't know. Curling into a ball on the bed, she drew the crumpled sheet to her chin and dared to think back on the fiery moments just ended. Driven by the attraction she'd felt for Jim from the start, she'd responded like an experienced woman-of-the-world . . . which she wasn't. Somewhere along the line, she must have made a mistake. She should have *known* she couldn't do it right. First with Pete, now with Jim . . . the bed was evidently a stage on which she was destined to fail.

But if she'd somehow let Jim down, he'd done no better, she argued with herself in a rush of anger. She'd wanted him, *needed* him, and he'd deserted her. Was it fair that he'd made her feel foolish for having offered herself so shamelessly?

Was it fair that he'd made her feel as inadequate as ever? Was it fair that he'd deprived her of knowing, once and for all, what she'd been missing in her lonely existence? Was it fair that he'd spoiled something that had promised to be so very, very beautiful?

Rolling restlessly to her other side, she stared out the window. The sun was bright now, the world wide awake. She felt chilled and tired and wanted nothing more than to dig a hole in the ground and bury herself. The peach orchard would be nice. Even the earthworms would be welcome company. *They* wouldn't leave her in the lurch the way Jim Guthrie had done.

Why *had* he done it? It was a question that threw her into a maelstrom of confusion which superceded both embarrassment and anger. She was sure he'd been aroused; that had been no Colt .45 she'd felt cocked against her thigh. She'd felt his tremors, had heard his gasps. Frowning, she tried to recall what he'd said when, instants before he might have possessed her, he'd withdrawn. "I can't do this," he had said. Then, "I should have known." *What had he meant*?

The force of sheer frustration brought her upright in bed. Throwing back the sheet, she sprang to her feet and headed for the bathroom. On its threshold she stopped, suddenly, as though for the first time aware of where she was, where she *wasn't* . . . and why. A sad sigh slipped through her lips as, head bowed, she sagged against the doorjamb. Dismay seeped through her like a dark and murky mist.

Not once in the time she'd been awake had she thought of what had brought her here. Her father was ill. And Jim was the sturdy pillar she'd leaned against since she'd found out.

But it wasn't the sturdy pillar to whom she'd responded earlier. It was purely and simply the man. All joking about the breadth of his shoulders aside, she'd clung to him in unequivocal passion, not despair. Beyond everything else in the world, she'd wanted him on an impulse that seemed to be the sole justification of her womanhood.

For those few moments of near ecstasy, she'd been a woman first and foremost. *That* was what she found so disconcerting now. She was a proven flutist and a devoted daughter. As for being a woman? Someone up there was trying to give her a message, she mused, raising her eyes heavenward. So, she decided, if she was lousy at love, she'd avoid it as she always had. Perhaps she'd inherited the disability. In her wild imaginings, she pictured a mother who was indeed alive, but who, other than the biological fact of Rachel's birth, had been unsuited to either marriage or motherhood. And yet, her father had fallen for this faceless woman and loved her to this day. All of which went to prove, she reasoned, that brilliant people could be fools as well. What saddened her more than anything was that she suspected her own folly had just begun. To swear off Jim Guthrie's appeal was one thing, to develop an immunity to it another entirely. If she was lucky, he'd stay away, but somehow she doubted he would.

Taking a deep breath, she straightened. All the brooding in the world wasn't going to get things done. She had to confront her father regarding the urgency of the operation and somehow convince him to let the doctor do it within the week. She had to meet with the doctor again, then hop on a plane to Indianapolis in time for the evening concert. Ron would have a car waiting. . . . Good, dependable, safe old Ron. No seductively golden gleam in *his* eye. No roguish smile, no magical hands, no inviting shoulders. And below the waist? She'd never really noticed. In a nutshell, that was that.

Accordingly, it wasn't good, dependable, safe old Ron who dominated her thoughts as she sat alone in a small restaurant on the edge of the campus shortly after noon. It was Jim.

She tried to concentrate on her father, but that loose end had been temporarily tied. After a marathon bargaining session during which she'd assured him repeatedly, if presumptuously, that Jim would be his watchdog at SCT, he had finally agreed to the operation. As a concession, she'd had to agree not to miss any of her concerts during these final three weeks of the tour. This would require an exhausting amount of travel, since she would have to come home in between gigs. But that was her worry, actually not much more than a technicality.

She had tried to concentrate on her meeting with Dr. Balkan so that she would understand his explanation of the medical procedure which was to take place four days hence; but once the decision had been made, she had had no more energy left to absorb all the information he was giving her.

Four days to go; this was already Thursday. She'd play Indianapolis tonight and tomorrow night, then St. Louis the following night, before flying home again on Sunday. Ron would make all the arrangements necessary for her altered schedule.

Her father's health was a momentarily closed book . . . which left just one tale that remained up in the air. And so, over soup and a salad and a cup of herb tea, she thought of Jim. She hadn't seen him since he'd stalked from her bedroom. Though her senses had been keyed up all morning, wondering when and where he'd appear, he'd remained nothing more than a vivid picture in her mind. Now, with little to do but pick at her salad and relax for the final few moments before taking a cab to the airport, she acknowledged that she missed his presence.

He'd made their hours together seem full; in contrast, these alone were strangely desolate. She should be furious with him. While he'd been a comfort when she'd been upset, in leaving this morning, he'd only magnified her distress. While he'd been a source of distraction from her worry, now she sought a distraction from the distraction. While he'd been warm and kind, he'd also been cruel. And stimulating. So help her, stimulating in every way.

Furious? If only she could be, instead she found herself wondering dolefully whether she'd *ever* see him again.

Suddenly the seat beside her was filled. Looking up in alarm, Rachel gasped. It was as though he'd materialized out of nowhere. Her heartbeat faltered, then raced ahead.

"Hi," he said, grinning shyly.

Helplessly, she did the same. "Hi."

"Do you . . . mind the company?" He had the grace to sound sheepish.

Her grin persisted. Beast that he was, he was a sight for sore eyes. "You're already here."

"I could go—"

"Don't."

Her soft-spoken plea held no hesitancy. In turn, Jim decided that he'd been right in coming. He'd agonized all day. Hell, he hadn't been able to get any work done anyway! "How was your morning?" he asked, but Rachel's mind was stalled elsewhere. She'd told no one where she was going, had simply wanted a few moments' rest before leaving.

"How did you find me?" The cocoa sheen of her eyes mirrored puzzlement.

"I have my ways," was his simple reply. "You

said it yourself. I'm the detective." His voice took a subtle downward shift. "I'll always find you."

She recalled the conversation well. It had taken place shortly after dawn that morning when, with their arms around one another, Jim had wondered if she'd vanish. Ironic, she mused, the turn of events. *He'd* been the one to run.

He must have caught the glint of accusation in her gaze, for he seemed to flinch almost imperceptively. But he wasn't ready to discuss what had happened, not quite sure he understood it himself, so he quickly caught himself and rephrased his original question.

"How did you make out with Tom?"

It took a bit longer for the accusation to fade from Rachel's brown-eyed gaze. But she was stubborn. And proud. *She* had nothing to be ashamed of. And she wasn't about to humble herself by begging for explanations. "The operation's scheduled for Monday morning," she stated succinctly.

Jim waited for her to elaborate. When she didn't, he prodded. "He finally agreed, then?" Rachel nodded. "No nasty arguments?"

"Oh, there were arguments. Not really nasty. He very patiently reminded me that he was the head of SCT and that it needed him right now, to which I very patiently reminded him that not only did he have a hand-picked executive board deeply involved in the company but that if he didn't have the operation soon, SCT might be without him permanently."

"Not bad . . ."

But she wasn't done. In some small way, she must have wanted to warn Jim Guthrie of her stubbornness. She'd certainly exhibited it for her father's benefit that morning. "When he continued to argue, I resorted to dirty tricks."

"Oh?" A dark brow jacked farther up his forehead. Rachel struggled to ignore its dashing appeal.

"I reminded him that since I was his only daughter and he the only parent I had, *I* needed him. I told him that he was being unfairly selfish to think only of SCT and that I didn't care a whit about whether *its* heart gave out, only his. Even if he doesn't care enough about himself, he has a responsibility to me."

The scene she'd painted was one of father and daughter closeness. A sinking feeling nagged at Jim's insides. Though there was no rational basis for it, he felt left out.

"So you let him have it between the eyes?" he teased, but his humor was shallow. Deep down he wished she'd let *him* have it between the eyes. Among other things, she had a right to be furious at him. But she was cool, damn it, very cool.

"Calmly and quietly."

"And he folded?"

"Let's just say he agreed." Folding would have implied unconditional surrender, which wasn't quite the case. She had no wish, however, to tell Jim of the concessions she'd had to make.

Jim sat back in his seat and let out a weary

sigh. His mission had been accomplished. One more smashing success to add to the Guthrie legend. But . . . he'd lost, hadn't he? Even now, she was far more interested in studying the vegetables in her salad than in studying him. Didn't she wonder why he'd run out that morning? Didn't she want to know? Not that he'd be able to explain, but at least he'd hoped that she'd be *interested*! For a while there, he'd thought . . . he'd thought . . . maybe . . . Ah, what the hell! He was a loner anyway. But, damn, if he didn't resent this . . . this hunger for her.

"So," he said with a generous sigh, "what now?"

She looked up sharply. "What do you mean?"

"I mean," he went on more gently, "where do you go from here? You are flying to Indianapolis later, aren't you?"

"Yes. My father insisted on it," she explained more defensively than she might have wished. "I'll be back for the operation though."

Jim nodded, then raised a hand to summon the waitress and order himself a cup of coffee. "Strong and black," he added, needing the boost. He felt uncharacteristically discouraged. Looking at Rachel, he thought he read similar emotion on her face, but it was quickly concealed beneath a veneer of utter composure. She took a sip of her tea, then sat back and eyed him quietly.

"Is there anything doing with Renko?" she asked evenly.

"He's booked a trip to Europe."

"Could that mean something?"

"Possibly. He's going with his wife in August. It'll be interesting to see if he inherits from a relative between now and then."

"You'll keep watching him?"

"Yes."

She nodded her appreciation, then the civil interlude gave way to silence. What had passed between them that morning took dominance over all other thought. They simply looked at one another. It seemed a battle of wills, each daring the other to look away. Rachel's endurance was a product of defiance; she wasn't about to let Jim suspect how he'd hurt her. Jim's endurance was a product of fascination; he just couldn't look away.

The seconds ticked by, but neither of them noticed it any more than they noticed the conversational hum surrounding them. It was as though each was delving into the other, seeking answers to questions that couldn't be aired. But there were no answers. Nor did their faces suddenly light up and break into smiles to signal all was understood and forgiven. Rather, after intense moments of visual communication, they seemed to reach a silent truce. Rachel read Jim's apology; he read her temporary acceptance of it. Almost simultaneously their expressions softened. By the time his coffee arrived, they were ready to speak again.

Their conversation was light and interesting, if noncommittal.

"Duke has a beautiful campus," Jim observed. "You went to school here, didn't you?" She nodded. "What was it like?"

She told him, then turned the question around to discover that the life of a student at the state university hadn't been much different. "They're both southern schools," she reasoned. "I think the pace of *everything* slows below the Mason-Dixon line. The conservatory in New York . . . that was something else."

Jim would have asked her about it had not she chosen that minute to look at her watch. "I've got to run," she said quietly. Ferreting her wallet from her purse, she withdrew enough money to cover both her lunch, Jim's coffee and a tip, then stood. Jim was on his feet beside her, silently answering the question she'd been asking herself for the past five minutes. She wasn't sure how far he'd stick with her, wasn't sure how far she wanted him to. Hitting the fresh air, she struck out in search of a cab, only to be steered toward the car Jim had parked nearby.

". . . Jim?"

"What, darlin'?" His voice, with its easily flowing endearment, did annoyingly familiar things to her. She steeled herself by pressing onward with her thoughts.

"Will you . . . keep an eye on him while I'm gone? I mean," she waffled, "I know that you'll be working on the case, but will you . . . will you watch *him* for me?" She hadn't wanted to ask it, hadn't wanted to ask *anything* of Jim. And it angered her that she should be asking this of him, rather than calling any one of that "hand-picked executive board" she'd spoken so highly of to her father. But . . . that was business. Jim was . . . strangely personal. Though she was sure that every member of the board had been in to visit her father more than once, she guessed that Tom Busek found more comfort in Jim Guthrie's face. They were similar, those two. Not only in build, but in character. Both were strong men with incredibly tender streaks in them—and both were bachelors.

"Sure, Rachel," Jim answered her. "I would have done that anyway. And . . . thanks for convincing him to have the operation. I know it's the right thing."

She didn't want his praise or his gratitude or that ensnaring tenderness of his. "Just as long as you don't steal those blueprints while he's anesthetized," she snapped facetiously.

He scowled at her, then quickened the pace. "Come on. You'll miss your plane at this rate. And I can't do much mischief while you're here, can I?"

You missed your chance, Jimbo, she thought, but stifled the words as being far too revealing. She'd done well, so far. She'd met him head on and hadn't so much as blinked. "And how would you know which flight I'm taking?" she challenged lightly.

"Same way I knew where you'd be for lunch." His eyes twinkled in self-mockery. "I'm a pro.

I've been training for this for years. I watch. I ask. I put two and two together. Since I knew that you had to be in Indianapolis in time for an eight o'clock concert, the field was narrowed to two possibilities. One phone call took care of it."

She cast him a withering glance, which, to her chagrin, bounced off a rakish grin. "And the grin? What's that for?"

"That's for you. Just . . . because."

She looked quickly away. "Just . . . because" made her definitely uneasy. There was too much she didn't understand about this man, too much hurt she still felt. He had come after her; she had to credit him with that. It might have been easier for him to hide out until she'd left. But he hadn't. Why?

Once at the airport, they sat quietly until her flight was called. Neither spoke; each was lost in thought. It was only when a mechanical voice announced that it was time to begin boarding that something happened.

Jim looked at Rachel. She looked at him. Their eyes were twin mirrors of anguish.

Rachel melted. The defenses she'd so hastily constructed that morning seemed to fall like a house of cards in the wind. All of the feelings she'd had for Jim came back—the ease of his presence, his strange familiarity, the overwhelming attraction she felt for him. More so than ever, she wished she didn't have to leave.

There was so much to be said, *really* said. . . . But it would have to wait. Her plane wouldn't.

Her tongue worked at moistening suddenly dry lips while she concentrated on controlling an unbidden tightness in her throat. Feeling she had to say something, if nothing more than a soft good-bye, she opened her mouth. But her words were dammed by Jim's forefinger, which pressed lightly while he shook his head. Then, bringing his finger back to his own lips, he entrusted it with a whispered kiss which it promptly carried to hers.

She pursed her lips for an instant, returning the kiss, and held his gaze even when he stepped back. Then, taking the strap of her bag from his out-stretched hand, she adjusted it on her shoulder and turned to the gate. She didn't look back, fearful that she might do or say something she'd later regret. It was enough that there had been the warmth of his finger with its second-hand kiss. Better to leave well enough alone.

Nothing had changed. She realized it even as she forced her legs to carry her steadily across the tarmac. There was still the memory of the morning's desolation. Perhaps given three days' time she'd be able to make better sense out of it.

Wishful thinking. That was what it had been. As the plane brought her back from St. Louis Sunday morning, Rachel was no closer to understanding either her feelings for Jim or his behavior on Thursday morning than she'd been when she'd left. And it wasn't for want of trying; she'd thought of him, it seemed, constantly.

The concerts were successes, as their advance sales had foretold. With a program that spanned light classical to easy listening, Montage seemed to have developed something of a cult following on college campuses in particular, where an evening of music performed brilliantly was a proven—and healthy—upper.

Rachel, too, found the concerts uplifting. It was when she played her flute, when she breathed life into notes that were nothing more than small black dots with tails, when she concentrated on the beauty of the sounds and the messages they carried, that she was in her element.

Yet each night she returned to her room, alone and, to her dismay, lonely. Now, as the plane made its approach to the runway, she felt more than a twinge of apprehension. She was frightened for her father, but she was frightened for herself as well. She wasn't sure why, couldn't put her finger on it exactly. But she knew that it had to do with Jim.

The plane landed smoothly, then slowed and rolled to the terminal. Tucked behind a large church group, she was one of the last to deplane. Eyes downcast, carry-on bag hanging from her shoulder, she made her way through the terminal and headed for the waiting line of cabs.

She never made it. Her peripheral vision detected the dark shadow of a man by her side instants before a steel vise seized her arm. Her senses froze.

"Don't breathe a word, miss," the deep voice ordered. "If you come with me quietly, there won't be any scene."

She doubted that she could breathe, much less say a word. One glance up at the sunglass-shrouded eyes and her insides turned over. She managed a faint "But . . ." before the already familiar voice became more gruff. It was close to her ear, well hidden from the world.

"No 'buts,' lady. You've got some answering to do."

Trembling all over, Rachel despised her weakness, but she was given little chance to wonder where she was being taken. It seemed to happen so quickly. No sooner had they turned a corner than her abductor looked quickly from right to left before squirreling her into a small utility room, where he pinned her to a wall and took his instant pleasure.

His lips were exquisitely gentle from the first, closing over hers, tasting and teasing, coaxing her response. She was helpless to resist. At least her body understood itself, even if her mind was lagging, and her mouth clung to his.

Unnoticed the weight of her bag slid down her leg to the floor, soon followed by her pocketbook. Freed from restraint, her arms found their way upward along the strong bands that circled her back, and found their niche around his neck. In the suddenness of the onslaught, she forgot all, save this gloriously potent, delightfully honest form of communication. Taken off guard, she was stripped raw, exposed and vulnerable. She gave him every answer he might have wanted.

When she could finally breathe again, her face was buried against his neck. The scent of him evoked a sense of home, much as did that of fresh mown grass on a humid morning or fresh-baked muffins on the windowsill. She stood on precarious tiptoes, and her entire body still trembled, but she had the utmost faith that she was secure.

"Jim," she gasped at last, "you're a rogue!"

His growl was muted by the soft swirl of blond silk. "Just a desperate man who was in no mood for playing pretty word games with a pretty lady."

Her fingers played in the vital locks of hair just above his collar as she tipped her head back to eye him. Reaching up with her free hand, she removed his sunglasses and let them dangle over his shoulder. She wasn't about to release him either.

"What if I'd screamed?" A mischievous smile danced across her lips. "What would you have done then?"

His eyes played golden tricks, looking so bright that they might have been love-blessed. "I think I would have kissed you quiet, out there, in front of everyone." His voice softened, his gaze dropped to her lips. "If nothing else, I'd like to think you'd have recognized my kiss."

"Anywhere." She breathed a telling admission. Then she stood quietly for a moment, refamiliarizing herself with his facial terrain. He looked healthy and hardy, if a bit tired. "You mean, it doesn't bother you to watch *other* people fly?" she teased, reminding him of his fear.

He squeezed her middle gruffly, but the resulting press of their bodies was far from punishment for either of them. "I'm the one who's supposed to be asking the questions."

"Okay . . . ask."

It was his turn to do the refamiliarizing then, as his gaze circled her face before touching each one of her features in turn. "How are you, Rachel?" His voice was suddenly less steady.

Pleased to know that she could affect him, she smiled. "I'm fine." Then her smile faded. "At least . . . I think I am."

Seeing that other world encroaching and wanting to forestall it just a little longer, Jim brought his hands up to frame her face and kissed each of the features he'd studied moments before. Then, drawing her into his embrace, he held her tightly. His cheek fit snug against the top of her head, and for a brief instant he closed his eyes and imagined himself in heaven.

"You will be," he finally murmured, then slid his arms down to hook them loosely over the small of her back. Her fingers, in turn, were laced behind his neck. Her upper body swayed away from him, giving her a clear view of his face. It held confidence and concern, an infinitely gratifying combination for Rachel.

"I hope so," she murmured. "I'd rather be coming home to any circumstances but these."

"I know. But it'll be fine. He's doing well. And he's good and strong. The doctors couldn't have asked for a better candidate."

"Well," she sighed, bringing her hands down to his chest as he released her. She let her palms savor the awareness of his strength for a final moment before severing the contact. "I guess we'd better be going."

When her chin fell, Jim tipped it up again. His eyes held the last word, a silent promise that all would be fine. Then, reaching for her bag, he hoisted it to his shoulder as she retrieved her purse.

They went directly to the hospital, where Rachel spent time with her father. If Tom Busek seemed subdued, it was understandable. In his presence, she kept up a confident front. As soon as she left his room, however, her confidence dwindled.

Jim respected her need for self-containment, and though he was there at her father's door to drive her home for a few hours before returning her for an evening visit, he kept a prudent distance. Things had gone well at the airport, far better than he'd hoped. He'd half feared that he would have had to make explanations there and then. Oh, he had them now. Three days away from Rachel had given him the time he'd needed to sort out his thoughts, to put things in perspective, to plot his future course of action. He would tell her, he'd decided. He'd be open and forthright and explain exactly *why* he'd left her bedroom in such a rush that morning. It had been despicable of him. Hell, had any woman dared take *him* that far and then renege, he would have been hard-pressed to avoid rape.

No, Rachel deserved an explanation. It was simply a question of finding the right time to talk.

By nightfall, though, she was drained. Jim drove her home, parked the car on the edge of the curved gravel drive and took her hand. "How about a walk?" he asked softly. When she nodded, he led her across the front lawn and around the house toward the peach orchard. Their steps were slow. They didn't talk. Rachel simply breathed in the warm night air and tried to relax. Jim's company helped, as did his total lack of demand. When, after more than half an hour, he turned and led her back to the house, she didn't argue. At the front door, he turned her to him and propped his hands loosely on her waist.

"You'd better go on in and try to get some sleep. Shall I pick you up at eight?" The operation was scheduled for nine.

"You don't have to—"

"Eight?"

"Jim, you've got work—"

"Or should I make it seven-thirty?"

She yielded gratefully. "Eight will be fine."

His smile was just reward for her surrender. "Good." He ran a finger along the line of her lip. "Eight o'clock, then."

Nodding, she watched him descend the walk and swing around his car. At the driver's side he stood still, waiting. Opening the front door, she stepped inside. Only then did he slide into his car and drive away.

It was long after his taillights had disappeared down the road that Rachel closed the door and headed for the stairs. "Try to get some sleep," he had said. *Try*. How apropos his words, she was to muse hours later. She couldn't seem to settle her mind any more than she could her restless body. True, she was worried about her father. But there was more. She thought of Jim—of the way he'd met her at the airport, taking her so unaware that she couldn't have resisted him, of the way he'd pulled back after that, letting her know of his presence without forcing the issue. God, but he *was* like Pete in that sense. After she and Pete had failed to make it as a couple, they'd become the closest of friends. To this day, he was like a brother to her. It had been he who, during these days in Indianapolis and St. Louis, had kept tabs on her to keep her spirits from sinking too low.

But Jim . . . a brother? She didn't want that, damn it! While with Pete it had seemed perfectly natural, indeed very right, it didn't with Jim. The physical attraction was there; she knew it was. Indeed, it was stronger now than when she'd left on Thursday. And, if the scene that morning at the airport had been any indication, Jim felt it too.

Over and over again, she asked herself what stood between them. Over and over again, she came up empty-handed. . . . And lonely. More than anything she would have liked Jim to be with her now.

But where her body continued to betray her with its haunted ache, her pride remained intact. She wouldn't beg for him.

And she didn't. He stayed with her through the wait Monday morning, sharing her tension, urging hot tea into her and an occasional bite of danish. He felt her relief when the doctor reported that all had gone well. He took her to lunch, then sat quietly in Tom's room with her until the patient was wheeled back late that afternoon. And not once did she reach for him. Not once did she betray anything other than gratitude for his presence—not until later that night.

six

It was nearly eight at night when Jim finally returned Rachel to Pine Manor. The hours of waiting had ended with Rachel's talking to a groggy Tom Busek, hearing his voice and knowing that he was on the mend. The greatest danger had been the strain of the operation itself; having survived it, his chances were good.

Only at Rachel's invitation did Jim come inside

where, in the study, he fixed them both drinks. Midway through a Scotch and water, Rachel put her head back and sighed. The next thing she knew, her glass was being lifted from listless fingers and Jim had drawn her to her feet.

"Come on, darlin'. Why don't you get up to bed," he said, an arm about her shoulder as he walked her to the foot of the stairs. "It's been a long day."

That it had, particularly given her lack of sleep the night before, and she didn't argue. Her smile held heartfelt thanks. It had been a long day for Jim as well, yet he'd stuck it out with her.

"Please stay, if you'd like. Finish your drink."

"I may," he said thoughtfully. "Actually, there are some papers I'd like to look through in the study. . . . If it's all right with you . . ."

"It's fine," she murmured, trusting him implicitly. She turned and leaning on the banister for support, she made her way to her room, where she took off the skirt and blouse that it seemed she'd put on an eon ago, took a fresh nightgown from the dresser and disappeared into the bathroom. A hot bath felt wonderful, imbuing tension-weary limbs with a decidedly pleasant languor. The thick terry towel in which she wrapped herself was no less luxurious, blotting up the worst of the water, leaving her skin feeling moist and fresh as she slipped on her gown. It was blue this time, diaphanous and dreamy, with thin straps on her shoulders and a single tie beneath her left breast to hold the fabric in place as it fell softly to the floor. She didn't bother brushing her hair, simply finger-combed its damp ends as she returned to her bedroom. Then, she padded barefoot across the carpet to the walk-in closet, took out a small black case, opened it and carefully fit together three shining silver pieces.

Never had she found a better spot for playing the flute than the window seat in her bedroom on a warm spring night. Bracing her back against its rich oak panel, she tucked her knees up, rooted her feet flat on the padded cushion, and raised the flute to her lips.

The breeze came softly through the open window, nearly as softly as her flute's first sweet sounds. Closing her eyes and resting her head back against the oak, Rachel let her mood direct her choice of song, moving from Sibelius' prayerful *Finlandia* theme to Chopin's "Minute Waltz" and then on to a Handel sonata that was light and full of hope.

Her father had done well. She felt infinitely relieved. For the first time in nearly a week of living with a cloud hanging over her head, she felt as though the future might yet hold fine things for Tom Busek.

Handel aside, she picked up the jaunty "Rondo" from a Mozart quartet, played it through, then found herself, quite without thinking, playing the more contemporary, more thoughtful "Bridge Over Troubled Waters."

What about her? What did *her* future hold? The past week had been an eye-opener in several ways.

There was the fact of mortality, for one thing. Her father wouldn't live forever. Had she been shortsighted in thinking that her life as it was now would be enough? When there came the day that she was truly alone in the world, would her flute-playing suffice?

And then . . . there was Jim.

Downstairs in the study, he stood in the dark at the window, his shirttails hanging out over his jeans, his sleeves rolled to his elbows. In his hand he held the drink he'd never finished, condensation dripping unnoticed to the thick auburn rug. Behind him on the desk were spread the papers he'd been in the midst of examining when her first sweet notes had drifted through the quiet night air.

Lord, she was beautiful—her body, her soul, the music that was an extension of her innermost heart. Had he tried to name any of the pieces she played, he would have struck out cold. But the sound—the sound and its feeling came through loud and clear. Her notes were buoyant, delightfully lighthearted. She was relieved about her father . . . and well she should be. It had been a tedious day, and she'd held up magnificently.

Rachel Busek was a strong woman. Despite the image of delicacy she conveyed, she was one hell of a fighter. She adapted . . . to her father's illness and the operation, to Jim's own rejection of her that morning in her room. She accepted

. . . and survived. He somehow imagined that she could do most anything she set her mind to.

No wonder he'd fallen in love with her. . . . It still astounded him.

Thirty-nine years a bachelor, and in one short week—no, it had happened that first night, he was sure—he'd taken a tailspin. The question was what he wanted to do about it. Rachel was an exquisite creature, different from him in so many ways. Could he ever hope that one day they might share a life?

His mood grew more melancholy with the music above. She was playing more current themes now, some that he recognized—"Bridge Over Troubled Waters," "The Sounds of Silence," and "Time in a Bottle." Jim Croce had been one of his favorites, yet it wasn't Jim Croce to whom his thoughts riveted. It was Rachel, upstairs, playing a new theme on her flute.

He heard unsureness now, and seeking. He heard loneliness and, yes, longing. Or was he simply feeling those things himself?

Suddenly he recognized "The Way We Were." He remembered the movie, and it brought back new memories of smiles and a kiss. The hauntingly beautiful "The First Time Ever I Saw Your Face" made him realize that she was playing for him.

Setting his glass down atop a pile of papers, he absently wiped his fingers on his jeans, left the study and, bidden by a force he could no longer deny, slowly headed up the stairs. On the uppermost step, he paused, haunted by the achingly sorrowful strains of "So Far Away." Without thinking them, the words seemed to materialize in his mind as, so very many times, they'd come to him on his car radio when he'd been only half listening. *You're just time away . . . holding you again . . . so many dreams . . .*

His feet took him down the hall. His hand opened the door without a sound. And then he saw her, on her window perch, silhouetted against the night, the moonlight casting its ethereal aura on her hair, her eyes, her skin, her flute. His heart seemed to squeeze tightly, then expand with a swell of love.

He didn't move, unable to do anything but watch, listen and adore her with every fiber of his being. Her flute grew softer, slower. "But you're so far away . . ." it offered its wordlessly plaintive cry, then an aching, broken, "It would be so fine to see your face at my door . . ." Suddenly, her lips trembled, her breathing faltered and her tone fell apart. With a mournful moan, she dropped her head to her knees, the flute forgotten in her lap.

Jim crossed the carpet soundlessly and sank down on the window seat before her. "Rachel," he whispered, his hands on her hair, stroking its natural softness and realizing that she was totally unadorned and more beautiful than ever. "Ah, Rachel . . ."

Even before she raised her head, she reached up to take one of his hands in hers. Holding it tightly to her neck, she lifted her eyes to his. She seemed stricken.

"It just . . . came out," she whispered, bewildered. "I was sitting here playing and then . . . there it was. I usually have some kind of control. But I didn't. Not any."

Her admission pleased him endlessly. Leaning forward, he brushed his lips against her brow. Then, so very close, he looked down at her. "It's all right, darlin'. You were playing what I was feeling. I only wish I had your way with expression."

Slowly, Rachel realized what had happened. It shouldn't have surprised her. Her flute had always been an outlet for her emotions. Yet this time, she *hadn't* directed it. Her heart had spoken without her permission, and she wasn't sure if she liked what it had said. Her grip on Jim's hand tightened, and she stiffened back against the oak panel. Instantly he sensed her withdrawal, and he ached.

"What is it, darlin'?"

"I'm frightened," she whispered soulfully.

"Of me?"

"Of *me*. Of what will happen if you walk out this time. I don't think I could bear that, Jim."

With an uncompromising reach, he drew her body forward once more. Her knees were still between them, and the muscles of her neck were taut, but she didn't pull back.

"I'm sorry for having done that to you, Rachel." His voice was deep and tormented, his sincerity unquestionable. "But things had happened so fast," he breathed, his lips working against her temple. "You'd thrown me for a loop."

"Me?"

He met her perplexed gaze. "Yes, you. I'd told you all about my lack of scruples. I'd openly declared I'd take advantage of you even when you were down. Then, when push came to shove, I couldn't do it. I just couldn't." His tone was as vehement as it had been then.

"But why?" she asked, so wrapped up in her own self-denigrating suspicions that she barely paused to listen, really listen to his words. "I was willing." She shook her head against him. "I've been trying to understand it since then, and I can't. Why, Jim? What did I do wrong?"

"*You* didn't do anything wrong! My God, Rachel! Is that what you thought?"

Tears gathered at the back of her eyes. "What else could I think? I wanted you so badly . . . and I thought you did . . . and then all of a sudden you stopped. . . ." A solitary tear trickled down her cheek. Jim bent to sip it, then framed her face with both hands and caressed her cool cheeks with his thumbs.

"I stopped," he explained, knowing that the time was finally right, "because I couldn't take you that way. Not when you were so vulnerable. Not when your guard was down." His voice was a deep caress. "I stopped because, in that one instant when I looked at you," he smiled lovingly, "when you were finally naked, so very beautiful and there for me, I realized that you meant far more to me than a fast lay." When she winced at his crudeness, he kissed her cheek. "Shhhh. Listen. That morning I felt like a bull in a china shop. When I saw you beneath me and you were so small and fine, I was scared. Scared about hurting you . . . physically *and* emotionally. But"—he put his arms around her back and drew her to him, knees and all—"I need you, Rachel. I'm still scared. Scared as hell. But, God, I need you!"

Hearing his fierce confession, Rachel felt as though the sun had come up. If it hadn't been her fault after all, maybe she still had a chance. She wanted . . . she wanted . . . oh, how she wanted to please him . . . More than anything, she wanted to be with him now. Perhaps, after all, there had been a purpose behind her failure with Pete. Now she could give to Jim what no other man had had.

"Oh, Jim," was all she could whisper through the relief that welled in her throat. Her arms went up to his neck and in an infinitely gentle move, Jim swept her to her feet in front of him. Her flute slid silently to the carpet, unnoticed.

Anchoring her between his thighs, he wrapped his arms around her waist and tipped his head up to eye her. His voice seemed to flow from his very depths. "What I wanted that night—what I want tonight—is to make love to you. Real love. Slow and easy, until neither of us can bear it any longer. Do you think . . . could you . . . trust me enough after that other time to be with me now?"

The warmth of his breath on her chin had begun to send tingling shivers through her. "I'm not sure trust has anything to do with it," she whispered in triumph. She knew it did, but there were so many other things going on inside her that trust seemed the least of it. "When you hold me, I'm . . . lost." She managed a weak chuckle. "A bull in a china shop, my foot. It's more like the sculptor with his clay. You seem to be able to mold me into something I've never been before."

"And do you like it . . . what I've molded?" he whispered.

She breathed as softly. "Yes."

"Then kiss me," he murmured against her lips. "Kiss me as if I've molded the one thing I've always wanted in life but never been able to find."

It wasn't hard, for the "as if" went two ways. Jim, himself, might have been the one thing Rachel had always wanted in life but had never been able to find. Not that she'd been looking, or consciously pining, or, for that matter, even aware of the lack . . . until now. But subconscious knowledge told her that life would never be the same without him, that he was . . . right.

It wasn't a big step to take; he was already there holding her, waiting. For a split second though, she wondered if she *could* be that one thing he'd always wanted. She was inexperienced; he was a man of the world. Her heart leapt to her throat, pounding in trepidation.

Then she felt the warmth of his hands on her back drawing her closer, and the fervor of his body reached out to her. Even beyond encouragement, it stirred in her all of those new and wondrous feelings, letting the inevitability of it all take over.

Lashes fluttering down, she tipped her head and leaned forward. Her lips touched his lightly, finding them firm but pliant, seeming willing to bend to her every wish. She feather-kissed him again, then again, held back not by shyness, but by sheer enjoyment of these initial sensations. It was dreamlike, this glancing of her mouth off his. Over and over she returned, helplessly drawn to his taste, barely realizing Jim's slow participation until his lips mirrored hers. Lightly. Parting more with each sampling. Until at last, their mouths were open wide in play, barely touching at times, but ever tempting and taunting.

It seemed perfectly natural, the feel of his tongue on her lips, adding its more moist exploration to the dizziness of the moment. Dazed, she savored its gentle flow, sighing at the delight of it, marveling at its simple pleasure. Bidden by the force of erotic curiosity, her own tongue emerged to touch his. Jim gasped, as though he'd been shocked.

"God, Rachel!" His hands worked more restlessly over the slender frame of her back. "It's so good . . . sweet. You know just what I want."

His words thrilled her as much as the sensuality of his velvet touch. Beneath his fingers she was a woman, molded from head to toe and from deep within. Perhaps she'd been wrong in thinking him a sculptor. He had to be a puppet-maker, whose skilled hands gave her life. For only at his touch did she come alive this way.

And alive she was. Every sense seemed suddenly sharpened, every nerve end receptive. It was as if her body would miss nothing of the man before her, not the muscled strength of the thighs that held her intimately, nor the leanness of the torso against which her own pressed, nor the sinewed form of the shoulders over which her arms lay in languor, nor the faint twist of Scotch on his breath.

His lips . . . those were something else. Light as ever, they seemed to take control now, lingering longer with each ghost kiss, making it real and heady and new. Her sigh of delight wafted into his mouth. Of their own volition, her arms tightened around his neck in silent urging.

"Oh, Jim . . ."

"You like that?"

"Mmmmmm. And . . . you?"

"Oh . . . yes . . ." he whispered, then took her mouth in a long, deep kiss that was infinitely gratifying and abundantly stimulating. Rachel felt tiny spots of fire ignite in forgotten corners of her body. Without realizing it, she squirmed closer, edging by instinct toward the only relief there was.

But the heat would get far worse before it got better, and worse was all the more exciting. When he ran his fingers up her spine, she trembled. When he caressed the smooth flesh of her hip, his hand swishing gently against the silken fabric of her gown, her stomach did flip-flops. And all the while his lips moved against hers in an ever-fluid interplay.

Then, suddenly his mouth was gone and he took her face between his huge palms. He was gentle, but vehement, and she could feel the thud of his heart by her breast. "Do you know what I'm going to do, Rachel?" he asked in a voice made hoarse by passion. Barely able to breathe, she shook her head. "I'm going to kiss you all over. Everywhere." She blushed, and he prodded. "You're so soft. So warm. And you taste so damned good."

Rachel could do nothing but cling to him, feeling frightened and titillated all at once. She knew that she'd let him do anything he wanted, knew she wouldn't be able to resist him. Jim was the sole occupant of her mind; she seemed created to be with him.

"Do I scare you?" he whispered, feeling the tension in her arms and wondering whether she was having second thoughts.

Her reply was as soft and forthright. "A little."

"How?"

"You've awakened all these feelings. I've never known anything so strong."

Eminently pleased, he crushed her against him. His face was buried in her neck, hers against his hair. She marveled at its thickness, at its clean scent and rich texture. Then, just as her hands began to stroke his nape, she felt his mouth at her neck. Moist kisses, one by one, pressed by ardent lips that seemed to nibble and suck, to taste just as he'd promised. A shiver passed through her, and he felt it at once.

"Cold?"

He seemed more than willing to talk, as though words were designed to draw out and enhance the beauty of lovemaking. Rachel took his lead. "No . . . excited. That feels good."

"I'm glad, darlin'," he crooned. "It feels good for me, too." His mouth moved against her pulsepoint. "Your heart's racing."

She smiled shyly. "I know. I can't seem to do anything about that."

"Nothing to do but enjoy." His lips continued their slow torment, moving from her throat to her chest, savoring the smooth warmth of her flesh in everdescending increments. Then his fingers were at the small of her back, sending darts of sensation shooting outward from that one touchpoint to the myriad of sensual receptors that seemed to have cropped up throughout her body.

Not only had she never felt anything like this, but she'd never even imagined it could be this way. Only in hindsight did she realize that anything she might have felt in a dating kiss, anything she might have thought she felt in Peter Mahoney's arms, was child's play compared to the near-overwhelming vortex of feeling in which she whirled crazily. Was it a roller coaster she was on, exhilarating and frightening in its ups and downs, gaining momentum, ever speeding to that final lunge? No, she mused. She was a tiny snowball at the top of a giant hill covered with ecstasy, gaining strength and size with each layer of excitement, moving inexorably toward the center of a huge, dark-haired, broad-shouldered oak against which she was sure to explode.

But there was nothing cold about the lips that now moved lower over the gauzy stuff that covered her breast. There was nothing cold about the skin beneath that cloth, or about the heat emanating from far beneath that. Straining forward, Rachel wondered if she'd hit that oak already and burst apart into little bits of sensation.

His name came in short wisps of breath, muffled against his hair as her hands held his head closer. She wanted more. She needed more. Yes, she did want him to kiss her all over. Her body craved it in some predestined sort of way. This gown . . . why had she put it on? . . . it was only in the way, when she wanted him to cover her instead. . . .

Jim felt her need in the instinctive arch of her body. Drawing his head back, he sought her eyes. Closed at first, they opened in question. But he smiled and cocked his head in an invitation for her kiss. She accepted it readily, momentarily as greedy as he. It was only when, breathless, they looked at one another again that Jim spread his hands around her waist and slowly, slowly inched them upward until the roundness of her small breasts fit into their vee. She gasped once.

"They're perfect," he crooned, letting his fingers explore the contour of each taut globe. "Perfect."

"They're small," she gasped, biting her lip against the sweet agony that seared her belly.

"Small and delicate and perfect. Like you."

Rachel gave a soft moan as his fingers passed over her nipples, finding them budded, stroking them to full, rigid bloom. "Jim . . ." she breathed, knowing what she wanted yet not having the courage to ask.

He seemed to know. Whether it was the clenching of her hands on the bunched muscles of his shoulders or the harsh working of her lungs or the straining of her breasts against his hands, he seemed to know what to do. Allowing several inches between their bodies, he set to work on the bow beneath her left breast. With a gentle tug it was untied. Then, sliding his fingers against her flesh, he spread the silken fabric to either side, revealing her nakedness to the moon and him.

"Oh, baby," he moaned, struck every bit as hard as he'd been the first time he'd seen her this way. Then, the sight of her had brought him to his senses. Now, her body plated silver by the moon, it inflamed him all the more. As though to assure them both that there would be no running this time, he slipped his hands inside the fabric and ran his palms from her hips to her armpits. His fingers skipped in back, over her rounded bottom, her waist and ribs, but it was his thumbs that seemed to hold the force of fire, drawing rapturous currents along the soft hollow of her hips, by her navel, along the sideswells of her breasts. When she thought she'd cry out at the torment, he gathered her into his arms, spread his thighs and pressed her snug against him. She felt the tremor that ripped through his limbs, but it was the undeniable hardness straining against her that spoke most avidly of his arousal.

"And this is really mine?" he murmured in awe. Once again, as though disbelieving, his hands explored her length, moving up and down her back, kneading her close to him.

Marveling at the bold strength of him, Rachel was awestruck by a similar thought. Was he really hers, this exquisitely virile man? Again, for a fleeting instant, she was frightened. She was a virgin, he a practiced lover. Though she'd done her share of reading and was intellectually aware of the act of lovemaking, the experience . . . ah, that could be far different.

"If . . . you want it . . ." she whispered, trembling badly.

Jim's voice was a low sizzle from the back of his throat. "I want it. I want you." Dipping forward, he touched his lips to her breast. "This . . ." he whispered, his tongue following to lightly bathe her skin before trailing a liquid path to the beckoning peak.

Rachel sucked in her breath, watching in fascination first as he touched the tip of his tongue to her nipple, then, when it strained forward for him, as he took the entire aureole in his mouth and drew on it.

She felt the pull deep inside, a tugging in her womb, and was as astonished by the sensation as she was by the sense of flow within. Lids drifting shut, she sighed, amazed to feel contentment in the midst of this passionate tumult. But contentment it was, and a sense of purpose. Not for a minute did she debate the morals of giving herself to Jim; nor did she give a second thought to the imminent loss of her virginity. These moments now, here with him, were too beautiful to possibly be wrong.

Bringing her head forward, she buried her face in his hair. Her body was a mass of tremors. "Jim? . . ." she cried at last.

"Mmmmmmm? . . ."

"I can't . . . I can't stand . . . much longer, Jim. My legs . . . feel like rubber."

When he raised his face, it was lit by a broad smile. Sweeping her into his arms, he carried her to the side of the bed, where he lowered her slowly to her feet, letting her body slide in sensual abandon down his. Looking at him barefooted and half-nude, she was struck by that distance, by the sheer height of him, by the towering span of his shoulders. Then he was bending to flip back the quilt, and a quiver of excitement lurched through her at the thought of their destination. When he stood before her again, he slipped his fingers beneath her straps. She thought she felt an unsteadiness in his touch but decided that it must have been an echo from her own body.

The gown fell to the floor in a pale azure mist. Curving an arm about her back and one behind her knees, he lifted her and placed her on the bed with care. Her blond hair spilled in riotous luxury on the pillow. He savored the sight for several long moments.

"There," he drawled softly, leaning over her with one hand by either hip. "Rubber legs remedied . . . Next problem?"

She fought her modesty for only a minute. "Your clothes," she whispered.

"Uh-huh?" He wanted to hear her say it.

Though not much more than mouthed, she did. "Take them off." When he smiled and shook his head in wonder, she misunderstood. "You won't?" she cried in dismay.

He was quick to reassure her. "Of course I will. I wasn't saying no. I'm just . . . amazed."

"Amazed?"

"Uh-huh." His amber eyes still held amazement as they traveled over her flesh. When she moved her arms to cover herself, he restrained her with a gentle hand. "No, darlin'. Don't do that. You're a rare vision, and I could watch you all day. But that I knew already. It wasn't that that amazed me."

"Then what did?" she asked urgently.

"You. Your words. A kind of freedom you have." He wound his fingers through the flaxen strands he'd admired moments before. His voice stroked her as tenderly. "I wasn't sure, Rachel. I've never known a woman like you before. I didn't know how you'd be . . . I mean, at times you seem innocent, like that first night in Chicago when you were dressed in white. You're so much more of an intellectual than I am. Yet, naked before me, you're very natural. Honest without being outright aggressive. Alluringly feminine without being passive. Just shy enough to turn me on all the more." He paused, and she could have sworn she saw a blush. But the room was too dim. It must have been her imagination. "What I'm saying," he went on, seeming more frustrated than ever, "is that I wasn't sure how you'd be in bed. But you please me, Rachel. You're so much more alive than I would have expected from a woman who's neither married nor attached." He caught himself, then growled, "Have I put my foot in far enough yet?" Even in the dark she could see the brow that arched high beneath the hair that had fallen so rakishly over his brow.

She grinned, both pleased and touched by his words. "No, Jim." Then, aware that the shimmering of her insides was as vibrant as ever, she whispered, "But you're still dressed. It's my honest opinion that those clothes will have to go."

Easing himself down with a roguish smile on his lips, he raised a hand to the center tab of his shirt. His eyes held hers, humor fast fading, as, one by one, he released the buttons and shrugged out of the cotton fabric. It fell on the floor, unnoticed by Rachel, whose attention was riveted to his chest. It was breathtakingly broad and solid. On impulse, she reached out to touch him.

His skin flamed beneath her, its texture bursting at her touch. Rising slowly to a sitting position, she set both hands to explore the wonder of his strength.

"You're very beautiful," she murmured without quite realizing that she'd spoken aloud.

Jim had returned his fists to the bed on either side of her hips, and would have seemed nonchalant had it not been for the fine shaking of his arms. He wanted to keep things slow, but the stress of constant restraint had begun to take its toll. His fists were clenched as much in confinement as support.

"I'm only so if I can pleasure you," he said in a thick voice. Taking a shuddering breath, he swooped forward to claim her lips unerringly. Like magnets meeting, the bond was instant and firm, a soulful linking that defied even Rachel's movement when she rolled to her knees. It was a kiss that fast evolved into a hungry slanting, a ravenous maelstrom of lips and teeth and tongue, accompanied by the fervid search of her hands up and around the masculine contours of his chest.

She couldn't seem to touch him enough. It was as though this was *her* proof of his presence, as though the feel of his skin was the reassurance she needed that he was there, not a dream about to fade. When her fingertips inadvertently grazed his nipples, he sucked in his breath and broke the kiss.

"Wait," he rasped, terrifying her for a split second as he set her back and left the bed. But the moonlight was her ally, illuminating his hands at work at his belt. Kicking off his shoes, he attacked the snap and zipper of his jeans, then, balancing first on one foot then the other, thrust the denim from his legs, taking his socks along in the sweep.

Rachel's breath lay suspended in her chest. Standing before her in nothing but snug-fitting white briefs which, in the moonglow, hid nothing of his fully aroused state, Jim held out his arms. She flowed into them as though coming home after the longest tour of all. Her breasts were flattened against his chest, but the pain was a pleasure not to be denied, as was the exquisite contrast of rugged tan and sleek ivory, muscle and curve.

"You're here, darlin'," he murmured, rocking her from side to side, then squeezing her with a force that threatened the well-being of her ribs. "You're here."

"Yes . . ." she gasped.

"Let me love you. . . .

"Oh, yes . . ."

His arms and hands seemed everywhere then, doing marvelously silky things to her insides. But silk began to smolder, then burst into flame, and patience became a tenuous thing at best. Backing her down to the bed, Jim was with her all the way, angling himself off only far enough to skim the briefs from his flanks before letting his body settle over hers.

For Rachel, there had never been a moment as filled with heat and expectation as was this one. Her hands were lost in the thickness of his hair, holding his head closer to her lips, her neck, her breasts. The coiling knot of need centered deep in her belly was no mystery to her, though it was a new and wondrously frustrating thing.

"Jim," she cried on the fragment of a breath he left her when his tongue retreated from the soft underside of her breast. "Please, Jim. My God . . . please . . ."

He didn't have to ask what she wanted. The abandoned writhing of her body told it all. And he didn't know how much longer his own tether would hold. But he wanted to touch her . . . there . . . and there . . .

"Jim!" Her insides were positively aching with the need for fulfillment, a need which his fingers did nothing to salve. "How can you do this to me?" she cried in agony.

"I want it to be good, so good, darlin'," was his hoarse reply. "But I'm not sure if I can wait. . . ."

With a determination verging on desperation, she dragged her hands down over his shoulders and chest. Just above his hips, she clasped lean muscle and pulled, urging him toward her in the most elemental way.

"Now . . ." she cried, ready to burst. "Do it now . . ."

At the tail end of his own control, Jim eased up her body, taking her hands in his and pinning them to the sheet on either side of her head. "Look at me," he whispered raggedly. "I want to see your face when . . ."

Through a daze of passion, Rachel looked into his eyes. There she saw the justification of their lovemaking, the reason behind the rightness of it all. She couldn't interpret, couldn't think straight, yet that look she took to her heart, unknowingly returning an identical one in her ardent upward gaze.

Then she felt a probing between her thighs. The rise and fall of her breasts grew faster with the pounding of her heart. Propped above her, Jim bent his head to kiss her. Then, recapturing the depths of her smoky brown gaze, he pressed forward.

At the very moment he felt a hint of resistance, she bit her lip. Then, fighting deeper, he paused . . . and knew. As he went suddenly very still, Rachel's eyes widened.

". . . Rachel?" Taking great gulps of air, he eased back, but she clutched his firm flesh and held him.

"Please, Jim!" she cried, barely knowing what she was saying. "Dear . . . God, not again! Not this time, when I . . . when I . . ." She couldn't say it. The words were in her heart, not yet in her mind, much less on her tongue.

There was sheer panic in her voice, stark horror in her eyes. Jim saw it all, even as he felt his own pulsing need so close to fulfillment. "It's all right, darlin'," he rasped, smoothing damp tendrils of hair gently back from her face. "I'm not going anywhere. I couldn't, even if I tried." He kissed the dampness of her temple, then gritted his teeth against the raw force of emotion. "I need you too badly. Oh, God, how I need you!"

In one magnificently powerful stroke he surged forward, then stilled to absorb Rachel's anguished moan, holding her tightly until her strangled gasps subsided. His arms never released her. His lips never strayed far. And all the while, buried deep within her, he murmured soft words of love and encouragement to make her feel warm and cherished.

She did. The pain had been a treasure in itself, signifying not simply her rite of passage into womanhood, but into Jim's arms, Jim's life, Jim's very being. With her arms wrapped tightly around his back to hold him close, she gloried in the realization that their bodies were one, coupled, mated. A thrill of excitement hastened the ebbing of her discomfort, shaking her body with an expectant quiver.

"Jim?" she murmured in his ear when still he hadn't moved. "Are you . . . is it all right?"

Arching his chest ever so slightly off her, he propped himself on his elbows. Looking down, he found that her features were soft and glowing, and the pulsing he had tried so diligently to contain burst on.

"I should be asking you that," he whispered through a smile. Muscles trembling, he leaned down to take her mouth in a short, deep kiss. "Are *you* all right?"

The broad crescent of her small, even teeth was snowy in the moonlight. "I'm fine." Her fingers worked through the damp sheen of perspiration on his back. "I'm fine. But . . . you're so still. . . ."

His amber eyes held the knowledge that she, for all the reading she'd done when she'd reached maturity, couldn't possibly have. "I'm tryin', darlin', I'm tryin'. If I'd moved at all, not only would you have been in mortal pain," he exaggerated, "but I'd have been all done way back then." Even now, he struggled to think of the recent hockey playoffs, or the upcoming heavy-weight boxing title bout, but it was useless. Rachel possessed him, body and soul. The knowledge that she'd given him her virginity was enough to make him swell all the more. "And I don't want to be done," he said more softly, lowering his head to take her lower lip between his teeth in a most erotic way while, shifting his weight to a single elbow, he ran his free hand from her throat down the moist valley between her breasts, past her navel to the harbor in which he'd finally found his mooring.

She caught in her breath, her senses tingling.

"Good?" he asked. His fingers worked slowly, massaging tenderly.

"Mmmmmmm." It was an understatement, but she couldn't think of producing more coherent words when her mind had begun to spin with her body. Jim tantalized her, then brought his hand back up over the dewy silk of her body, teasing her navel, taunting her ribs, positively tormenting her breasts with a lover's hide-and-seek until, at last, she cried out for mercy.

Only then did she feel him move within her, slowly at first and gently as he seasoned her wounded flesh, then with greater boldness as their breaths mingled more quickly. Mindful now of her novice state, he gave her whispered hints now and again. "Wrap your legs around me, darlin' . . . ahhhh, that's it," and "The rhythm . . . find it . . . there," and "That's right . . . you can touch me there. . . . Oh, God! . . ."

For Rachel, discomfort became a thing of the past. She'd begun to experience things that no innocent could have possibly read about and fully understood. There was the rush of blood through her veins, now with a molten cast. And the low, slow burning in her loins that had her arching, meeting his thrusts in an age-old reach toward fulfillment. And the exquisite sense of emotional delight, the joy of knowing that she was with the one man in the world who was her salvation. For he was, she knew. They'd been fated to meet that night in Chicago, just as they'd been fated to make love now. It was ordained. It was infinitely right.

As the slow whirlwind within her picked up speed, all thought fell aside. Her every sense centered on the tension building, building to a great mass of fire at that spot where man and woman were destined to meet. She cried out, tiny sobs of frustration escaping her throat.

"It's all . . . right, Rachel." The best Jim could produce was a grating whisper. "It's good, darlin'. . . . Let it come. . . ."

She arched then, straining against his body as though it were a pinnacle from which she was hanging. There was a moment of sublime suspension, then an explosion of exquisite sensation that rattled her body with spasm after spasm of ecstasy. Her sobs now were of astonished delight, echoed instants later by Jim's triumphant cry as his great body stiffened, then shook, before finally collapsing on her as he gasped madly.

"Rachel . . . Rachel . . ." His ragged voice held a wealth of pleasure and brought a smile to her passion-flushed features. "Oh, Rachel . . ." His arms tightened about her until she thought she would burst, then his breathing began to slowly quiet and his limbs grew rapidly languorous. "Rachel . . ." he whispered, and she wondered if he was falling asleep there and then.

A smile of sheer feminine satisfaction blessed her face as she stroked the dampness of his skin from the breadth of his back to the taut muscle of his buttocks. His weight was a delicious burden which she would have willingly carried longer, but, with a spurt of energy that took her by surprise, he hoisted himself up and rolled to her side, bringing her along to face him. His fingers explored her features one by one, as if to memorize the feel of them. Then, not satisfied with feel and suddenly frustrated by the sheen of the moonlight alone, he reached behind him, groping for the lamp.

"What are you doing?" she whispered, then closed her eyes against the light and her own innate modesty.

"I want to see you, Rachel." The voice was one of determination. "I want to look at you and know that you're really here."

"I'm here," she countered shyly, fascinated by the slow smile that lit the manly face before her.

"You are," he breathed, as though believing it only now. Leaning forward, he kissed those features he'd touched moments earlier. Then, with one arm propped beneath his head and the other hand tracing the fine line of her ear, he held her gaze. "That was something else." Leaning forward, he touched his lips ever so lightly to hers, then repeated the words against them. "Something else."

Her heart swelled, the overflow of happiness bringing tears to her eyes. "I thought so."

As she watched, his expression grew more concerned. "I'm sorry if I hurt you, Rachel. That was the last thing I ever wanted to do."

"You didn't hurt me. I mean, there's hurt . . .

and there's hurt. What I felt . . ."—her voice cracked—"just now was worth every little pang."

"Every little pang, eh?" He gave her a lopsided grin.

"Uh-hmm."

For a second longer their gazes clung, saying far more than either dared speak aloud. When she felt she would burst with it, Jim drew a fierce, shuddering breath, thrust an arm beneath her shoulders as, rolling to his back, he drew her into the niche of his arm. She lay on her side, her legs straddling a long, sinewed thigh. Her hand rested atop the flat plane of his stomach, with her ear to his chest. She felt comfortable, fulfilled and happy.

They lay quietly for a time, each simply savoring the other's presence. Far from being tired, Rachel was aware of every sensation, from the curl of dark hair by her cheek to the scent of love-warmed manskin by her nose, from the latent power of the leg between her thighs to the slow, strong sound of her lover's heart.

Lover. This added a new dimension to her life, giving her the kind of depth that she now realized had been lacking. Her lips moved against his flesh in a spontaneous kiss.

"Rachel?"

"Um-hmmm?"

"Tell me about it."

"About what?" she asked, but she knew.

He spoke slowly, carefully choosing the words to tell her that he meant no criticism, simply wanted to understand. "About what happened before . . . why you nearly panicked when you thought I wouldn't go through with it . . . why you were a virgin."

She shot an anxious glance up toward his face, then looked quickly back to study the swirling pattern of hair on his chest. After what they'd just shared, she felt that he had a right to know. Indeed, now that her confidence had been boosted by his evident enjoyment of her, she had nothing to fear.

"I never really dated much when I was younger," she began softly, her breath barely stirring those lightly matted curls. "You know, during high school and college. I was always too busy studying, practicing." With a light snort, she contradicted herself. "Actually, I suppose I could have made the time. God only knows Dad was after me enough. But there wasn't anyone who interested me. There wasn't anyone who could compete with what I had with my flute." She looked up timidly. "Does that sound perverted?"

"No. I can understand it." He paused, waiting, knowing there was far more to the story.

Snuggling back to his chest, she sighed. The very masculine scent of his skin gave her a measure of encouragement. "Well, anyway, I was happy enough. I guess I convinced myself that there were other goals in life . . . like the conservatory, and a professional career. It was only when I finally began touring with Montage that I wondered. I was nearly twenty-four. I told myself that it . . . it wasn't *normal* for a woman my age not to have . . . not to have done it." The hand that skimmed the silken span of her back was ample reassurance that she was all right. The eye she cast downward over Jim's sinewed body, knowing what he'd done, what *they'd* done, stirred her in further proof.

"Go on, darlin'," he urged, unaware of her meanderings.

She took an unsteady breath. "There was a man who had been . . . good to me." She didn't have it in her heart to reveal his name; loyalty and protectiveness were fierce things. "We grew close, and I thought, maybe this is right. Maybe this is what I've been waiting for." She paused, thinking how right *this* was, how *it* had seemed what her life had built toward.

"And? . . ."

"It wasn't. It, uh, just didn't work." She tucked her cheek lower. "After I'd debated and debated, finally deciding to . . . go to bed with him, it didn't . . . he couldn't . . ."

"He couldn't get it up?"

"God, you're blunt," she whispered.

"But that was the gist of it."

"Mmm. He kept saying that it wasn't my fault. That it was him. But I did blame myself. It was devastating. After all it finally took for me to make the decision. . . ."

He understood then why she'd come close to panicking. Not once, but *twice* he'd nearly done it, first that morning when he'd left her on her bed, then tonight, when she feared he'd do the same. His arms closed around her in a breath-taking squeeze, then slackened.

"Rachel?"

"Um-hmm?"

"Tonight . . . what did it take for you to make the decision tonight?"

Sandy brows dipped low in bemusement, she looked up at him. Stunned by the question, she didn't answer at first. "I . . . uh . . . it didn't." She glanced away, then back. "Tonight just . . . happened."

"Without any thought?" He knew what he wanted to hear and prodded with his detective's skills. The easiest road to confession, he'd learned over the years, was to insult the confessor's sense of pride.

Indeed, she looked wounded. "Of course there was thought—"

"That it was just . . . happening?"

"That it was *right*! *Inevitable*! That I could no more stop it than I could the rising of the sun!" Her voice lowered, glazed with that deeper emotion. "That I wanted it, more than anything else in the world." Her breath caught, broken, her eyes large and luminous.

Jim caught her up to him, his hands beneath her arms shifting her until she lay on top of him. His strong fingers served as corded combs to keep her hair from her face. "I wanted to hear that," he murmured, his voice a husky murmur just inches from her lips. "I needed to hear that." He lowered her head until their mouths met and he wordlessly told her how much. By the time he released her, she had no doubts. Hurt had vanished, replaced by a wondrous trembling.

"Jim? . . ." she whispered in amazement, realizing in the instant that the trembling was his as well.

"I know," he rasped, pressing her body against him in all the right, telling places. "I know," he gasped, then kissed her again.

It was right. Inevitable. Passion was at their fingertips, warm and heady. A look, a touch, in this case with the force that acted as a potent prod, emotion and need burst over them once more. If the time before had been slow and long and filled with the newness of exploration, this time was faster, harder, governed by a sense of fate, of a need so intense as to burn them from the insides out until, after paroxysms of fire and light, they collapsed on the bed, bodies enmeshed, sweat-slicked and spent.

Words came slower this time, though all the sweeter for anticipation.

"I love you," Jim breathed, unable to hold it in a second longer. The most gentle forefinger tipped her face up for his adoration. "I love you."

"And I you," Rachel whispered without hesitation.

The hesitation would come moments later.

seven

"Say it again," he commanded in a breathless whisper.

"I love you." The words had just . . . popped out. The look on her face was something to behold.

"And you mean it?" Jim asked, studying her brown-eyed incredulity.

"Oh, my." A slow smile curved her lips. "I guess I do." Amazed still, she shook her head against the hands that held it. "You have this way of taking me off guard and making the weirdest things come out. Only they're not all that weird, are they?"

This time he was the one to smile. "No, darlin'. They're not weird. I think that you're just such a disciplined person that I have to catch you with your pants down"—he had the good grace to grimace—"to get at the wonderfully spontaneous woman you are."

She feigned a pout, buying time to assimilate what he'd said, what *she'd* said. "Then the rest of the time—when my pants are *up*—I'm boring?"

"The rest of the time you are a beautiful, intelligent, warmly fascinating and caring person . . . whom I adore just as much but who does . . . intimidate me just a little."

"Intimidate? *Me*?" She thought of how the reverse was true, of how there had been something from the start in her attraction for him that had frightened her. That little inkling of fear was there now, buried in a recess of her mind.

As though to nudge it forth, Jim went on. "Yes, you. Your life is so"—he searched the ceiling for the word—"upper crust. You're such a lady. A lovely vision in white. Fragile." He held up a hand when she would have protested, and begged, "Indulge me," then went on where he'd left off. "Refined. Delicate. Ethereal." Though his voice was soft and gentle, his eyes were a golden amalgam of intensity. "I sometimes think that you'll slip right through my fingers. Or that I'll crush you trying to hold on. Or that some other guy, more cultured and highbrow, will step right in front of me and steal you away."

"That wouldn't happen—"

"Then marry me, Rachel."

His words hung in the air, suspended on threads of desperation. Rachel's eyes went wide, her heartbeat faltered.

"Will you?" he prodded.

"I don't . . . know."

"How can you not know?"

"I just don't. Things have happened so fast."

"But you say you love me."

"I *do* love you." It was the one thing of which, at that moment, she had no doubt whatsoever. This feeling of wanting to absorb and be absorbed, wanting to give and be given to, wanting to share anything and everything with Jim had to be love. But the future . . . she simply couldn't conceive of it.

"Then marry me. Marry me now. Today. Or three days from now. Whenever the law will allow."

"I . . . I can't do that. . . ."

"Why not?"

"Because I . . . there are too many things happening. . . ."

"Like what?"

"Like . . . my father. And the tour. I've still got to finish it."

"Two weeks. We can be married then."

"But there's next year . . . and the next. And your work." She grasped at anything within reach. "Weren't you the one to say that it could never work between us? That you spend most of your time in a car while I spend mine on the road? How could a marriage possibly survive under those conditions?"

"I've got no idea, damn it! But I can't let you go."

Her expression softened as she looked at him beseechingly. "No one's saying you have to, Jim. I wouldn't want it either."

"Then what you want is just an affair?" Something dark in his gaze sent a shiver through her, making her quick to deny his claim.

"An affair sounds tawdry. What I want . . . is time."

"To do what?"

She shrugged and looked down. "To . . . be together. To get used to the idea of love. Perhaps, for me, to know you in a time of my life that isn't all topsy-turvy."

It was the last which got to him. She was right. They'd known each other for less than a week, all under the pressure of Tom Busek's precarious health. It had been, and would continue to be, a trying time for Rachel. She didn't need his pinning her down. It was far better that they spend their time loving rather than arguing, he reasoned, convinced that in time she'd come around.

A magnanimous sigh broadened his chest all the more. "Okay, darlin'. You win . . . for now. If you want time, time you'll have. But it's only temporary. I won't wait too long." Then, pausing, he eyed her more speculatively. There was the barest hint, just the barest hint of humor astir at the corner of his mouth. "If I'm lucky, you'll get pregnant. Then you'll *have* to marry me."

Another shocker. Something inside Rachel crinkled electrically,then went suddenly dull. She wouldn't be pregnant. She wasn't meant to be a mother . . . any more than her own mother had been.

"I wouldn't *have* to marry you," she argued softly, "but I won't get pregnant."

"You're sure?" Still that flicker of amusement, now in his eyes. He rather liked the idea of Rachel bearing his child.

Using his chest for leverage, she pushed herself up and lowered her feet to the floor. Her back was to him, her hands on the edge of the bed flanking her hips. "I'll see someone tomorrow."

"And if it's already done?" When she glanced sharply at him, his amusement vanished. "It is a possibility, you know."

Refusing to recognize that possibility, she simply repeated herself. "I'll see someone tomorrow." Then she moved to get up.

Jim caught her wrist. "Where are you going?"

Her chin dropped to her chest. She shrugged. "I don't know. The bathroom, I guess."

Pushing himself up until he was propped against the brass of her headboard, he gently hauled her back into the circle of his arms. Despite the threads of tension holding her together, her supple lines conformed to his with that same rightness of which she'd spoken.

There was more, far more he wanted to say on the matter of children, but he knew that it wasn't the time. His own fear surfaced; he would do nothing to jeopardize what they'd found. "Stay here, darlin'." He pressed her head to his chest and began a slow massage of her back. "Just relax. You'll have all the time you want. . . . Okay?"

It was only after what seemed an agony of forever to him that he heard her whispered "Okay" and allowed himself to relax. More so even than that word, her warm nestling against him spoke that all was well. His hands worked lightly over her back, feeling her softness, hearing her sigh of repletion.

"I love you," he whispered.

"Me, too," she whispered back, her breathing even, her mind solely on the delight of being held soft and naked against the equally naked but far more rangy and rugged body of Jim Guthrie. There would be time to think of marriage and . . . babies. Some day . . .

Jim closed his eyes, thinking that nothing could be more peaceful than holding Rachel like this. Minutes later, snapping from the first clutches of sleep, he realized precisely how peaceful it was.

"Rachel? . . ." he murmured, forcing himself to speak, to think, when all he wanted to do was to burrow on and on in serene oblivion.

She was in much the same state. "Hmmmm?" The sound was little more than a faint hum against his chest.

"Should I leave?" he whispered. "I mean, a minute more and I'll be asleep. Would you rather I go?"

Her lips moved in languid protest. "No . . . no . . . stay."

"But Mrs. Francis . . . will she be too disturbed to know I've spent the night?"

"You did once before," came the drowsy reply.

"That was different." He felt a smile against his chest.

"I know."

"Rachel? . . ."

"It's all right," she pacified him sleepily. "I'm

a big girl." Then she moved innocently against him to make herself all the more comfortable. "I'm so tired. It's . . . been a . . . long . . . day." Each word was a little more distant than the one before. Looking down over the golden crown of her head, he saw that her eyes were closed, her limbs limply entwined with his. Had he not been as exhausted himself, he might have risen to the occasion. But, as she'd said, it had been a long day.

Sliding down against the headboard until his head hit the pillow on the bed, he settled Rachel snugly and pulled a sheet to cover them. There would be time aplenty to talk tomorrow.

Tuesday, however, proved to be tedious. Tied up with work, Jim wasn't able to join Rachel at the hospital until early evening. After letting a pain-doped Tom know that he'd come and that he was taking Rachel off for dinner and a good night's sleep, he led her into the hall, where he hugged her properly.

"How are you, darlin'?" He freed his lips to ask, leaving his hands to hold her body in contact with his.

"I'm tired." She smiled. "But better now . . . Dinner and a good night's sleep?"

A dark brow arched mischievously. "Only if you're feeling up to it . . ." His words trailed off suggestively.

"I'm up to it," she said softly, moving her hands ever so slowly over the smooth fabric of his shirt. He felt warm and solid, very comforting. When he shifted her to his side, they began to walk. "Dinner?"

"For starters." He looked down at her for a breath-stopping moment during which she felt his nearness as a heady stimulant. Each touch-point of their bodies—their hips, their shoulders, arms, waist—seemed suddenly ultrasensitive, honed to acute awareness by the sexual dynamism raging between them. So engrossed were they in each other that they barely saw the elderly couple who'd been walking that much more slowly until they were nearly on top of them. Just in time to avoid a collision, Jim steered Rachel to the side. Then he cleared his throat. "Dinner . . . I've got just the place in mind."

It was a restaurant midway between Durham and Raleigh. The food was good, the wine and easy conversation were the relaxants Rachel needed. At her prodding, Jim told her more about himself.

"You worked for the FBI?" she asked excitedly, duly impressed, knowing how selective the agency was.

"For only two years."

"You didn't like it?"

He twirled the stem of his wineglass, daring the amber liquid to escape. "It was too structured for me. I wanted to be nearer the action, really involved with people. Somehow working for the government like that I felt more constrained." He shrugged at the simplicity of it. "So I left."

"And opened your own agency?"

"Yup."

"Why here?"

"Why not? I'd gone to college here and was familiar with the area. My parents were both dead, my brothers and sisters spread all over the place. I had no ties to keep me in New York. Besides, the triangle area was promising." The corners of his lips twitched as he spoke in distinct Brooklyn-ese. "It needed a good private investigator."

"Oh?" She smiled at his good-natured immodesty, finding it as endearing as the rest of him.

"Oh." He echoed her, but he was serious. "So much of success is being in the right place at the right time. I was suddenly here and available."

"And the clients came . . . just like that?"

He chuckled, recalling those early days. "Not quite. It was slow at first. I walked the streets, hung around in every bar and courthouse around, made myself a very visible entity. Then I managed to pick up one or two cases, which, with a little luck, I solved. They were stinkers, sticky ones." His lips twisted into a facetious half-grin. "When you're green and just starting out, you get the ones with all the odds against you. It's like the client says, what the hell, I'm gonna lose anyway."

"But you didn't."

"No," he went on, as surprisingly modest now as he'd been immodest moments before. "And when one gets results, word spreads."

"So that's how you get most of your clients—word of mouth?"

"Among lawyers, yes. Your name gets established as the one who's winning so-and-so's cases for him, so you get other calls. The legal community, *and* the criminal community spread the word. Most of the other cases though—missing persons and domestic cases—come through an ad in the yellow pages."

She sat back in her seat. "You're kidding."

"Nope. It's not so strange, when you stop to think about it. I mean, it's not as if a guy who's hired me to track down his promiscuous wife is going to brag to the other guys at the office. And in the case of missing persons, you're often dealing with families that have never needed a lawyer, much less an investigator."

"Interesting . . . Would you let me watch you work some time?"

He shrugged, his massive shoulders effortlessly denoting equivocation. "I don't know. You'd probably be bored."

"Come on. You've heard me play, and I could have said the same to you. *Were* you bored?"

"Of course not. That was *you* playing. It was beautiful."

"So? . . ." She smiled, her point made.

But Jim wasn't ready to yield. It wasn't so much that he feared she'd be bored. Rather he thought of the often coarse talk, lewd photographs, seedy sites. Not for a minute would he expose her to that.

"We'll see," he said in dismissal. "And speaking of your playing, tell me what you've got to do in Des Moines. . . ."

As Jim had promised, dinner was followed by a good night's sleep. To Rachel's delight, he'd stashed his shaving gear and fresh clothes in his car . . . just in case. And, nestled warmly against one another, they did sleep, waking to a slow, mellow awareness of each other, a delicious dawn passion that warmed and heated, then exploded with the first rays of the sun.

Wednesday was, in its way, harder than Tuesday had been, for Rachel wanted to spend time with Tom and to speak with Ray Balkan before catching an afternoon flight to Des Moines. Jim dropped her at the medical center in the morning, then returned at one to take her to the airport. With a long, lingering kiss he put her on her plane.

" 'Til Sunday," he murmured, holding her close and tight as he studied the upturned face that just reached his shoulder. Her eyes were round and love-filled, her lips soft and waiting. He kissed them again, once more . . . for the third time.

" 'Til Sunday," she whispered, her gaze now bearing regret. She never imagined that parting could be this difficult. She felt as though she'd be torn apart the instant she walked away from Jim. When she would have told him as much, however, she caught herself. It would be the perfect invitation for him to launch into an argument for marriage. And she wasn't ready to think about that, much less talk about it.

Stiffening her upper lip, she managed to force a smile. Then, lest she be forced to speak through the grand lump in her throat, she turned and, eyes straight ahead, handed her boarding pass to the stewardess.

Four long days. Three enjoyable, if demanding, concerts. There were hours of free time during each and every one of which she wished that she was home, home, with Jim.

"Rachel?"

"The soft voice across the table from her brought her out of her reverie. "Hmm? Did you say something, Pete?" It was just the two of them, lingering for a few final minutes over dinner. The others had already gone to dress for the evening's concert.

"Is everything all right?"

She smiled in affection and appreciation of his concern. "Everything's fine. . . . Why?"

"You seem distracted. You have since you've been back."

Her slender hand gave a horizontal waver in a gesture of iffy-ness. "Oh, you know, I'm just . . . worried about Dad." She hadn't quite had the courage to tell Pete about Jim and felt very much the coward for it.

"He's doing all right, isn't he?"

"He's doing fine." That, from the patient

himself, as well as from Jim. "It's just that . . . you know . . . I feel so far away. . . ." Stricken, she looked away. *So far away . . . it would be so fine to see your face at my door, doesn't help to know you're so far away . . .*

"You're going back tomorrow, aren't you?"

She nodded, swallowing hard. "I'll join you guys again on Tuesday." Her breath quavered into a sigh. "Hard to believe it's season's end." Then she laughed at herself. "I take that back. I'm exhausted. It feels like we've been on the road for years, rather than months."

"And this summer . . . anything special planned?" he asked cautiously.

Rachel met his gaze then. They'd discussed their summer plans many times. She wondered if she was that transparent, then realized that, despite the inauspicious start of their relationship, Pete Mahoney knew her better than most. He was, in a way, her best friend.

Her smile held a more sheepish twinge at the edges. "I don't know. I'll stay pretty close to home until Dad's on his feet. And then . . . I don't know."

"You'll be seeing . . . him?" There was no doubt to whom Pete referred. She nodded. "You like him." Again she nodded, this time more slowly. It was with a wave of relief that she saw Pete smile. "I'm glad. You should have someone like him, Rachel."

"How do you know what he's like?" she teased. "You met him for all of thirty seconds."

Pete's shrug was appallingly different from Jim's version of the gesture, yet no less meaningful. "Gut feeling, perhaps. You'll think I'm crazy, but the two of you *look* good together."

"Now *that's* a solid basis for a relationship," she drawled.

Again he shrugged, more shyly this time. "We'll see," he said knowingly, then cocked his head toward the door. "Come on. We'd better get ready." When she was by his side in the hotel lobby, he spoke again. "You've been coming directly back after concerts. Does he call you then?"

She shook her head, eyes on the forward movement of her feet. "No. He works."

"Works? At eleven o'clock at night?"

"He's a private investigator," she said, looking up, prepared to defend Jim against the trace of cynicism in Pete's voice. "Most of his surveillance work is done at night."

"Not much of a life for you."

"I have my life."

At Pete's gentle urging, she stepped into the elevator. He pressed their floor. "But if something develops with Guthrie, where'll you be?"

"Nothing's developing with Guthrie," she drawled, mocking Pete's words in the hopes of convincing herself. "We've both got our eyes open. We know how impossible it would be to make a life together, given our particular careers." Jim had said they'd find a way somehow. He didn't know how, but somehow.

"Well, I just hope you won't be hurt."

"I'll be fine," she said, but wondered as she let herself into her own room, closed the door, and began to dress for the evening's concert. Thinking of Jim, she walked pensively to the window.

Made from the warmth of his own bed, Jim's calls came each morning, waking her up in a most entrancing kind of way. Even now, she grew flushed as she recalled that morning's conversation.

"What are you wearing?" he'd asked softly.

"What kind of question is that? I'm still in bed!"

"That's why I want to know. Tell me. Is it blue? Green? High-necked? Long-sleeved?"

"It's yellow, very sheer and very skimpy." Only the first was true.

"You're being very unkind, Rachel," he'd said with just a hint of desperation behind his grave declaration. "Do you have any idea how uncomfortable that makes me?" They both knew his discomfort was very personal and very physical.

She shrugged. "You asked. . . . Got any more good questions?"

"Do you miss me?"

Her breath lingered an extra minute in her lungs. "Oh, yes," she whispered. "And you?"

"What do you think?"

"What are *you* wearing?"

"Nothing."

"You always sleep that way?"

"Haven't I always with you?"

"It's only been twice . . . and that was because . . ."

"Because what?"

She heard the smile in his voice and blushed. But fire deserved fire. "Because we were making love, warm, passionate love. Our bodies touching everywhere," she cooed, delighted to hear the way he sucked his breath in harshly at the other end of the line.

"Christ, Rachel! What are you trying to do to me?"

"You started it," she'd sing-songed back, her face alight with a smile. The mornings seemed to be special times, when they were fresh and rested and looking at the world through love-drenched eyes. It was appropriate that Jim should call her then.

With a sigh, Rachel turned from the window and finished dressing. It was Saturday night. One more day. Less. Twelve hours. Then she'd see him again.

The plane ride Sunday morning seemed endless. This time, she was one of the first to deplane, and her head was up, her eyes seeking from the instant she entered the terminal.

She didn't have far to look. Jim was there, lounging against a wall not far from the gate. She halted for a minute, her breath stolen by the sight of him. Wearing his typical jeans and a short-sleeved denim workshirt with epaulets at the shoulder, he looked all legs, lean and rangy, all shoulders, broad and sinewed. All male. Definitely all male.

The slow smile that spread across his tanned face was enough to set her legs in motion. One foot after the other, then more quickly as he straightened, then at a trot when he began to move forward . . . and suddenly she was in his arms, being swept into the air and around, crushed so tightly she could barely breathe. But she loved it, every minute of it.

"Ah, Rachel," he growled thickly. "It's good to have you back."

Setting her down at last, he gave her a thorough once-over. She had purposely chosen to wear a chic pair of plum-colored linen pants, a plaid blouse with its short sleeves rolled high, and a matching plum sweater vest. "You look great," he purred. "As always."

"So do you," she murmured, and raised her lips to meet his.

The perfection of this reunion was only the beginning.

"Hey," Jim began as soon as they'd reached the privacy of his car, "I think I've got a lead."

"In our case?" If possible, her eyes lit up even more

"Possibly. A pattern. The same name written on pieces of paper tossed into Renko's wastebasket . . . Landower. Mean anything to you?"

"Landower." Rachel scanned her brain, but

the name was foreign. Frowning, she shook her head. "But how can you be sure it means something?"

"I can't. But I've cross-checked it with every name that does mean something to the man, and it doesn't fit."

"How about my father? Did he recognize it?"

For the first time, Jim was hesitant. "I haven't run it past him yet. He's still pretty weak. I hate to risk upsetting him. I'm going to check it out further. . . . At least it's something."

Rachel grinned. "That it is."

But the news was fast forgotten in the pleasure of seeing Jim. What followed was three days of bliss for Rachel. When Jim worked, she visited with her father. When Jim was free, they spent time together, just the two of them, ambling about Pine Manor, shopping at a mall near Chapel Hill, sitting quietly in one another's arms on the back porch of Jim's house, a decidedly modern cabin of sorts overlooking a pond in a wooded spot just outside Raleigh.

They talked about small things, pleasant things, memories from their childhoods, tales from their more recent pasts. When words were spent, they lay quietly together. When that too was spent, they made love. Or was it the other way around? Rachel was to ask herself when she awoke in his bed on Wednesday morning.

Jim was still sleeping, one long, sun-bronzed arm thrown across her waist, one even longer and more sinewed leg draped across her thigh.

Turning her head on the pillow, she looked at him and knew that she had never loved him more.

She watched his muscle flex when her finger lightly traced the shadowed line of his jaw. She watched his nose twitch when that same finger sampled the smoother texture of his upper cheek. She watched his lashes flutter once when her thumb got into the act and lightly strummed its thick dark fringe. She watched as his eyes opened; then she smiled.

"Good morning," she whispered.

He closed his eyes again, opened one to spy her sleepily, twisted his head to see the clock on the nightstand. "Okay, pretty lady," he muttered in mock anger, "what's the story? It's not even seven o'clock yet. There had better be a damn good reason for this."

"There is." She grinned, rolling over until it was her arm around his waist, her leg across his thigh. Locking her fingers with his on either side of his head, she sought his mouth and kissed him sweetly. Her breasts were full and budded against the warm hair of his chest, their message further clarified by the faint and innocently provocative undulation of that part of her straddling his thigh.

"A virgin not so long ago?" he teased against her mouth, then held her back to appreciate the blush that stole across her cheeks.

"Goes to show what a good teacher can do," she rejoined smartly, if softly, her eyes twinkling.

His grew smoky. "Doesn't it just."

"Are you . . . having regrets?"

"Does it feel like I am?"

"Not really."

"What *does* it feel like?"

"It feels, oh, warm. Kinda hard. Maybe needing a little TLC?"

"Maybe," he admitted, his voice more strained. "Will you give it?"

Letting her knees slide to the mattress on either side of his hips, she pushed herself upright astride him. Then, astonished by her boldness, she grew still.

"Come on, darlin'," he urged, his own boldness now a throbbing force. "You wouldn't keep me in suspense . . . would you?" Then, realizing how new she was at it all, he gave her a helping hand. Strong fingers curled into the silken flesh of her hips, gently lifted her, then even more gently lowered her until she'd enveloped him as they both wanted.

Rachel closed her eyes and let out a soft moan of pleasure. "Mmmmmmmmm, Jim. How did I live before you?"

"I don't know," he panted, his fingers biting more deeply with the first of the rhythmic beats.

Catching the tempo, she fell forward to brace herself as she began to move on her own. Her lips whispered over his, becoming a willing captive when his mouth opened hungrily. Her breasts brushed his chest, back and forth, her nipples hardening with the contact. Her belly slid against his, feeling the heat from below as a tangible thing. And all the while his body responded in kind, until it bore a fine sheen of sweat and strained against passion's force.

"I love you, Rachel," he whispered urgently, his hands moving to her breasts now that her hips knew their work. His fingers cupped her fine-shaped fullness, his swiveling palms a tormenting caress on her ever-tautening tips.

She felt it coming, a slow building within her that quickened and grew hotter and threatened to shatter her. But she wanted it to linger. She wanted to feel more, to know more. She wanted to be forever part of Jim, and he of her.

With the arching of her body she rose to a sitting position, eyes closed, head thrown back, blond hair a mantel about her shoulders and down her back. She was the image of feline delight, with soft purring sounds coming from her throat and a half-smile of pleasure on her moist, parted lips.

Jim watched her, feeling that same delight, that same pleasure, plus an even deeper appreciation of her womanhood. She'd burst her bonds of virginity to become a deeply passionate lover. Thanks to his tutelage? No, though he may have been the catalyst for its escape, it had been in her all the while. Above him now, her body undulating with a slow and breathtaking grace, she was a study in devotion. Just as she could lose herself in her love of music, so she could lose herself in this.

As though hearing his thoughts, she slowly tipped her head forward and opened her eyes.

They met his without doubt, their message on her tongue in the instant. "I love you," she gasped, feeling fiery tingles sizzling through her bloodstream when he swelled all the more inside her. "I love you, Jim."

His hands possessed her hips, then slid up her body until their gentle urging brought her downward. Her lips parted for his, their tongues meeting first in a fluid duet before being relegated to play in the darkness of each other's mouths when the kiss was sealed.

It was a kiss that spoke more loudly of love than had any of the other words uttered that night. Suddenly there was no time to spare. It seemed imperative that their bodies should know the end of this sweet, sweet torment. Wrapping his arms about her back, he rolled her beneath him in one fast move, then thrust quickly. She groaned at the fierceness of him, at his rock-hard strength straining deep inside her. His strokes were long and heady, the friction of him driving her higher until she could see nothing but a blinding array of spotlights surrounding a stage afire with passion.

It was an eternity of gasping and sighing before either of them could speak. When, at last, his body drained and limp, Jim rolled to her side, he reached up to smooth clinging tendrils of blond hair from the dampness of her cheeks.

"You've got to marry me, Rachel," he whispered without preamble, taking her by surprise with this first mention of marriage since she'd been home. His eyes shimmered. "I'm so afraid of losing you. . . ."

"You won't lose me," she answered softly. "You *couldn't* lose me. I'm not going anywhere."

"But you've discovered yourself now." The image of her as she had been moments before, riding him confidently with her head flung back and her breasts shifting seductively, came as a prod to his peace. "You've become a full woman. Passionate. Aware. You'll see men, and their stares of appreciation will suddenly have more meaning for you."

"I've seen men before. None of them interested me."

"You didn't know what you were missing then."

"What you're saying is that you think you've unleashed a sexual she-cat on the world?"

"It could happen."

"It won't."

"How can you be so sure?"

"Because I love you. *You.* Because with all the men I've run into over the years, not a one had the where-withal to turn me on . . . until you. Don't you see, Jim?" she pleaded, addressing herself to his original proposal. "You don't need a piece of paper to tie me to you. I'm *here.*"

"But if you love me and say you'll never leave me, why not marriage?"

For the first time, Rachel grew unsteady. "*Why* marriage? What is the need?"

His gaze held hers unwaveringly. "I want the

world to know. I want you to know. I want every goddamned man who walks up to you with a glass of champagne in his hand and a leering smile on his lips to know. . . ."

"That's jealousy. And it's unnecessary."

"I know. But I can't help it . . . any more than I can help wanting to know that you're my responsibility, legally in my care."

"I'm not helpless . . . or dependent," she returned, her tension mounting side by side with dismay. "You make me sound as though I'm a little lady in distress, needing that knight in shining armor."

"But you don't need me, do you?" he asked, his voice laced with an underlying sense of defeat. "You *are* successful and independent in your own right." He paused for a minute, then went on more pensively. "Maybe that's why I need marriage, Rachel. Maybe I'm insecure enough to *need* that piece of paper for my peace of mind."

Rachel's eyes were warm, limpid pools of brown, her voice a fluid extension. "Oh, Jim," she breathed, "you're so wrong." She touched the grooves by the side of his mouth, grooves she'd never seen before. But then, she'd never seen him in defeat, and it hurt. "I need you more than I've ever needed another living soul. Success and independence are only relative. Do you have any idea how my life has changed since I've met you?"

"Yeah. Your father has had a triple by-pass

and you've lost your virginity." His lips thinned. "Two cuts. Appropriate."

"You're awful," she said, aching at his hurt. Then anger mixed with hurt, and the emotions brought her upright. "And if you don't understand what I mean when I say that my life has changed, maybe *that's* why I won't marry you." She started to get up from the bed in a huff, only to be snagged by the long fingers which curved around her waist and hauled her back to the mattress. Jim was suddenly above her once more, his shoulders looming wide.

"Don't run from me, Rachel. Argue! Tell me that your life has grown fuller, richer. That the nights alone may be much more frustrating but aren't half as lonely because of the knowledge that tomorrow, or the day after, we'll be together. Tell me that for the first time you can see the future, that you *dare* see the future and it's something warm and wonderful. That's how *my* life has changed, Rachel. Tell me it's been the same for you."

Tears welled in her eyes, brought forward by the painful swell of love in her heart. "It has, Jim. Damn it, it has!" she admitted grudgingly, her voice rising, broken and frightened. "And I don't know what to do," she cried, the tears spilling freely down her cheeks. "Because it scares me. The force of it scares me. The thought of losing you scares me. But . . . marriage scares me most of all!" She shook her head, sobbing quietly. "I . . . don't know . . . what to do!"

With the slow dawning inspired not only by her words but by the crushed expression she wore, Jim realized that there was more to her resistance of marriage than the newness, the suddenness she'd originally claimed. There was something deeper, something he couldn't yet understand. And he suspected that she didn't either.

"Shhhh," he crooned, setting aside his own anguish to comfort her. For that was what he wanted to do. Comfort her. Be there for her. Love her. "It's all right." Slipping his arms beneath her back, he brought them both to a sitting position, then rocked her gently against him until she'd stopped crying. "It's all right, darlin'. Everything will work out."

"You . . . say that," she hiccoughed, "but you haven't . . . said how. I don't . . . want to lose it. . . ." Her tears resumed. "And . . . I've got to . . . leave this afternoon . . . and I don't want to!"

It was as close to a commitment as she was ready to make. Sensing this, Jim held her all the more tightly. "You won't lose it. *We* won't lose it. We can't. It's too damned good."

Those were the words that stuck with her during the flight to Omaha. They gave her hope to counter-balance the enigmatic cloud that seemed to hover in the back of her mind. She could think of herself being with Jim forever as his friend and lover. But wife? And mother to his children? For, without a doubt she was sure he'd want children. He was a man with too much love to give to be denied them. All too vividly she recalled a kind of primal satisfaction in his gaze when, after they'd first made love, he'd suggested she might be pregnant. Oh, no, he wouldn't mind. But could she handle it?

As happened now more often than she wished, she thought of her mother and wondered if she'd ever know the truth. Just as Jim had hesitated broaching a Landower connection to Tom, she hesitated mentioning her mother. Yet the uncertainty of it all gnawed at her, muddling her attempts to envision her future with Jim and in turn upsetting her all the more.

It was Pete who once again saw through her attempts to keep up a front through the final concerts in Omaha on Thursday and Friday nights, then Oklahoma City on Saturday night and Sunday afternoon. There had been an early dinner to celebrate the tour's end. At its conclusion, he approached her.

"You're leaving in the morning?"

"Actually I was toying with the idea of stealing away tonight. There's an eight o'clock plane I may try to make."

"You must be looking forward to being home for a while." His gentle statement held a wealth of understanding.

She nodded, feeling queer knots of numerous kinds in her stomach. "My father will be coming home from the hospital in the morning. It'll be good to be home with him."

"And Jim?"

Her hesitation was momentary. "Him, too."

Putting a brotherly arm about her shoulder, he guided her from the restaurant to begin the short walk to the hotel. "Will you marry him?"

"*Marry* him? Whatever put *that* thought into your head?" Her voice was too high, her words too quick for nonchalance.

"You. The look on your face when you think no one is looking." He studied her for a minute as they walked. "You love him, don't you?"

For an instant she pondered a denial. But to Pete, after all they'd been through together? "Yes," she whispered. "I do love him."

"Does he love you?"

"Yes."

"Has he *asked* you to marry him?"

"Oh, yes," she drawled in a so-what-else-is-new tone of voice. "He's asked."

"And you've answered—"

"No. I don't want to get married."

Turning a corner, he gave her a squeeze. "Is it the thought of those long nights at home alone that frightens you?"

"No. We could work around that." In her heart, she knew they could. With the conviction of his love, she could wait hours and hours, if need be, for the sake of those spectacular few together.

"Then what?" Pete countered in confusion. "I mean, *I'd* like to see you with a guy who'd be there all the time for you. But if his working habits don't bother you, what does?"

She studied the pavement, counting each seam. "I don't know," she murmured at last. "Maybe it's *my* working habits that would be hard to get around. Being on the road for so many months a year could strain even the best of relationships."

They walked in silence for a time before Pete spoke with greater hesitancy. "You could always look for a position with an orchestra or a chamber music group nearer home."

"And leave Montage?"

"If being with Jim meant enough to you."

She shook her head. "I don't know, Pete. Montage has been so good to me. I don't know if I'm ready to move on yet."

"You're ready musically, Rachel. You're an accomplished flutist who can carry her own just about anywhere. Mind you"—he squeezed her again—"not that I'd particularly like letting you go. But . . . it's hard seeing you unhappy."

"I'm not unhappy."

"Then . . . maybe lonesome is a better word. Your thoughts are with him more often than with us. And that's the way it should be, if you're in love with the guy." He took a deep breath and released it in a sigh. "Well, you've got the summer to decide, at any rate. Why don't you think about it. Maybe look around at the opportunities while you're home."

"Peter Mahoney," she eyed him askance,

teasing him by way of her own diversion, "if I didn't know better, I'd say that you're tired of duelin' the banjos with me."

"Oh, no, Rachel. Never that. You're the best thing Montage has going for it. We'd be in big trouble if you left. But I'm not Ron, and my concern for you is as much personal as it is professional." He stopped walking and turned her to face him. "I want you to be happy. I want you to fulfill all your dreams. Montage has been one. And you've done it already." He smiled in gentle reminiscence. "Do you remember when you first signed on, how frightened you were, how strange everything was? But you wanted it so badly and it worked out. Well, maybe that's how you're feeling about Guthrie right now. What you have to do is to decide what you want . . . and how badly you want it."

Rachel gazed at him sadly, then threw her arms around his neck. "I do love you too, Pete," she managed to say before she choked up completely and simply held on to him.

"Then do me a favor?"

Drawing back, she eyed him through misted lashes. "What?"

"Get your pretty little behind on that plane and go to him. Maybe *he* can talk some sense into you."

That was what frightened her. And excited her. As the taxi approached Pine Manor late that night she pushed the former to the back of her mind, letting the latter fill her with smiles and small ripples of anticipation. She knew that he'd most probably be working tonight, so she planned an early morning surprise. Paying the cabbie, she stood aside while he set her large suitcases inside the front door. Then, being as quiet as she could so as not to disturb Mrs. Francis, she took her smaller bag and crept up the stairs.

Everything was dark. Stealing down the corridor to her room, she slid inside the partially opened door and crossed the carpet to reach for the light.

"Don't . . . do . . . it . . ." came a low growl from somewhere in the far reaches of the room.

She froze.

eight

In place of the snap of the lightswitch came a click that had the uncanny sound of the trigger of a gun. A tremor scissored through Rachel's limbs, and she took a deep breath to speak, only to have the breath knocked from her without a touch by the return of the low rumble from the corner.

"Very, very slowly"—the words fitted the command—"lower the bag to the floor. Don't . . . make . . . a sound. . . ."

Very, very slowly she did as ordered, sliding

the strap of the bag from her shoulder and lowering its weight carefully to the floor. She didn't . . . make . . . a sound. . . .

"And the purse."

It slid from the other shoulder to follow the fate of the bag. Her knees felt much like its ultrasoft leather and would have similarly conformed to the shape of any support offered. None was.

"Now," came the voice, deadly quiet but determined, "take off the sash."

Rachel's insides quivered wildly with the first understanding of what was to be. For an instant she hesitated and looked again at the dark blob which was the lamp. Sensing that her fate wouldn't change with it on or off, she momentarily took the road of least resistance. Bowing her head, she set her fingers to the task of untying the knot at her waist. The sash fell silently to the floor.

"The skirt next. Slow and easy."

Her fingers couldn't seem to obey, insisting on fumbling shakily with the five buttons that descended the seam where a zipper might have been.

The command was repeated, more thickly this time and with a mild shot of impatience. "The skirt."

"I'm try—"

"Just . . . *do*. . . ." He lowered his voice again. "And don't talk. I'll do the talking." With her back to him, he couldn't see her rebellious smirk when her fingers continued to fumble. "Come on," he had to urge her again before the skirt was finally free to follow the sash in a swish to the floor. "Now the shoes. Step out of them. Slowly . . . That's better."

Rachel held her breath, her heart pounding. She knew what was coming. Somehow, standing there in her blouse and slip, she still felt covered. Once they were gone though . . .

He had no pity. "Unbutton the blouse. . . . And don't be all day about it." His voice sounded thicker and had a corresponding effect on Rachel. There was a strange aura of carnality in the air. Fighting its pull, she applied herself to the buttons. Soon the blouse lay open. She stood erect, waiting. "Take it off," he barked.

The night was quiet, save the sounds of his low commands, her shallow breathing and the murmur of each piece of clothing as it left her body. One shoulder was bared to his sight, then the other. Though the air was warm, she shivered as she let the blouse fall to the rug.

"Now the slip," came the taut rumble in the dark. "Over your head."

It took her no more than a minute to realize how provocative it would be to remove the slip that way, rather than simply take the straps down and push the silk over her hips. He wanted his pleasure. Her only recourse was to do what he demanded while her mind reeled with thoughts of revenge.

Gathering the thin fabric upward from her hips, she slowly lifted it past her waist. By the time the negligible material left her breasts and cleared her shoulders to slide over her head, her arms were extended above. Allowing him only a brief glance at the seductive pose, she let the article slither from her wrists to the floor.

She thought she heard the harsh expelling of a breath before his voice returned with remarkably leashed force. "The pantyhose. Get rid of them."

Again she could picture the sight she would make. Emboldened by a burst of perverse pleasure, she took her time hooking her fingers beneath the waistband and slowly inching the clinging mesh from her hips, her thighs, then off one leg at a time. By the time she straightened, she wondered if she'd gone too far.

"You're asking for it," came the feral growl, then a long pause during which she could do nothing but pray to control the leaflike shaking of her limbs. Her body was astir with memories of the last time it had been bared to a man, memories of *his* body, so clean and long and athletic. Then she'd felt coddled. Now, standing in nothing but her bra and panties, she felt bare, exposed and helpless.

He only had two choices. "Take the bra off."

Head bowed, she could see the rapid rise and fall of that sheer nothing he'd called a bra. When she hesitated, the simmering voice came again.

"Strip it. . . . Now."

She toyed with the idea of forcing him to do his own bidding, but the growing raggedness of his growl suggested that she'd be better not to incite him further. Tremulous fingers reached back to the single book and released it.

"Off."

She slid the shoulder straps forward and eased the lace from her rounded flesh. When again there was a long pause, she gritted her teeth. Revenge. He'd get his for this.

The voice was softer, less imperious this time, if tautly strained. "Slip the panties off. Real easy."

Real easy? He'd get that, she vowed, biting her lower lip in frustration. Moving in slow motion, she hooked her thumbs at the waistband of the small bit of silk and slowly, shifting her hips from one side to the other, slid the panties down her legs. When she stepped out of them at last, she wore nothing by the pale reflection of the moon. With a quivering breath, she straightened, drawing her shoulders back, her head up. Every one of her senses was alert and pulsing wildly in response to the eyes she felt rake her flesh.

She heard a quiet rustle and knew that he was rising, only then realizing that he must have been sitting in her favorite rattan chair as he'd watched the show. Oh, he'd get his, all right. One day . . .

His voice was nearer, a series of rasping chops from far back in his throat. "Your hair. Let it down. Every pin. I want it free."

Her body a mass of jangling cells, she began to protest. "Please—"

"Take . . . it . . . down. . . ."

Her head fell forward. Slender fingers approached the pins that had been so carefully placed that afternoon and, one by one, drew them out. They fell in a random array atop the clothing that had been discarded on the floor. Her blond tresses spilled as haphazardly over her shoulders. She shook her head once to free any knots, then forced herself to stand still, awaiting further command.

"Very slowly"—the voice came from directly behind her—"turn around."

She swallowed hard, took a deep breath, then, steeling herself for further torment, turned. Looking up, she met his eyes, then watched as they lowered to examine the pert thrust of her tightening breasts, the subtly feminine flair of her hips, the nest of flaxen down at the juncture of her thighs. Even darkness couldn't shroud the smoldering golden gaze that seared her body at every touchpoint.

"This is how I dream of you," he said in a choked voice. "Naked in the moonlight."

She licked suddenly parched lips. Her breath came even faster, giving added life to the breasts to which his gaze had returned. When his eyes finally rose to meet hers again, she could restrain herself no longer.

"My God, Jim," she ground out a whisper, "if you don't touch me soon, I think I'm going to die!"

A silver of white slashed across his face. "I think you're not the only one," he moaned, opening his arms and taking her in with a vengeance. "Rachel, Rachel. It seems like it's been forever."

She might have been happy to stay in his arms for another forever had it not been for the erotic scene he'd orchestrated instants before. She was too aroused to be satisfied with a hug. "And you're still dressed!" she whimpered, pushing herself only far enough away to go to work on the buttons of his shirt. Amazing what fingers could suddenly do so very efficiently, she mused with a feline smile. Tugging his shirt from his jeans, she pouted. "You've ruined my surprise. I was going to wake you up early tomorrow morning. How did you know I'd be coming tonight?"

"I didn't," he said, his voice strained to its limits by the feel of her hands undressing him. He spoke quickly, expelling the words with an effort. "If I had, I'd have met you at the airport. I just happened to be working downstairs earlier. When I was done there, I turned off the lights and came to sit here for a while. It seems the only place I can get any peace." He let her push the shirt off his shoulders and was turned on all the more by her aggressiveness.

She took but a moment to give her hands a hungry taste of the solidness of his flesh, running them across the warm muscles of his chest and around his shoulders before she went to work on his belt. "You mean, your gumshoe instinct didn't tip you off to my need to be home?" The belt was undone. He stepped out of his loafers as she unsnapped and unzipped the jeans. Then, with a greediness that would have startled her had she been a fly on the wall, she knelt to tug the denim down his legs, and, with his hand on the top of her head for balance, off one foot then the other.

Catching her breath but barely, Rachel ran her hands up his legs. They were strong and hard to the touch, so long that, from her position on her haunches, his face seemed an eternity above her. Reminded of the distance yet to go, she savored the very masculine hairiness of him for an instant longer before reaching up to tug at his briefs. Given his state of arousal, it took quite a tug. When the soft cotton fabric had finally joined its companions on the floor, she slid her hand back up one leg to the very top of his thigh, where she wavered, studying him in open awe, until he took her fingers and drew her slowly to her feet.

As he had done moments before, so now she stood back to look at him. He was magnificent, gleaming in the moonlight with only that manly covering of hair on his flesh, spreading broad across his chest before tapering to his navel and beyond. It was the beyond to which her gaze was drawn again, then, more timidly, her hands. She'd never touched him there before, had never been so bold. Now, aware of the wildfire raging through her veins, she needed to know of his.

It was hard and hot and pulsing, visibly straining for her. She felt a warm rush of liquid within her and knew that, for all its invisibility, she was as ready for him.

"Come here, Rachel," he gave a soft snarl,

taking her arms and securing them around his neck, then sliding his hands beneath her bottom and lifting her clear off her feet. As though there were no other possible course for them, her legs curved naturally around his hips. There and then he entered her. Their sighs of satisfaction were in perfect unison. "God, have I missed you," he rasped against her hair. "And this. I don't think I'll ever get enough of it."

Rachel clung to him, eyes closed, savoring the feel of him filling her everywhere. "Nor I," she whispered, deliriously happy. "See what you've made of me. To strip brazenly before a man with a gun . . . the gun . . . where is it?"

"It was a beer can," he muttered, holding himself locked deep within her as he lowered her to the bed, "and it's on the rug by the chair." When her back hit the cover, his lips pressed her deeper. "You don't really think I'd ever hold a gun on you, do you?" His voice was a punishing caress against her mouth.

"I don't think I'd care," she whispered, "as long as it was you with a finger on the trigger." A sigh of bliss escaped her lips when his hand moved upward on her body, settling at last on her breast. "That finger does such wonderful things. . . ." she began, then drifted into a less verbal enjoyment of rapture as his back bowed and he thrust. A moan of shameless pleasure filled the air; she wasn't sure whether it was hers or his, and didn't care. It was a time for exquisite appreciation, not analysis.

And the appreciation was indeed mutual. Jim set the pace with ever deepening strokes. Rachel met his thrusts, her breath coming faster, her body fueled and ready for the inevitable combustion that never failed to mark their joining. The low, fierce sound of his voice was as stimulating as the hardness of his man's body spearing her again and again. "Yes, Rachel . . . ah, yes . . . there . . . aaaah, it's so good . . . yes, faster . . . oh, God!"

Whirling into frenzied circles of oblivion, they found their height together, reveled in it, clung to it as long as was physically possible, then slowly, reluctantly, collapsed in one another's arms. Jim's arms clung to her long after every other part of his body had gone limp. "I love you. . . ." he whispered at last.

She turned her lips in toward his sweat-dampened cheek and, with the gradual steadying of her breath, kissed him. "I'm glad."

How long they lay like that, limbs entwined as were their hearts, neither knew. Rachel only knew that the happiness she felt was like nothing she'd ever known before. It kept getting better, their love. She couldn't believe it, but it kept growing. Bigger and deeper and demanding every inch of her being. She felt as though she were being swallowed alive . . . and loved it.

"You're mine, now, you know," Jim said. She opened her eyes and tipped her head up to find that he was studying her intently. "For the whole summer. Forever. It may take you a while longer to realize that, but you'll be my wife. So help me, Rachel, you will."

Seeing the determination on his face, knowing where she'd just come from herself, she half believed him. It was . . . nice . . . to hear him say it. Strangely nice. Unsettlingly nice. "Let's not talk about it now," she whispered, reluctant to jeopardize the pleasure of the moment.

But either Jim wasn't as sentimental, or his need to settle the matter was simply that great. "Then when? As it is, your father's coming home tomorrow morning. *He's* bound to ask."

"Ask what?"

"When we're getting married."

"Why would he ask that?"

"Well, maybe he won't ask it, but he'll certainly be wondering. I mean, when a father sees his daughter having an affair under his nose—"

"It's not an affair!"

The smile that curved Jim's lips was very masculine and very knowing. "What *would* you call it?"

"We're in love!"

"Are you going to tell Tom that?"

"If he asks."

"And when, as he's bound to do, he then goes on to ask when we're getting married, what will you tell him?" They'd come full circle. Rachel was cornered.

Lowering her eyes, she whispered, "I don't know."

"Why don't you just say . . . next week. Or

next month." His voice softened to a loving plea. "What's so awful about that?"

"Nothing's *awful* about it," she drawled, mocking him. "It's just that I'm not . . . ready. Marriage is a big step."

"So is giving your virginity to a man at the age of twenty-nine. You didn't spend long dilly-dallying about that, did you?"

It was a rhetorical question, which Rachel proceeded to ignore. Her mind was occupied in sorting out her thoughts. This was what she'd feared about coming home. She'd known that Jim would try to pin her down. But just as she couldn't deny herself his loving, she was unable to commit herself to a future as his wife. To be a wife . . . and mother . . . was something foreign to her existence. She felt threatened and insecure.

"Give it time, Jim," she begged softly. "Please?"

"And what *do* we do when your father gets home? Kiss each other good-night at the door?" He gave a harsh snort. "You know as well as I do that that would be impossible."

Recalling an earlier conversation they'd had, she grasped at solutions. "Weren't you the one who said that my father wouldn't mind?"

"Won't *you* mind? Won't it bother you to spend the night with me, knowing that Tom is right down the hall?"

It certainly was a new twist to her life. "I . . . don't know."

"Well, I do. I know you, Rachel. Mrs. Francis

may be one thing. Your own father is another. You wouldn't sneak me in behind his back, that's for sure." He shook his dark head and inhaled deeply. "No, the only hope we have of being together is for you to tell him about us. He may not be thrilled that in the matter of weeks he's been hospitalized I've managed to weasel my way into his daughter's bed. But he seems pretty level-headed, and I know that he loves you dearly. He certainly won't *force* you into marriage, if you're that much against it."

His voice held hurt. Rachel felt it in turn. Stroking his face with the back of her hand, she looked up at him beseechingly. "It's not like that, Jim. I'm frightened. That's all." She tried to explain. "When I think of marriage—to *anyone*—I start to shake."

"You wouldn't be marrying *anyone*, Rachel. You'd be marrying me."

With a sigh of frustration, she turned her head away. "I know," she whispered, then in defeat, "I just need time."

In the silence that followed, confusion gnawed at her. If she didn't understand herself, how could she possibly explain her feelings to Jim? And, increasingly, she *didn't* understand herself. If she loved Jim, why *shouldn't* she marry him? Why shouldn't she be elated? Just because she'd never had a role model didn't mean she couldn't do it. Many a woman whose mother had died very young later grew to be wonderful wives and mothers themselves. Why not she?

Bits and fragments of her father's sleep-talking flitted in and out of her consciousness. Again she wondered about her mother. Did she dare ask her father about it? But she couldn't, not when he was so weak. The last thing she wanted to do was to upset him, she concluded, for what had to be the umpteenth time. No, she vowed, if she'd waited this long, she could wait a little longer.

"You know," Jim began, slipping his large hand beneath her shoulder in a gentle caress, "if I didn't love you so damned much, I might tell you what to do with your plea for time. . . ."

"But you do love me."

". . . So much." To make his point, he kissed her quite thoroughly.

He'd given her a temporary reprieve.

Tom Busek returned home the following morning, accompanied by a nurse who would be spending a week at the house. Though Jim had insisted on driving Rachel to the hospital to pick them up, he left for work soon after he'd seen his friend comfortably settled in bed, though not before he'd tossed out the Landower name with as much nonchalance as he could.

"Landower?" Tom repeated, seeming suddenly tired by reminder of the trouble at SCT.

For an instant Jim regretted having mentioned it. But he'd been hired to do a job and his detective's instinct told him he simply couldn't wait much longer. "Mean anything to you?"

Tom shook his head, his lips tight. "No," he sighed as he closed his eyes.

Without further word, Jim took his leave of Tom. Rachel walked him to the front door.

"Will you come for dinner tonight?" she asked, wondering whether his work would extend into the evening. "I mean, I'm sure that Dad won't be joining us, but Mrs. Francis is bound to cook something super."

His arm hooked about her waist, Jim set aside darker thoughts to grin down at her. "With the promise of a home-cooked meal, how can I refuse?"

"So that's it," she teased. "That's the way to lure you from work?"

"Actually, I'll probably have to eat and run. But . . . I'll be back." With a kiss to the tip of her nose, he was gone, leaving her standing, wondering whether this warm, silky feeling would be part of seeing him off to work each day. Shaking her head to free herself of the thought, she turned to change and see what she could do for her father.

It was very little. The nurse kept close watch on him, trying to limit both his phone calls and his visitors while enforcing adequate rest and exercise.

Rachel made a point of spending time with him, often to take him on those slow walks around the yard, but for the most part she was free to unpack, to catch up on her own sleep, to play the flute, to look forward to being with Jim. As for pondering the future either in terms of her career or of Jim, she avoided it like the plague.

That first week, the issue of the shift in Rachel's sleeping habits never did arise. For starters, Jim was particularly busy with a new case, a criminal investigation that demanded much of his time. On those nights that he was able to stop by Rachel's, more often than not it was at an ungodly hour of the night. Using his key to quietly let himself in, he would find that Rachel had fallen asleep on the den sofa waiting for him, would pick her up and carry her to bed with as much privacy as they'd ever had. He was up and gone in the mornings before anyone was the wiser save Rachel, whose warm, pink cheeks and tingling body kept her aware of him long after his car had pulled from the drive.

It was during the next week, with the nurse gone and her father making remarkable progress, that the fact of their love came out. Jim had managed to stop by and join them for lunch on the back patio. When he'd gone, Tom turned to her.

"He's a good man, Jimbo is."

Rachel was in high spirits. Not only did the warm June sun feel wonderful on the skin bared by her sundress, but Jim had just announced that he'd hired another assistant. Tonight would be theirs—hers and Jim's—completely.

Her lips twitched at the corners. "So you've said."

Tom's eyes narrowed in speculation. He hadn't been blind to the softness in his daughter each time she looked at Jim, nor to Jim's when he returned the glance. "You seem to believe it."

"I do," she said more softly. "I love him."

Her father broke into a smile. "That's what I was hoping. And Jim? What about him?"

"He feels the same."

"Good!" Tom brought his hands together in a great clap of satisfaction, then sobered almost comically. "So what are you going to do about it?"

Jim had warned her. Typical Tom Busek. "We're going to spend every free minute together. We're going to enjoy one another . . . and our love."

"And marriage? What about that?"

Rachel tipped her head to the side and shrugged, unable to meet his eyes. "Maybe. We'll see."

"What do you mean 'we'll see'?"

"Shhhh! You're supposed to stay quiet."

He lowered his voice once again and spoke through what she suspected were gritted teeth. "What about marriage, Rachel? He's asked you, hasn't he?"

"Yes."

Tom eyed her in disbelief. "And you've put him off?"

"For now," she answered quietly, perplexed by her father's reaction. He seemed actually . . . angry.

"For heaven's sake, *why*, girl? He's a good man and you say you're in love. Isn't marriage the logical next step?"

"It may be, but the time isn't right."

"You're waiting for a cure for the common cold?" he muttered with barely cloaked sarcasm. "Where's your sense, Rachel? Grab him! Tie him down! Don't risk losing what you've got!"

Rachel had no instant reply in the face of her father's vehemence. She'd expected excitement and pleasure . . . not this. She couldn't quite understand him. He seemed to be pressuring her almost out of fear.

"You sound as though I may never get another chance," she murmured at last, unable to completely hide her hurt. "Did you think I was such a lost cause that I have to grab at the first man to come along?"

"That's not it, sweetheart," he said, his voice softening instantly. Leaning forward, he took her hand in his. "It's just that, well, love is sometimes a tenuous thing. We think we have it in the palm of our hands and then . . . something happens and we lose it."

"You're talking about . . . mother." The word had never come easily on her tongue. Even now it emerged only with an effort.

It was Tom's turn to shrug. "Perhaps."

Momentarily giving lip service to the premise that her mother had simply died at her birth, Rachel went on. "But that was different. Things like that don't happen as often nowadays. I think

Jim and I would be making a worse mistake to rush into something we're not one hundred percent sure of."

There was an element of defeat in her father's eyes. He spoke more slowly. "What's not to be sure of, if you're in love?"

"Our careers, for one thing. We'd have to make some alterations to ensure ourselves time together." It suddenly struck her that that was exactly what Jim had done. Between Pat and this new assistant, he'd be that much freer in the evenings.

"You can do that."

"I suppose."

"Then . . . do it!"

Rachel looked up, a hint of rebellion in her expression. "Is that an order?"

Tom shook his gray-thatched head and sighed. "No, sweetheart. You're much too old to take orders from me. It was simply a suggestion spoken with a father's concern. I like Jim. I trust him. I think he'd make a good husband and father. And you're in love. Now"—he held up a hand to still her imminent protest—"I know that sounds very old-fashioned. But I'm not *so* old-fashioned"—he arched a brow—"that I can't imagine what you two do when you're alone." When Rachel's cheeks flamed wildly, he smiled. It was a warm, melancholy smile, bearing a score of poignant memories. "Hell, it *is* old-fashioned. Your mother and I did it way back then." Very slowly, his smile faded. "But the most natural outcropping of that is children, and your children should be protected."

"*I'm* protected," she blurted out, then grew all the more red and would have bit her tongue had she not realized that she wanted her father to feel completely at ease about her spending time with Jim. If he was constantly worried about her becoming pregnant, that ease would be elusive. "I mean, we have to come to terms with marriage before we can start thinking about raising a family."

Tom nodded, then grew pensive, his gaze meandering out toward the peach orchard. "Well," he sighed, "I can't argue with that. But don't be too long about it. You're not getting any younger."

"My Lord, Dad," she laughed, feeling suddenly relieved, "you sound as though I'm *really* over the hill."

"Give yourself a few more years. . . ." His voice trailed off, then picked up more softly and with a hint of mischief. "And Rachel?"

"Um-hmm?"

"Tell him to sleep a little later in the mornings." Tom shook his head. "I mean, dawn is damned early. My God, but the man must be exhausted!"

"He said *that*?" Jim asked in amazement when after dinner was over he found himself alone with Rachel in the den. Then he threw back his head and laughed openly. "The fox. So he's known all week?"

"I didn't think it was so funny," Rachel scowled, then softened. "Not at the time, anyway." She pushed herself from the sofa to put a record on the stereo.

"What else did he say?"

"Pretty much what you thought," she murmured, her back to him.

"About marriage?"

"Uh-huh."

Jim broke into a broad smile. "I knew I could count on him! He made the pitch, did he?"

Rachel turned, her hands on her hips, a look of exasperation on her face. "It didn't do *him* any more good than it did you. I told him I had no intention of rushing into anything."

"Shame on you, Rachel . . . robbing a sick man of such simple pleasure."

Her eyes widened in amusement. "Uh-huh. So now you're saying that I should marry you to please my father? That's a new twist to a love triangle."

"It's been known to happen." He held out an arm and welcomed her back to his side. She slid in quite comfortably, tipping her head back to eye him speculatively.

"Wouldn't it bother you if I agreed to marry you for my father's sake?"

"Not a bit."

"Jim! That's awful."

"Not really. I know that we love each other

and that it's only some peculiar hang-up of yours that's keeping us apart. Our marriage would be good. Knowing that, I could very easily enter into it under false pretenses."

"You are without conscience."

"No. Just honest." He looked toward the stereo, from which slow, soft chords had begun to emerge, and screwed up his face. "What's that?"

"Berlioz's *Symphonie Fantastique*. What's the matter?" she teased. "Don't like it? See, how could we ever make a go of a marriage when you can't stand what I like?"

"I didn't say I couldn't stand it. I just wanted to know what it was."

"Then what was the face for? Come on, where's that honesty now? You hate it, don't you?"

His brow furrowed and he tipped his head to the side. "I don't hate it. It just seems . . . disjointed . . . to me. All classical music does."

"That's because you don't understand it."

"Then . . . explain."

At his ardent expression, she caught her breath. "You're serious."

"Very! Tell me about what I'm hearing."

Rachel eyed him closely for another minute, deciding that indeed he was serious, then settled her head back into the crook of his shoulder and began to speak quietly. "When Berlioz wrote this in the 1830s, he was madly in love with an actress who didn't even know he existed. He wrote it in large part for her, to get her attention. In that sense it's autobiographical." She paused, listening to the music for a moment longer before continuing.

"According to the composer's own notes, the symphony tells of a young man, an unstable, lovesick musician who tries to poison himself. Under the effect of opium, he proceeds to have a series of vivid hallucinations, each involving the image of his loved one." Rachel turned her head against Jim's chest until she could look up into his eyes. "Listen. This is the first movement. The musician is having all sorts of dreams of his life as it was before he met the woman with whom he'd become obsessed. Listen."

Doing just that, they sat quietly. Jim held her closely as he tried to focus his energies on the music.

"What do you hear?" she prompted.

He waited to answer, trying desperately to find something intelligent to say. "What am I supposed to hear?" he finally asked, coming up short on the interpretive end and feeling unduly frustrated.

"You're supposed to free-associate. Tell me what the music brings to mind."

Again he listened. "Different things. Sadness. Happiness. Confusion." He threw a hand up. "Hell, Rachel, I don't know!"

"But you're right!" she returned enthusiastically. "Those were precisely the things the young musician was feeling. In a drugged state, he saw his life passing before his eyes. Sadness.

Happiness. Confusion. He'd experienced all those things. Now . . . listen." She held her breath. "There," she instructed. "That." Her eyes grew more luminous. "Do you hear it—that particular melody?"

Jim snorted. "It's the first thing I would have actually called a melody."

"That's the *idée fixe*. The fixed idea. It's the theme of his beloved. Listen to it now. Then you'll be able to hear it in each of the other movements."

Together they listened, Jim with a skepticism that was tempered only by Rachel's eagerness. When the second movement began, again she gave a brief and patient narration.

"The musician dreams he's at a ball now. Listen. The dancing. The waltz tempo. The excitement of whirling around the floor." She quieted for several minutes. "Now . . . hear it?"

"The beloved?" Sure enough, he thought he did. At least the tune sounded vaguely familiar.

"Uh-huh. He can't seem to escape her."

"Poor guy," Jim murmured, nuzzling her forehead. "I know the feeling."

Rachel turned inward, draping a leg over one of his, an arm across his waist. With her head tipped back, she smiled at him. "I wouldn't exactly call you unstable."

"Yeah, that's what scares me. I don't need hallucinations to conjure you up." His head dipped and his lips caught hers open and warm.

His hand pressed against the small of her back, molding her closer.

"I'm here," she whispered when at last he'd freed her lips. Her hand strayed across his chest. "You don't need to conjure anything."

"That's what I find so hard to believe at times," he murmured, kissing her again, shuddering as he squeezed her tightly, then settled her more comfortably against him. "I sometimes think that it *is* a hallucination. That I'll wake up and you'll be gone."

"Never."

"Then marry me."

Breaking contact with his eyes, she lowered her head, brushing her cheek against his chest, catching her breath. "Don't, Jim. Not tonight. Not when we've finally got time to enjoy what we have."

He caught her chin and lifted it. "You do enjoy it?"

"You know I do."

"Tell me," he demanded in a hoarser whisper, then held her gaze unwaveringly. "Tell me what it is you enjoy."

She couldn't have looked away if she'd tried, so intent was his eye-lock. "I enjoy being here with you, here at home, knowing that I don't have to take the next plane out. I enjoy telling you about my music, sharing something that's been part of my life for so long." When she hesitated, he prompted her.

"Go on. . . ."

"I enjoy curling up next to you like this. Feeling safe. Protected." She slid her hand across his chest, inching her fingers between the buttons of his shirt. "I like the feel of you. So warm and hard." She buried her face against his neck. "And your smell." She inhaled deeply, releasing the breath in a sigh of pleasure.

"Go on. . . ."

Her gaze met his again, reading a masculine smugness that only added to his appeal. "You're enjoying this, aren't you?"

"Um-hmmm." His lips struggled to contain a grin. "Do go on."

There was only one way to fight fire. Her hand began to move again, working at the buttons of his shirt, releasing first one, then another, spreading the fabric aside as she leaned forward and touched her lips to his chest. His faint squirm was ample encouragement.

"I enjoy the texture of you, hair here, smoothness there." Her mouth sampled each as her breath warmed his chest all the more. "I enjoy the way you tighten up when I do this . . . and this. . . ." His nipple was rock-hard by the time her tongue had finished with it. She angled her face upward, watching his expression as her hand moved downward. His amusement had grown ardent. "I enjoy the way you break out into a sweat when you get excited. There's something . . . animalistic about it." Her fingers worked at his fly, lowering the zipper, slipping inside. She savored the way his breathing had quickened, the way his body strained toward her. Her voice was a seductive rasp. "And I enjoy the way you respond to me." Her hand captured him and stroked him as he'd taught her. "The way you swell and arch"—she did the same, bringing her lips to his, her tongue darting against the corner of his mouth—"and need me . . ."

A deep growl slithered from his throat. "Speaking of animalism, you're gonna get it on the floor in a minute if you don't stop that."

"You don't enjoy it?" she asked sweetly, feeling a heady power as she continued to caress him.

"Enjoy? Oh, I enjoy, all right. I also . . . do . . . need you . . . right this minute." He looked up, momentarily distracted. "There she is again!"

Rachel eyed him in confusion, realizing that his excited gasp held both passion and . . . triumph. "What?"

"The beloved! The fixed idea!"

Sure enough, she had appeared. Rachel moaned, in truth as turned on by her manipulations of Jim as she thought he'd been. "I can't believe you were able to hear that," she accused him, having herself been oblivious to the music that had set the background for her sensual assault. "I must be losing my touch."

"You're not losing your touch, Rachel," Jim crooned, suddenly serious. "You could never do that, it's such an inborn part of you. I just want you to know that I am learning. That I want to learn." He kissed her very gently, tasting her lips as he would something fine and subtle and new.

"Teach me more," he whispered, and kissed her again.

Rachel felt herself in a daze of delight. Her voice came in sweet murmurs between the most tender of kisses. "The fixed idea is something . . . like a variation on a theme. . . . The composer picks his theme . . . then works with it to change its shape and texture . . . while the heart of it remains the same."

"Variation on a theme?" Jim breathed against her lips.

"Mmmmmm. It's . . . a fascinating phenomenon. . . ."

It was only the first of the fascinating phenomena they explored that night.

"Good news, Buseks!" Jim burst out as he appeared on the patio the following noontime. Rachel and Tom had been about to have lunch. She rose immediately and went to put an arm around Jim, adoration in her upturned gaze.

"Give," she urged.

His own eyes held the masculine version of that adoration. A variation on a theme. "A kiss," he murmured, "or my news?"

"Okay, you two," Tom interrupted with a good-natured growl. "Kiss and get it over with, then let me hear my news. After all, I have a heart condition. Suspense isn't good for it."

The kiss was short and sweet, the news likewise. "We've got the contact nailed down," Jim announced, drawing a chair up to the table and downing Rachel's iced tea while the two Buseks eyed him in anticipation.

"The contact?" Tom echoed quietly.

"Renko's. Pat was on it last night and managed to photograph a meeting of Renko and another man at a restaurant not far from Renko's house."

Rachel sat forward. "But how do you know it was the contact?"

"A package was exchanged. Then, this morning, Renko deposited five grand in a money market account." Tom remained strangely silent, his grim expression giving Jim a moment's pause before he continued. "The fellow was driving a rental car, spent the night in a motel, then returned to the airport this morning and flew out. The rental was charged to a New York-based organization—the Landower Foundation. Landower. The bag man." He shot a glance at Rachel and explained, "The one carrying the money was registered as Richard Landower."

Landower. Hadn't Jim suspected? "A high man on the totem pole there?" Rachel probed. "Surely they wouldn't have sent someone that important."

Jim shrugged. "That's the next step—finding out why this particular man came. He's a vice-president, son of the president of the foundation. Not very old—mid to late twenties. It's odd." He turned his attention to Tom. "You're sure the name means nothing to you?"

Pensive for a minute, Tom frowned. "I'm sure."

Rachel's attention was riveted to Jim. "If it was a rival to SCT, we would have heard of it. Any idea what it's in?"

Jim's lips twisted. "You're not going to believe this. The Landower Foundation is the parent organization for several, uh, shall we say, smaller conglomerates." His brows dipped in puzzlement. "There's a division that works almost exclusively with charities. A real estate division. And . . . Landler Drum."

"Clothes?" Rachel exclaimed. "I've been in their stores many times. They're all over the country. But what in the world would such a corporation want with SCT's irrigation chip?"

"*That* is the sixty-four-thousand-dollar question," Jim drawled, obviously as stumped as she.

Tom was no better, his expression blank. It was Rachel who seemed to be representing his interests. "It doesn't sound as though this Landower Foundation would want *anything* from us. . . . You're sure Richard Landower is the contact we've been looking for? Maybe he had some other kind of relationship with Renko."

Jim sighed and shook his head, eyeing Tom almost apologetically. "Something happened at the plant several nights ago. Renko was working late that night." He held up a hand when he saw Tom grow more tense. "Nothing critical. Just minor vandalism. Shuffling of papers. Messing up of stuff. Enough to mean the loss of several days' work without really losing any information."

"Another delay," Tom groaned. "Why didn't anyone tell me?"

"There was no point. It's pretty much cleaned up by now, and there was nothing at all you could do."

Rachel spoke up once again. "But what you're saying is that the timing is too perfect for it to be anything *but*. You'd suspected Renko before. He was there on the night in question. He needs money."

"Some," Jim qualified. "I'm sure that last night's payment represented only part of the total take. This is the first time we've been able to peg it down as neatly, though."

Tom sat back in his seat, his eyes bleak. "What now?"

"Now I fly to New York to learn what I can about Richard Landower."

Rachel suffered through the flight as though it were she on the plane terrified for her life. Though she'd tried to convince Jim to let her go with him, he'd been adamant that he'd be better alone. Two long, lonely nights seemed to prove him wrong. When he returned on the third day, however, their reunion more than made up for the separation.

Tom Busek commented neither on the significant gap in time between the landing of Jim's plane and the couple's arrival at Pine Manor, nor on the fact that they both looked newly showered and that Rachel's cheeks were the softest, most gentle shade of pink, her lips as naturally rouged. Rather, he was business through and through.

"What did you learn?"

Jim took a deep breath. It hadn't been the most productive of trips. "I learned that Richard Landower is twenty-seven years old, lives with his new wife in a wing of his parents' estate on Long Island, is wealthy in his own right, and has no apparent reason to diddle with our man Renko."

"And SCT?" Tom asked tautly.

Jim replied with a shrug. "Beats me. I went through a string of records on the Landower Foundation. There's no *hint* of anything involving microelectronics *or* irrigation. I'm drawing a blank."

"So what's next?" Rachel asked as she walked him to the door moments later, her elbow linked through his, their strides in easy syncopation.

"I'll keep on it. Pat and Wayne will keep on it." He frowned, frustration etched in his features. "There's got to be *something* tying Renko and Landower. I know in my gut that an exchange of money at this particular time isn't pure coincidence. There's got to be *something*. . . ."

At the front door they stopped and Jim drew Rachel toward him. Wrapping her arms loosely around his neck, she looked up. "Will you be over for dinner?"

He glanced at his watch. "I'm not sure. I've got to check in at the office. A new case came in while I was gone, and I may have to take my turn working on it."

"Let me come."

"No."

"Why not, Jim?"

"Because it might be dangerous."

Her gaze narrowed. "I think it's a macho thing. You just don't want a woman around."

"You're right." His arms tightened possessively. "It's far better for my peace of mind to know that you're safe and sound here."

"Safe and sound, bored to tears and lonely."

He nipped at her pouting lips. "Play your flute."

"I have. For the past two days and nights." She'd also had a talk with a friend in the music department at Duke, but she hadn't come to terms with that yet. "And I'd rather be with you."

"I'd rather that too, darlin'," he whispered, "but I'd be too nervous with you around. Not to mention distracted. And if I'm not paying attention to what I'm watching for, not only would I be shirking my responsibility to a client, but I'd be shirking my responsibility to you. If anything ever happened . . ."

"Nothing would ever happen," she drawled, then cut the discussion short with the realization that his mind was set. So was hers. She wasn't about to spend the evening alone. "You'll let me know about dinner?" she asked, managing to sound sufficiently resigned.

"I'll call you," he said against her lips, giving

her a long, hungry kiss that belied the passion they'd shared at his house an hour before. "I'll call you."

He did, and he stopped by for a light dinner before heading out in his car at dusk. Rachel made a point of saying good-night to him when he was just finishing up a discussion with her father.

"Since you won't stay and you won't let me come," she teased, "I'll leave you to your lonely dreams." Placing a mischievous kiss atop his nose, she turned and made a regal exit. Two pairs of male eyes watched her go.

"She's a good girl," Tom mused aloud, thinking how well she seemed to adapt to Jim's erratic work habits.

Jim, though, wasn't as convinced. She was up to something. Was she going out herself? On a *date*? Lord, she wouldn't be so spiteful. Besides, she loved him. He knew she'd be waiting for him when he finally finished for the night. He *knew* it . . . or *hoped* it?

Rising abruptly from his seat, he would have gone after her had not Tom stopped him. "She'll be fine, Jim. Take my word for it. She's a stoic in her way."

Torn as he was between reason and emotion, Jim stood still for a moment, hands on his hips, eyes glued to the empty doorway. Finally, knowing that to follow Rachel would only invite a rehash of the arguments for and against her accompanying him, he yielded. Saying a begrudging good-night to Tom, he headed for his car.

It was nearly dark. Since as a matter of course he'd removed the overhead light that would illumine his face if he opened the door on a stakeout, he slid behind the wheel and reached to pull a small penlight from the glove compartment to study the notes on a pad of paper he extracted from beneath the passenger's seat. One glance, though, and he thrust the pad down in frustration. Damn it, he wanted to be with Rachel. He could actually *smell* her. So much for professional detachment. It was going to be one hell of a long, hot night.

Starting the car with a muffled oath, he headed toward Durham, stopping only for a six-pack of cool beer and a fresh tin of tobacco. Cruising slowly, he turned down a narrow street on the outskirts of the campus, a street crammed with houses in turn crammed with students. He knew which one he wanted. Wayne had tracked the man in question here last night; Pat had likewise followed his comings and goings throughout the day.

Now, as Jim approached, Pat conveniently pulled from a space into which Jim then eased the Camaro. The guard changed without a word.

Killing the engine, Jim slid down in his seat, reached for a can of beer and deftly opened it with his thumb. Tipping his head back, he took a long swig of the cool fluid . . . then nearly choked when something long and lethal stuck suddenly into his ribs.

nine

"If you don't give me a drink of something cool quick, you'll be in big trouble, mister."

"Damn it!" Jim sputtered, coughing furiously, then gasping for the air he seemed to have lost. He managed a hoarse "Rachel!" as his hand snaked back and closed around the wrist by his ribs. "What in the hell . . ."

Responding to his tug, she uncurled herself from the crouched position it seemed she'd held for hours. "My God, Jim, but I'm dying of thirst! It must have been that corned beef Mrs. Francis made. What are you drinking? I'm parched!"

Jim had twisted around in his seat to eye her. "What are you doing here? I thought I told you—"

"I know, I know. Danger and all." She looked around him and started to reach for the can he'd set on the dashboard when he grabbed her by the waist and tugged her bodily between the bucket seats and forward.

"You minx!" he growled, sorting out arms and legs to set her firmly on the seat beside him. "I'm working!"

"I don't believe you," she challenged pertly. She'd never done anything quite like this before. "From what I can see, you were just going to sit here and drink." She made it successfully to the can and took several short gulps. "Ahhh, that feels better."

Jim sat, still half-turned, with one arm across the back of his seat, the other along the wheel. "I don't *believe* you!"

She grinned. "That was my line."

"Rachel, do you know what you're doing?"

Unable to tell whether he was angry or simply recovering from the fright she'd apparently given him, she grew momentarily contrite. "I do, Jim. I want to be with you."

"And that . . . that *thing* you stuck into my ribs? . . ."

She reached back to recover the item in question. "My comb. It's really terrific. See, the top half is the comb part and the bottom half has this skinny pointed handle." Her voice grew higher in a plea for compassion. "Great for getting a little fullness here and there . . ." She gave a timid demonstration, then paused and spoke more softly. "Don't be angry, Jim. I just want to see what you do."

He stared at her for what seemed an eternity, his expression fathomless in the dark. Then, turning his head forward, he shook it gently. "Rachel, Rachel, Rachel . . . what am I going to do with you?"

"Just talk with me. Tell me why you're here on this street, what you're looking for."

He speared her with sharpened eyes. "Your father will be worried sick."

"My father won't know. He's been preoccupied lately." She frowned, then shrugged, at a loss to solve that puzzle, among others. "Anyway, I told Mrs. Francis I'd be with you and that if my father asked, she was to say I'd gone out for a long walk. I've done it many times and ended up just sitting in the orchard. He won't worry. After all," she added facetiously, "he knows how lovesick I am." Her own gaze sharpened on the houses on either side of the street. "What *are* you looking for?"

Jim said nothing for a minute, still disbelieving. When at last he spoke, it was with grudging acceptance of her presence. "Nothing *there.*"

"Then where?"

"Here." He pointed to the rearview mirror which very conveniently reflected the front door of a house behind the car.

Rachel nodded. "Very clever. Hard on the eyes, though, isn't it?"

"I'm used to it," he murmured, casting a studied glance into the mirror, as though just then remembering his mission. Reaching to take the can of beer from her hands, he drank slowly, his eyes ever on the house.

"Jim?"

"Mmmm?"

"You're not angry, are you?"

"Angry? I should be."

"Are you?"

Trying to muster an ounce of disgust, he looked

at her and grimaced, looked at the mirror, then back. "No. I'm not angry."

"Good. Then . . . tell me what we're looking for."

"*We're* not looking for anything." He put a large hand atop her head and pushed her several inches down in her seat. "I'm the one who's looking. *You* are going to become invisible and remain that way for as long as it takes me to see what I want."

"What's that?" she whispered, caught up in the air of adventure she associated with his work.

"That," he sighed very quietly, "is the appearance of a young woman whose parents are frantically trying to find her."

"How did they lose her?"

"She was coming home from a boarding school in Connecticut when she . . . disappeared."

"Disappeared?"

"Took off, it seems." Settling more comfortably in his seat with his eyes glued to the mirror, he explained in a voice low enough not to carry beyond the car. "We got a call two days ago from the parents. They've been having trouble with the girl for a while now. Actually sent her off to school to get her away from this guy she'd been dating here." Rachel could sense the tongue in his cheek. "Seems he's not exactly the type of fellow they'd have picked for their daughter's true love." He cleared his throat. "Anyway, they thought distance had cured the infatuation. When the daughter didn't show on the plane she was supposed to, they called the school. Under threat of expulsion her roommate confessed that not only has she been writing to the guy all year, but he's been up to see her more than once."

"What does he do?"

"He's a perennial student. Quite a bit older than my clients' daughter. The poet-type?" He arched a meaningful brow, his question inviting her to draw her own conclusions, which she did.

"Ah. Head in the clouds."

"Sounds it. Good-looking as hell, it seems. And a real charmer. Hasn't ever done anything close to earning a living though. At least, that's what my clients claim, and since their daughter has a tidy little sum of money coming to her in time, they're concerned that she'll be used."

Rachel twisted in her seat to look at the house. A street lamp very conveniently lit its door. "So . . . what do *you* do?"

"I wait until they come out. Or rather, I wait until *she* comes out." He reached over to return Rachel to her invisible position. His hands lingered a second too long on her arms. "Damn," he muttered in a broken whisper, "I knew I smelled you. I thought it was just my imagination. My wanting to be with you."

"You *smelled* me?"

"You always smell clean . . . like springtime."

"Lavender. It's body lotion. And I never knew you noticed."

"Oh, I noticed. . . . Body lotion?" Imagining the application of a warm cream to her butter-smooth skin, he sucked in a ragged breath. "Damn it, Rachel," he grated. "This is going to be difficult."

"Why?" she whispered, sensing what he was going to say, wanting to hear it. It was some solace to know that Jim had wanted to be with her, even more to know that she could distract him so thoroughly.

"Because I want you in my arms." Leaning forward, he touched his lips to hers lightly, then with greater force as one taste inspired another. His large hand closed around her neck, his thumb caressing the sculpted line of her jaw. "I don't want to be here working," he whispered against her mouth. "You've got to know that. I always had such patience on stakeouts . . . until I met you. Now all I want to do is finish up and get home . . . or in this case sit here and neck all night."

Rachel's lips parted and she kissed him with all the love his words had brought forth. "But necking wouldn't be enough," she breathed at last. "And believe it or not I *would* feel guilty about distracting you. I didn't come here for this."

"No?"

"Well, maybe not directly. I mean, I'm sure I'd hoped for a little kiss every so often. But I'd be happy enough just to sit here with you."

Jim pulled back, a lopsided grin on his lips. "And not touch?"

Shrugging, she looked down to her lap. "We

could hold hands. That wouldn't be too distracting, would it?"

He chuckled and shook his head in awe of the myriad of small and wonderful things this woman did to him. Now she seemed so innocent, so beseeching that he would have gone along with just about any suggestion she made.

"I suppose not," he conceded, settling her hand in his. "But you're supposed to be invisible. Remember that. And I'm supposed to keep my eyes on that house. It'll be up to *you* to make sure that I do."

"I will," she whispered, feeling eminently satisfied. Slipping down in her seat, she closed her eyes. "While you watch, tell me more. How will you know the right girl?"

"I've seen pictures. She's a cute little thing. Blond, like you. Slim and small for a seventeen-year-old."

"And she was lost somewhere in midair between Connecticut and North Carolina?"

"She boarded the plane at LaGuardia. We've got a boarding pass and witnesses to attest to that."

"Then she must have put on a wig and dark glasses and marched directly past her parents."

Jim let his eyes stray from the mirror only long enough to cast Rachel an admiring glance. "Not bad, for an amateur. That's precisely what she must have done. She had a carry-on bag with her and left her other luggage for her parents to pick up."

"And you think you'd see through her disguise if she came out of that house?"

"She won't be in disguise."

"Why not?"

"Because the novelty of that will have worn off. She's rebelling. Besides, it's my hunch she'll reach a point when she'll half want her parents to find her."

"Oh?"

"She's used to living in luxury. Her parents have put a hold on her bank account. When she realizes that, she's apt to have second thoughts."

"So you just wait until she does?"

"Not me. My job is simply to find her. We've got the guy nailed down. I have to hand it to him; he was very careful not to put a return address on any of his letters, and my clients never did know a last name, much less where he lived. But the daughter is a doodler. One look through her school papers and we picked up most of the information we needed." He chuckled. "I have to sympathize with her. She must have hated Latin. That's where we got the best stuff."

"Such as? . . ."

"His full name. And address. Even several rough sketches of him. She's got art ability, I have to say that much. Police artists should be as good."

Puzzled, Rachel pondered what he'd said. "It all sounds very simple. Couldn't her parents have handled it themselves?"

"Her parents were far too emotionally involved

to even think of looking through her notebooks. Since they felt fairly sure that she hadn't been abducted against her will, they didn't want to go to the police for fear of creating a scandal. They're rather," he cleared his throat, "prominent members of the community. Besides, I'm not sure they know exactly what to do with her when they find her. By hiring an investigator, they can quietly locate her and *then* decide what to do."

"And your job is over when you call them with her address? Can't you already do that?"

"I haven't seen her yet."

"She hasn't come outside?"

"Not yet. She may even be somewhere else. That's why we've been trailing her man, here. But he's only gone to class and the grocery store. There's been no sign of the girl. Pat and Wayne even doubled up today so that one could follow him while the other watched the house. Nothing."

"Don't you get frustrated?"

He cast her a pointed glance and rubbed her hand along his taut thigh. "Frustrated?" he growled. "What do you think?"

"That wasn't what I meant," she chided. "And *I'm* trying to behave myself. I was talking about your work. What do you do while you wait and wait and wait?"

"I think and think and think."

"About what?"

He was suddenly very sober. "About where else that girl could be. About what other things might have happened to her. About any clues we may have misinterpreted. About any clues we may have *missed*. About what that girl might be thinking and what her next step might be. About how her parents, faults and all, must feel worrying about her." He paused, more pensive. "How would you feel if it were *your* daughter and you felt she might be on the verge of throwing her life away?"

Taken off guard, Rachel was momentarily tongue-tied. Looking off into the darkness, she spoke slowly. "I'd be worried too."

Jim faced her then; she could hear it in the directness of his low voice. "Do you want to have children, Rachel?"

She swallowed hard. "I've never really thought that much about it." It wasn't quite the truth.

"Well, I have," he countered with every bit of the conviction she lacked. "I want children with *you*. *Our* children. And I want them nearly as badly as I want *you*." He slammed a hand against the wheel. "God, Rachel, I feel hamstrung! I can solve most every mystery but this one. What is it that's holding you back? If you love me—"

Her fingers pressed against his lips to silence him. "I do, Jim. I do."

"Then marry me! Have my children!" His hand left the wheel and slid across her stomach, its intimacy sending wrinkles of hunger through her. "Don't you know how beautiful it would be?"

Her gaze locked with his in the dark, just as

her fingers found his and twined with them. Her mouth felt dry. She spoke falteringly. "One part of me does," she whispered timorously, "then the other part begins to quake. I've never pictured myself as a wife or mother. I don't think I'd be very good at it."

"Bullshit!" His hand slid up to cover her heart. "It's all in here, Rachel! You've got the feelings—the kindness, the patience, the caring, the love. If you've got the desire, you're all set. And don't tell me you don't know how to cook, because I do. And we'd learn how to change diapers together. I mean, this is ridiculous! We're all but married anyway!"

"Then why change things?" It was the wrong thing to say. Jim came back all the more vehemently.

"Because I want my ring on your finger. Because I need that bit of security. Because I want our children to be legitimate."

His words struck something raw within her and she blanched. She knew, she just knew that there was some mystery involving her mother. Among the many unhappy thoughts she'd entertained was the distant possibility that Tom Busek had never been married. Which would make Rachel, herself, illegitimate. An excruciatingly painful thought.

"Oh, Jim," she whispered, her eyes filling with tears. She heard his urgency, felt his hurt and she wanted desperately to ease it. But there was a hurt of her own that gnawed at her. She was the one who felt hamstrung, unable to share the worst of her fears with Jim, unwilling to confront her father.

Lifting a tentative hand, she traced the hard line of Jim's mouth, willing it to soften. More than anything, she needed his support. "I do love you. And, yes, I want your children. I never thought I'd say that, but I do." Tears rolled down her cheeks. "I mean, I probably would make an awful wife and an even worse mother—"

"Shhh!" Cupping his hand beneath her hair, Jim brought her head to his chest. "Don't say that again," he commanded in a whisper.

"But . . . I have to. . . ."

He stroked her ash-blond crown, pressing her closer to his heart. "Why?"

"Because . . . because . . . my own mother . . . never made it!" she sobbed quietly, realizing what she'd blurted only when the deed was done.

"Shhhhhh." He rocked her gently. "That wasn't her fault. Death happens. You have no idea what kind of a mother she would have been." He spoke softly, soothingly. "And I'm sure that, for as long as she was with him, she was a good wife to Tom."

Rachel shrugged, trying desperately to control her tears.

"He must have talked about her."

She shook her head.

"You must have asked."

She took a shuddering breath. "Not much more than a "What did she look like?" And then he'd get such a . . . a vulnerable look on his face that I was too unsettled to ask more. It was hard enough for him without my questions. He's been such a wonderful father *and* mother." Her eyes were round, her lashes wet as she looked up at Jim. "I've always avoided it. Hated to ask. Hated to risk causing him pain by suggesting that I wasn't satisfied with just the two of us. It somehow seemed . . . disloyal. Does that . . . make any sense?"

For all his frustration with the situation, Jim felt his admiration grow. "Knowing you, it does." He used both thumbs to smooth her hair back from her face. "It's what I've been trying to tell you. You're warm and considerate. You'd put another's well-being before your own." He kissed her slowly, lingeringly, drinking the last of her tears. Only at length did he raise his head. "But if you think you're protecting me by putting off our marriage, you're making a mistake. *I* have no doubts that you'll make the best wife in the world. If anything, I should be the one worrying whether I can fit the bill." When she opened her mouth to protest, he went quickly on. "But that's another matter. And right now we're talking about you. Maybe it's just the thought of making a commitment for the future that frightens you, given what happened to your own mother. But, Rachel"—his voice grew pleading—"*I want you as my wife.* I can't worry about how long you'll live. Or about how long I'll live, for that matter. I want you for as long as that will be!"

Sitting in Jim's car, cushioned by the night's silence and his marvelously supportive presence, Rachel felt herself waver for the first time. She wanted so to be with him forever and ever. . . .

Suddenly a man's voice came quietly through the open window. "Jim?"

Stiffening instantly, his arms tightening protectively around Rachel, Jim twisted his head around. "Pat!" he muttered in a whisper. "What are you doing back here?"

In the darkness, Rachel could just make out the dark form bent toward the car. Her ear was pressed to Jim's chest, giving her a vivid indication of his startled state.

"I got home and checked in with the answering service," Pat murmured. "There was a call from Mrs. Francis."

Rachel bolted upright. "Mrs. Francis?"

Jim's arm restrained her, drawing her back. "What is it, Pat?"

From where Jim held her, Rachel couldn't see either the painful expression on Pat's face or the worried glance he sent her way. Jim could, however, and his arm around her tightened all the more.

Pat struggled to break the news as gently as possible. "I think I'd better take over here. You're wanted at the medical center. Mr. Busek wasn't feeling well, so they brought him there."

"My God!" Rachel cried. "What's wrong?"

Jim already had her back in her seat and was

starting the car. "We'll see in a couple of minutes, darlin'." He looked at Pat. "Thanks."

He said nothing more until they were on their way and he'd taken her cold hand in his. "We'll be there soon, Rachel. Just try to relax."

"But I thought he was doing so well! He seemed to be getting stronger every day!"

"It may be nothing serious. With surgery such as he had, the doctors are bound to be cautious."

She brought his hand to her lips, closed ten fingers around it, and held tightly. "I hope that's all," she whimpered. "God, I hope that's all."

It wasn't. They arrived at the medical center to find that Tom had suffered a major heart attack and had yet to regain consciousness.

"It was my fault," Rachel whispered, numb and distraught, sitting with Jim and Mrs. Francis in the waiting room.

"That's not true, darlin'." Jim wrapped an arm around her shoulder and drew her closer in an attempt to lend her his warmth.

"But it was. If I'd listened to you and stayed home . . . if I'd been there . . . he's been upset about something . . . he must have worried after all. . . ."

It was Mrs. Francis who put her mind at ease. "No, he didn't, honey," she said softly, coming from the window to reassure Rachel on a matter of fact. "He was just sitting on the patio watching the moon rise over the orchard. It was early. I'm sure he didn't even know you were gone. I looked in on him once and he was fine. No more than fifteen minutes could have passed before I went to check on him again. He was already unconscious by then." Her voice cracked. "If anyone's to blame, it's me. Perhaps if I'd checked on him sooner . . ."

Jim spoke gently. "It's no one's fault. None of us had any way of knowing that this would happen." He looked down at Rachel, so fragile-looking and pale. "Self-recrimination won't solve anything. All we can do is to wait until Balkan gets here. Once he sees Tom, he'll let us know what's happening."

Rachel's large brown eyes met his for a minute. "Will it be soon?"

"He's on his way. But the doctors in there now are excellent. I'm sure they're doing everything they can."

She nodded, then closed her eyes and took a shuddering breath as she sat back against the hard vinyl sofa. It was the beginning of a long night, an even longer day. Tom was moved to the intensive care unit, his condition critical. Rachel refused to leave the hospital, wanting to be there when and if he regained consciousness. Jim refused to leave her side except to make an occasional phone call or to bring food from the cafeteria. Not that he had much luck peddling the latter. Stunned and worried, Rachel felt far too queasy to eat.

The prognosis was grim. At the end of twenty-four hours, Tom was barely holding his own. Rachel agreed to go home to sleep that second night only on the condition that the private nurse she'd hired would have her called with the slightest change in his condition.

Jim drove her home, took her to bed and held her through the night. Even asleep in his arms, she seemed troubled. His own worry was as much for her as for her father.

The next day promised to be a repeat of the one before, long hours of waiting, of wondering, of worrying. The doctors allowed Rachel to sit by her father's side, holding his hand, willing life back into his limp body. By mid-afternoon, it seemed to have worked. Rachel held her breath as Tom's eyes fluttered, opened a slit, closed, then opened again.

"Rachel?" he whispered, lacking the strength to move anything but his lips and eyes.

Her heart thudded wildly as she squeezed his hand and smiled. "I'm here, Dad," she murmured softly. "Just rest. I'm not going anywhere."

When he closed his eyes for another minute she sent an excited glance toward the nurse, who nodded and quietly left the room to notify the doctor on the floor that the patient had regained consciousness.

As she studied his ashen features, Rachel saw a frown cross his brow. Then he opened his eyes again and looked at her with an intensity she would have thought impossible given his condition.

"Rachel . . ."

"Shhh. Just rest."

"No. There's something . . ." He stopped to gasp and Rachel felt her own heart falter. That he was in pain was obvious. She stood to reach for the call button, but he stopped her. "No," he rasped. "Let's be alone . . . for a last minute. . . . I want you to . . ." His voice trailed off and he coughed, then closed his eyes. Rachel was on the edge of the bed, leaning over him, her eyes wide and filled with tears.

"Rest, Dad," she begged brokenly. "Please, rest."

"I can't . . . not until you know. . . ."

"Know? . . ."

He struggled for an uneven breath. "I . . . suppose I . . . should have . . . told you years . . . ago. But now that I'm going to die . . ."

"You're not! Don't say that!" Tears slipped unheeded down her cheeks.

"I am, sweetheart. I . . . never believed it . . . 'til now. But I'm tired. . . ." He coughed again and Rachel felt a shaft of raw fear spear her. She held her breath, trying not to sob aloud. She knew what was coming, wanted to hear it, didn't want to hear it. But her father was dying. She knew that also. And if he needed to free himself of the burden, she had no choice but to take it up.

"What is it, Dad?" she whispered, her face so very close to his.

The effort it took for him to produce the words was crushing. His lips worked first, the sound slipping out in a grating murmur. His eyes remained closed, his nostrils taut with the exertion of speech. "Your mother . . . go to her . . . go to Ruth . . . I loved her. . . . You should have the chance . . . to know . . . her. . . ."

Crying softly, Rachel could barely speak. Biting her lip, she sniffled helplessly. At the moment she could think of nothing but this man who'd meant everything to her for so very many years. "Don't die," she sobbed softly. "Please . . . don't die."

Tom Busek said nothing more, lapsing back into unconsciousness as suddenly as he'd emerged from it. Only Rachel knew the purpose for his brief return to her. Only Rachel knew. And she kept it to herself through another two days' vigil, through the grief brought by that last, inevitable phone call in the middle of the fifth night, through the funeral service and burial, through the calls and visits from well-wishing friends and business associates.

She kept it to herself . . . but Jim felt it. He'd seen her face that afternoon, when he'd returned with sandwiches and drinks, and he'd never forget it as long as he lived. She'd just spoken with Tom, but he was again unconscious. The nurse had returned with the doctor on call, only to find the patient all the more weakened. Rachel had stood slumped against the wall by the door, her arms wrapped tightly around her middle, her cheeks tear-stained. On her face had been an expression of such helplessness, such utter anguish that Jim had thought he'd fall apart himself.

But he hadn't fallen apart. He'd remained strong for her, staying with her constantly, doing whatever he could for her through the ordeal that seemed to take its hourly toll on her. And all the while he worried about her health. All the while he debated confronting her. All the while he wondered what it was that seemed to make her grief that much more intense.

He didn't mention marriage again, sensing the timing to be off, sensing Rachel's need to come to terms with her father's death before she could face the future again. So many times he thought of that last minute in the car—when he'd been certain that she'd been about to agree to become his wife. So many times he'd wished that Pat had shown up one minute, five minutes, ten minutes later. If only he'd gotten that commitment . . . but he hadn't. All he could do now was to be there for Rachel, to show her his love in all the small ways he wanted, to convince her without a word that marriage to him would be right.

For the first few days after the funeral, Jim worked only in bits and snatches, infinitely grateful to have two associates to cover for him. When things finally quieted down at Pine Manor, he could ignore the office no longer. But he informed Pat and Wayne that the evenings would have to be their responsibility. His was to be with Rachel.

"Do you miss it?" she asked one night as they sat in the peach orchard at sunset. Jim's back was against a tree, Rachel's against him. Though tired, she felt more relaxed than she had in the two weeks since her father's heart attack.

"Miss what? The evening duty?"

"Mmmm. I feel a little guilty monopolizing your time this way."

He smiled against her hair and teased, "Am I complaining?"

"No." She tugged his arm more snugly around her middle. "And I love your being here. You know that. I just . . . wondered if you miss it."

"I don't."

"But you spent so many years of nights in your car following people around. You enjoyed it, didn't you?"

"Then I did. But then I didn't have someone like you to come home to." He nuzzled her ear, wanting to whisper "Marry me," not having the guts. It had been so long since she'd lain as comfortably against him. Oh, they'd made love. Far more than he'd have expected, given what she'd been through. He half suspected that she'd needed the escape into oblivion, and in this case, knowing that she did love him, he hadn't minded being used. "It's so nice being here with you, Rachel," he murmured, then more boldly, "I think I can be satisfied being the brain man during the day and letting the others do the footwork at night."

She tipped her head back to study his features.

Etched in gold by the setting sun, they were straight, strong and rich. "Spoken with just the right amount of modesty," she teased, then grew more serious. "But can you? Can you be satisfied doing that?"

"It's the best part," he answered without hesitation. "The analysis of the puzzle, the placing of the pieces. There will be times," he cautioned, "when I will have to work at night interviewing witnesses who may be unavailable during the day. But, no, I won't miss the hours of nighttime surveillance. And, yes"—he gave her a crooked smile—"I can be satisfied focusing on being the mastermind. By the way, did I tell you that our little runaway boarding student finally went home?"

"No!" Rachel sat up to face him. True to Jim's prediction, Wayne had spotted the girl in question marching boldly from the house the very afternoon after Tom had taken sick. With concrete evidence of her presence, Jim had dutifully turned the case back to her parents, the work of his associates and himself finished. "When did she do that?"

"Just yesterday, from what her father told me when he called this morning. He was pleased."

"Then they took your advice to leave her alone for a while?"

"Oh, it wasn't just my advice. They consulted a psychiatrist and a social worker. I have to admire them. I really thought they'd storm in there and snatch their poor baby up. But patience triumphed. She came home on her own."

"Will she stay?"

Reaching out, Jim drew her back into the cradle of his body, wrapping his arms about her just below her breasts. "I doubt it. But it's possible that she'll be less impulsive in the future. And it's possible that her parents' patience with her will have taken the wind out of her sails of rebellion. At any rate, she's their worry now." His expression grew more troubled. "I only wish I could come up with something more between Landower and Renko."

"Still nothing?"

"Nothing. No more vandalism. No more money passed. It's odd." Dark brows dipped over the amber of his eyes and his lips thinned. "Almost as though your father's death put an end to it. I mean, for a while there was trouble at least once a week. Now the project is moving ahead full steam, and there's nothing. I wonder if it could have been some kind of personal vendetta after all. Someone from the outside who used Renko to do his bidding." He shook his head slowly. "Landower. Damn it, it means nothing!"

At his suggestion, Rachel's stomach had begun to knot. "You think it could have been personal?" Her voice sounded very far away.

Hearing the distance, Jim studied her pallor. "Maybe," he said more lightly. "We'll know sooner or later. But . . . how are *you* feeling?"

"Me?" She met his gaze in surprise. "I'm fine."

"You still look tired. I thought you were going to nap during the day."

She shrugged. "I'm sleeping well enough at night. You know that."

"I have to take your word for it, since I don't really know what happens when *I'm* asleep."

A smile tugged at her lips. "You wear me out. I sleep soundly."

He looked down at her wan features. "Soundly may be pushing it a little." He didn't sleep so soundly himself that he was unaware of the tossing and turning she did. "But I'll let it pass. What about the weight?"

"What about it?"

His hands moved across her stomach and slid over her hips. "You must have lost a good five pounds. Don't you eat at all during the day?"

"I haven't been terribly hungry."

He took the chance, trying to sound nonchalant. "Maybe you should see a doctor."

"What for?" she asked in alarm. "I'm fine. It's just . . . that I've been through a lot in the past few weeks."

"That's what worries me. Maybe you need vitamins. . . ." He couldn't demand that she see a doctor, any more than he could demand that she marry him or, for that matter, demand that she tell him what was bothering her. He knew that there was something and knew that it went beyond her father's death. Her face took on a strange look at times, a distant look, a look of brooding, of fear, of equivocation. And if he caught her looking that way when he was around, he could just imagine the greater extent of her preoccupation when he was at work.

"I'll be fine," she murmured softly, sinking into a silence that told him he'd lost her momentarily. But he wasn't about to put up with it for long.

"Play for me, Rachel."

"My flute?"

"Uh-huh."

"You don't really want that. . . ."

"I do. It's been so long since I've heard you play."

She gave a tremulous laugh. "I play for hours during the day. It's a release. When you're here with me at night, though, you're all the outlet I need."

"But your playing is so beautiful. Would you do it for me?" She spoke through her flute. He needed some clues to her thoughts, her fears.

"You *do* want to hear?"

"Yes."

She thought for a minute, then nodded and held out a hand for Jim to draw her to her feet. She brought him to the attic solarium, beautiful and dim lit now at dusk. There she played as she had once before, closing her eyes, letting the music take the lead. Then, she'd played out her love for Jim even before she'd admitted it to herself. Now, she needed him as badly, but in a very different way.

All the songs were slow tonight, starting with

an expression of the love she felt for Jim. There was "Songbird" and "Long Long Time," then "Lara's Theme" and "Evergreen." She played from the heart and her notes were crystal clear and hauntingly beautiful. From where he sat across the room from her, Jim felt touched to his very core.

Then the tempo grew even slower and more melancholy, and the notes took on a more lonely sound. He listened, waited, tried desperately to interpret the message of several pieces he didn't know, then sat back and tried simply to free-associate as she'd taught him. He heard sorrow and fear, the same as he'd seen in her eyes. But more. He heard a yearning, a needing, a crying out for something far beyond him.

When her lip trembled and gave way this time, he held back. For the first time, he didn't know what she wanted. He saw her drop the flute and bury her face in her hands, and he wanted to run to her. He heard her soft crying, and he ached all the more. It was only when at last she called him that he was able to move.

"Jim? . . ." she sobbed, then raised her head as he crossed the room and knelt before her. He took her face in his hands and smoothed the tears from her cheeks.

"What is it, darlin'?" he whispered, already furious at anything that could cause her such unhappiness.

"I need your help, Jim."

"Anything, Rachel. Just tell me what it is."

She bit her lip to stem its trembling, but her eyes refused to dry. "Hold me," she whimpered, needing that last bit of encouragement.

Jim took her in his arms and held her as tightly as he dared. Her tears wet his shirt, her fingers bit into the hard muscle of his back. Very, very slowly, her crying ceased. For an instant he feared that his comfort would only help her push whatever it was to the background again. Then she raised her eyes and looked at him and he held his breath.

"Help me find my mother, Jim," she said, her voice suddenly strong in conviction. "She's out there somewhere. I need to find her."

ten

"Your mother?" Jim's voice was riddled with disbelief. For an instant he wondered if the strain of Tom's death had taken its toll on Rachel in the form of self-delusion. "But your mother's dead. She died when you were born."

"That was what I always thought," Rachel went on with surprising calmness. It was as if the making of the decision had brought her strength to add to the relief of sharing her thoughts with Jim. "Then Dad started talking in his sleep."

"When?"

"Off and on during the last year. The last few

months especially, though I wasn't home all that often. There were only fragments that I could pick up, but they were enough to suggest that things weren't as I'd assumed."

Stunned, Jim reached to stroke her hair, his mind working, working to put the pieces in place. "He said something to you in the hospital, didn't he? That time he regained consciousness for just a few minutes?"

It was her turn to look stunned. "How did you know?"

"I saw your face afterward." He drew a tender finger across her cheek. "I knew there was something. I could feel it in you through everything that happened later." He faltered. "I . . . wasn't sure if you'd tell me."

Her gaze fell to the floor; then, with conviction, slowly climbed back to his face. "I wasn't either. Half of me just wanted to forget it, to look the other way and hope it would simply . . . disappear." With a sigh, she rose and walked to the sloping window to gaze at the night sky. "But there are some things that don't just . . . disappear. Like the stars. Like love." She turned slowly. "Like this." She looked down again and brought an unsteady hand to her forehead in a gesture suggesting her discomfort with the confession.

"You know," she went on sheepishly, "for years and years, when I was a child, I used to dream she'd come back. I used to imagine that she'd been taken away to some secret place to be cured of whatever it was that had killed her." Her laugh was a self-conscious one. "I used to picture the day when my father would present her to me, and she'd be so beautiful, healthy and full of love. . . . Silly, wasn't it?"

Jim had risen and crossed the room silently. Taking her hand, he drew it from her face. "No. It would be a very natural thing for a child, even an adult, to do when she wanted something as badly as you must have wanted a mother."

"I did," she whispered, her eyes caught by his. "I did want one."

"And do you still? Is that why you want to find her?"

Rachel frowned, her light brows knitting, her eyes clouding, her lips pinching at the corners. "No." Then she shook her head more conclusively. "No." When she looked up again, her eyes were clear, clear mahogany beaming directly into Jim. "I gave up on those dreams long ago. And I've certainly learned to live without a mother. I doubt I'd know what to do with one now. . . ."

"Then why the search?" From the pit of his stomach, he feared what she might find.

But she had her mind set and her argument hit home. "Because I realize what's been hanging me up with *us*, Jim." She raised her hand to his shoulders, slid them along the sinewed cords of his neck in a way more earnest than seductive. "It wasn't just not having a model to learn from. Well, maybe at the beginning it was. Maybe for all those other years it was the perfect excuse.

Then I met you and fell in love. But by that time I'd already heard my father's sleep-talking. I already had doubts about my mother, that she'd *left* rather than died. And I'd already begun to ask myself why. Dad certainly loved her. He said that more than once in his sleep. He even told me so when he regained consciousness for those few minutes." Her voice cracked, but she forced it to resume. "The only conclusion I could reach was that she hadn't wanted to be a mother . . . or a wife. That she wasn't cut out to be one."

Jim picked up the narrative, his voice gentle and aching. "Add that to your earlier feelings, and you managed to convince yourself that *you* weren't cut out to be one." When she nodded, he wound his fingers through her hair and brought her closer. "But that *just isn't so*!"

"So you keep saying and I almost believe you."

"Almost?"

"That's why I want to find my mother." Her arms coiled around his shoulders with the same urgency that underscored her words. "I want to see, once and for all, what she's made of her life. Perhaps if I can find her, talk with her, I'll be able to understand why she did what she did." She stopped talking, her eyes glued to Jim's. His expression was unfathomable, his amber eyes shrouded. When he said nothing, she prompted him in a whisper. "Will you help me, Jim? I don't think I can do it without you."

Still he didn't speak as he struggled to sort out his feelings. It was only the appearance of a sudden fear in her eyes that goaded him on. "I love you, Rachel. I want you to be my wife and the mother of my children. I'll want that whether your mother turns out to be an exquisitely classy woman or a seedy madam." When Rachel flinched, he held her tighter. "No, listen to me. I could have said whore . . . or drug addict. I mean, there's always that possibility. There's also the possibility that once you go through hell to find her, she'll either refuse to talk to you or completely deny your existence."

"Why are you saying these things?" Rachel gasped, her eyes filled with hurt.

"Because I love you." He ground out the imperative, his hands holding her shoulders firmly. "And because this is my business. I've been through it before. I've helped people locate long-lost parents, and I know that things don't always come up roses. If you seek out your mother, you've got to be prepared for what you might find. *I* don't care what she turns out to be, but you might. What will happen to us then, Rachel? What if she's everything you've been fearing for the past few months? Will you still love me? Will you agree to become my wife then? Or will it only convince you *not* to marry me?"

Rachel's vision blurred and she struggled to swallow the lump in her throat. "But what if she's good?" she countered, answering one question with another equally as valid. "What if she has an entirely different story to tell? Either way then I can come to you *whole*. Don't you see? I need to know, one way or the other. *I need to know.*" She caught her breath and waited a minute before speaking. "Will you help me? It's right in your line of work. If I have to do it on my own, it'll take that much longer. And I don't think I can wait." The last was added in a hushed tone, one that sent a pointed shaft through him.

He had no choice. This was the only thing that stood between them, that would always stand between them. She did need to know where she'd come from. He understood that now. If he refused to help, she'd only go ahead on her own. He didn't think he could bear the time that would take, much less the strain it would put on her, on *them*.

"Of course I'll help you, love," he said, laying aside all fear and reluctance for the sole purpose of serving her. "You know that I'll do anything I can." Lowering his head, he kissed her gently. Relief and the wave of desire that was never far from the surface flooded her being. She wrapped her arms more tightly around him, only to be held back for a minute. "But on one condition."

"One condition?" she asked, suddenly wary. "What's that?"

He wanted to say, "That you marry me," but he restrained himself and took a more circuitous route. "That you start eating properly. That you try to get more sleep," he said, looking down at her devotedly. "That you relax and let me do the legwork."

"I thought you were going to be the mastermind," she quipped. She felt lightheaded and full-hearted, as she hadn't since her father's death.

"In this case," he growled, "I'm doing it all."

"On one condition." Rachel turned the tables, suddenly serious.

"What's that?"

"Your job is to find her. *I'll* be the one to approach her."

Jim's voice was a quiet murmur. "I figured as much, darlin'. But let's take it one step at a time." He slung an arm around her shoulders and drew her beside him as they walked toward the door. "First you have to tell me everything you know. Everything you remember your father saying. Anything else you may have picked up about her over the years."

It wasn't very much. "Her name is Ruth."

"No family name?" Slowly they walked downstairs.

"Dad never mentioned one to me."

"Where did he meet her?"

"I don't know."

"Where were they married?"

"They may not have been."

"Why do you say that?"

"I don't know. I just . . . feel it. Dad never once mentioned the word divorce. And if all these years she's been alive somewhere . . ."

"Did your father ever travel?"

"Not very often. When he did, it was on business."

"Do you remember where he went?"

"Atlanta, Washington, Philadelphia, New York . . . he was usually looking for funding for one project or another."

"And he never said anything about visiting friends in any of those cities?"

"No." She came to an abrupt halt on the bedroom threshold. "What if we can't find her, Jim? There's always that possibility, isn't there?"

"Heeeeeey, you're talking to the best." He nudged her inside and closed the door with his foot. "We'll find her. It may take time, but we'll find her."

Over the next few evenings, they poured through papers and files and letters both in Tom Busek's study and the basement storage room. Though Jim had ruled that Rachel shouldn't do any of the work, she seemed to respond to the sense of purpose the search had given her. Relenting, he left behind an assignment for her each morning, one that was demanding enough to involve her for a portion of the day without exhausting her.

There were large boxes of correspondence dating back to the earliest days of SCT, Tom's personal records and letters, and scrapbooks of Rachel's childhood to be looked through. All were interesting, if void of any hints as to the identity or whereabouts of Rachel's mother.

"He must have thrown everything out!" Rachel exclaimed in discouragement after they'd gone through the last of the packs of papers. "It doesn't sound right, does it? For a man so in love to wipe out all signs of his lover's identity. You'd think he would have kept something . . . some small token . . . a note or keepsake. . . ."

"We don't know the circumstances, darlin'. . . . You don't remember anything else?"

She squeezed her eyes shut. "I've tried and tried to come up with something. But he never *said* anything." When she opened her eyes they were fraught with frustration. "I mean, there had to be some other person involved. In his sleep, Dad would say things like, 'It'll work out. . . . He's wrong about that.' But I have no idea who the third person could be. Or what he was wrong about."

"He never muttered another name?"

"In his sleep? No. Just Ruth."

Jim rubbed his hand along his jaw, frowned at the last packet of papers in his hand, then tossed them to the desk and turned to sit on its corner. Needing his support, Rachel came to stand between his thighs.

"What now, Jim?" she asked in such a small, uncertain voice that he bounced back instantly.

"Now I start looking for official records. There's got to be a marriage license somewhere."

"*If* they were married . . ."

"We'll start on that premise." He shook his head. "It's too bad that your birth certificate didn't tell us more." He frowned for a minute. "I take that back. I'll start with the birth certificate. It was a copy. You say your father got it when you first filed for a passport?" When she nodded, he went on. "Ruth D. Busek. It's possible that there's an elaboration of the D. on the original which your father managed to have shortened on the copy. Usually the mother's full name is required. Since it was a small hospital in the western part of the state, the administrators there may have let something slip . . . but it's worth checking out. I'll make some calls and see what I can find."

It was the first concrete clue. Sure enough, sitting clearly on the original of Rachel's birth certificate. Ruth Drummond Busek.

Unfortunately, a marriage license was nowhere to be found. Jim searched records departments throughout the state, then departments in the cities to which Rachel had known her father to travel. There was nothing. And Drummond was a common enough name to make dialing numbers from the telephone book without even a targeted city a fruitless endeavor.

Jim wasn't to be discouraged. In truth, Rachel began to suspect that he was enjoying the chase.

"You like doing this," she accused him one night as they lay in bed discussing his latest frustration of seeking out Tom's oldest friends and subtly questioning them.

"I suppose I do. Not that I wish, for your sake, for *our* sake, that I couldn't solve it quickly, but it's cases like these that really tax the mind. And I do rise to a challenge."

He rose to other things as well, things at which Rachel had become quite adept over the weeks. And if, as he ran his hands over her body each night, his intensity verged on brooding, she knew it to be his very personal frustration at her continued resistance to his ever-open marriage proposal.

The first week in July had come and gone before Jim made a significant breakthrough in his search.

"I think I've found something, darlin'," he reported excitedly, calling her from work one morning. "How about if I pick you up in an hour and we'll go somewhere for lunch?"

"Tell me now, Jim!"

"An hour."

She was dressed and waiting within half, in a state of keyed anticipation by the time he finally arrived. "What is it?" she asked as he ushered her to the car. He'd traded the silver blue Camaro in for a more sporty Mazda and made sure she strapped herself in before he put his foot to the gas.

"One of those early business contacts. Outside of Boston, actually." He drove carefully, mindful of his precious cargo. "A fellow who knew Tom when he was first starting out. It seems they had something in common. Hans was an immigrant as well. He and Tom collaborated long-distance on several of SCT's earliest projects. Hans represented the supplier for some of the materials Tom needed."

"What about my mother?" Rachel prodded impatiently. "Did he know her?"

"He didn't know her. And he claims that Tom was as close as a clam when it came to his personal life."

"Then how did he ever—"

"The inevitable. Man's Achilles tendon: a night on the town."

"They went drinking together."

"Seems that way." Turning off the main road, Jim headed the car west. "Are you too cool?" Though she shook her head, he reached to lower the air-conditioning.

"What about her, Jim?"

"I'm getting there. From what I understand, your father wasn't much of a drinker. It may have been this affinity he felt for Hans that made him agree to join him for dinner, or simply the loneliness of being away from home. Anyway, they got going, drinking, talking, drinking, eating, and Tom got looser as the evening wore on."

"What did he say?"

"When Hans asked whether he'd ever consider establishing himself in New England, he shook his head and grew melancholy. It seems that he had fallen in love with a woman from New York, that it hadn't worked out, that he didn't think he could bear to be so close but not close."

"*Where* in New York? Did he say?"

Jim turned into the parking lot of a small

restaurant and drew the car to a gentle stop. "No. Hans remembered his saying that she was elegant and refined. At the time he thought it might have been the voice of love speaking. Neither he *nor* Tom considered themselves particularly classy at that point, though it sounds as though they *both* more than made up for that in recent years."

"What else? Did he know where they met?"

"No."

"Or whether they ever married?"

"He didn't know."

Rachel paused, then spoke more hesitantly. "Did Hans know about me?"

"Very much so. You were very young then. Tom raved about you."

"Yet he never spoke of a wife?"

"To Hans? No."

Not knowing whether to be encouraged or discouraged, Rachel gave a painful grimace. But Jim was fast to lift his hand and smooth the pained expression away with long, gentle fingers. His amber-eyed gaze caught her darker one.

"Cheer up, darlin'. The news is good. We know that she came from New York and that she was probably well-bred. It's *something* to go on."

"I suppose." She gave a voluminous sigh. "So, where to now?"

Jim cocked his head toward the restaurant. "In there."

"I doubt you'll find clues in there."

"I know. But I want to make sure you eat. *Then* we'll decide what's next."

He had several ideas up his sleeve. Later that night, while Rachel slept, he lay awake for long hours evaluating them one by one, setting out the pieces of the puzzle, twisting and turning them to see where they might fit together.

The facts were few. A woman named Ruth Drummond, twenty years of age at the time, had given birth to a child in a small, no-name hospital in a rural area of North Carolina twenty-nine years before.

The near-facts were as scant. Ruth Drummond appeared to have come from New York, from a family of good breeding, and had evidently resisted legally marrying Tom Busek.

From there, the hunches took over. Things had been far different twenty-nine years ago. A young woman in trouble would more probably have stolen off to have her baby in secret than have rushed to have an illegal abortion at a fly-by-night clinic. Very probably her parents would have been angry and embarrassed. Very possibly the "he" of Tom Busek's nightmares was the father of the young, wayward daughter.

As Jim thought about the case, he formed a picture of a Ruth Drummond whose socio-economic background was so completely different from that of the newly naturalized Tom Busek that her family had balked at the thought of any permanent liaison with the immigrant . . . or the child they had seen to be so carelessly conceived.

There were several roads Jim could follow. He pondered searching the files of hotels, motels and boarding houses near the small hospital where Rachel was born in the possibility that her mother may have spent a period of time prior to the birth hiding away there. For the time being though, he avoided this road on the suspicion that, given the conditions as he'd pieced them together, Ruth Drummond would never have registered at such a hideaway under a real name. Which left only the chancy memory of a clerk or a landlord who may have dealt with a pregnant young woman at the time period in question. It was *very* chancy, a true long shot.

Then there was the possibility of systematically calling each of the Drummonds listed in the various New York directories. That, too, seemed an exaggerated effort.

If Jim's hunch was correct and Rachel's mother was in fact from society's upper crust, so that an adoring Tom Busek would agree—in exchange for his child—neither to contact her nor divulge her identity, it was possible that the right people in the right places might give Jim the answers he sought.

It was too simple. He received the news the following afternoon in one heart-wrenching call. Too simple . . . yet still an enigma.

Leaving the answering service to guard the office, Jim swung from the parking lot and headed for Pine Manor, taking a long, time-stalling detour along the way, finally arriving with a myriad of doubts at Rachel's door.

She'd been playing her flute. He could hear it as he walked along the drive from his car to the front steps. Hands thrust in the pockets of his jeans, head bowed low in thought, he nearly turned and left. But she ought to know. She had a right to know. In his mind there was no longer doubt but that their relationship was secure. It was the anticipation of her hurt that gave him pause.

He lifted his finger to the doorbell, wavered, then finally pressed it. The sweet sounds of the flute, lighter and more gay than they'd been in days, stopped instantly. Jim could imagine Rachel breaking from her musical reverie, twisting on her window seat and spotting his car. Sure enough, Mrs. Francis had no sooner opened the door than Rachel appeared at the top of the winding staircase.

Involuntarily, Jim caught his breath at the vision of the delicate, blond-haired beauty high above him. She was wearing faded jeans and a long cotton shirt, looking no more than twenty herself with her blond hair falling free to toy with the shards of gold cast by the late afternoon sun through the window behind. Her face broke into a smile, its features soft and glowing. Barefooted, she ran down the stairs.

"Jim!" Her movement was light and graceful, flowing toward him with the rightness of a rippling brook into a surging stream. His arms took her as naturally, holding her for a long minute until she raised her head for his kiss. "What a lovely surprise," she murmured, eyes closed, lips responding to his. "I hadn't expected you 'til later."

He could have kissed her forever. She seemed happy. What he wouldn't have given to be able to guarantee that happiness. . . .

"I had to see you sooner," he began.

She opened her eyes to drown in his, only to find the waters more murky than desirous. An instant frown materialized on her face. "Something's wrong," she whispered. ". . . Jim?"

"Come. Let's go sit in the den." Curving an arm about her waist, he started her forward.

"What is it?" She studied his beloved features, able to read them now as easily as she could the score of her favorite symphony. She stopped in her tracks and went pale. "You found her."

Without a word, Jim cocked his head toward the den, took her hand and led her there, speaking only when he'd settled her on the sofa and come down on his haunches before her.

"Yes."

"How?" It was as if she, too, were putting off the inevitable.

"Going on the hunch that her family was high up there in society, I put in a call this morning to a colleague in New York."

"An investigator?"

"Yes. We often do each other favors." His lips twitched at one corner. "Saves the airfare." When he saw her holding her breath, he went on. "Anyway, I called and asked him to go back through microfilms of the *New York Times* society pages starting three or four months after you were born." Jim's voice lowered on an even keel. "He didn't have to go far. Six months after you were born, Ruth Drummond was married. It sounded like a lavish affair. The highest of society present. She married into a family nearly as wealthy as hers, apparently a good match. They've been married ever since, have a son and two daughters."

Stunned, Rachel looked away. A half-brother and two half-sisters?"

Jim stroked her cheek with the back of his hand. His voice was as gentle.

"So it's really good news for us. Things might not have worked out with Tom, but your mother was certainly capable of being a wife and mother."

She raised her eyes, meeting his with surprising strength. "But there's more, isn't there?"

He stared at her, then gave a sigh of resignation. "Yes."

"What is it? . . . Tell me, Jim."

He swallowed once, wishing there were some easy way to tell her, wishing he understood it all himself. But there wasn't . . . and he didn't.

"She lives with her husband and children in

the family estate on Long Island. The daughters are in their early twenties, the son is twenty-seven. He married recently. He and his own wife live in a wing of the estate."

It had begun to sound too familiar for comfort. Rachel felt her breath catch in her throat and only with effort managed to whisper a final question. "My mother's name?"

"Ruth Drummond Landower."

When Rachel closed her eyes and seemed to sway, Jim reached to steady her. "No, I'm all right," she murmured, distracted and confused. "Dad knew, didn't he? That's what he was brooding about those last days—" Her voice broke.

Jim held her hand tightly. "He may well have known, despite his denials. Maybe . . . maybe he didn't want to believe it. Maybe he thought it would just end at some point with no one the wiser. Whatever he knew, he must have agonized over how much to tell you."

She moaned for the pain that shouldn't have been. "But why? Why would my . . . why would her son want to hurt my father?"

Jim didn't have to ask what she meant. "I don't know. That's what we're going to have to find out."

She stiffened. "What *I'm* going to have to find out. We agreed that I'd be the one to approach her. I'll fly up tonight."

"Tomorrow. We're not racing into some fancy

estate at ten o'clock at night claiming that you're the woman's long lost daughter."

"All right. Tomorrow. But *I'm* the one who's going."

"I never agreed to let you make the entire trip on your own. You said 'approach her.' You may be the one to walk up to that door, ring that bell and face her, but I refuse to be any further than a rental car on the drive."

"But you hate flying!" she pleaded, in need of argument as an outlet for the maelstrom of emotions that surged through her with frightening intensity.

Jim, though, was no more cool or calm than she. "And I hate *worse* the thought of your making that trip alone. I'm going, Rachel! There's no way you can stop me!"

She didn't try. Underneath it all, she didn't really want to. Jim had become too much a part of her being to leave him behind when another part of her was a pulsing void of anxiety. She needed him. He seemed her one refuge of sanity in a world that had turned topsy-turvy in two short months.

Throughout a long night's tossing and turning, then a taut flight to New York, the reality of it all hit her. This was her mother she was going to see. *Her* mother. A woman who had turned her back on her once before. A woman who, as Jim had suggested, might slam the door in her face rather than admit her existence.

There was a point, as the plane touched down at LaGuardia, when she would have opted to remain in her seat for a return flight. Ironically, it was Jim's pale face, his need for fresh air and terra firma that gave her the momentary push.

Once in the car, with Jim at the wheel and a map and explicit directions written out on a pad of paper on her lap, she seemed to run clear out of stamina.

"Are you all right, honey?" Jim asked softly, studying her weary pose. He pulled her closer across the bench seat until she was enclosed in his own seatbelt.

"Just tired," she said, laying her head against his shoulder. ". . . And scared." She didn't have to elaborate. He understood.

"I love you," he whispered against her brow as he started the car. "You know that, don't you?"

She gave a wan smile. "It's the only thing that's keeping me going, I think."

"Naw. You're one hell of a strong lady."

"I don't feel it right now."

"That's because you're such a terrible flier," he teased, and headed the car eastward.

The traffic was too light, their directions too good. All too soon they passed through the center of the exclusive Long Island town harboring the Landower estate. It seemed to be only minutes until they arrived at the start of a surprisingly short drive.

"It's strange," Rachel murmured shakily. "I'd

have expected locked gates and dogs and at least a mile-long drive."

Jim gave her an indulgent smile. "It's not all that different from Pine Manor, is it?"

It wasn't. Though the landscaping was northern rather than southern, the overall effect was of understated elegance and style. Where Pine Manor was older and more stately with its broad veranda, high windows and open spaces, the large home before them was a study in ivy-on-brick sophistication.

Jim pulled up along the circular drive, drew the car to a halt before the front door, and turned off the ignition. Rachel's world seemed to have gone suddenly silent. She looked at Jim, her eyes large brown saucers carefully rimmed with proper shades of lavender liner, shadow, mascara, but holding a ragged assortment of emotional split ends.

He smiled sadly. "Can I go with you?"

She shook her head and mouthed a silent "No."

Thinking how positively beautiful she was in her cream-colored suit, how thoroughly stunning in her love, her courage, her determination, he leaned forward and pressed a gentle kiss to her cheek. "Go on, then. I'll be waiting here."

She took a breath—"Jim?—" wanting to tell him that she was frightened, that it didn't matter after all who this woman was or what she'd done, that maybe she shouldn't have come here. But he shook his head.

"You *need* to know. So do I. . . . Do it for *us*."

He kissed her once more on the same spot, his face lingering beside hers while she breathed in the essence that would give her strength. Then, as he sat back, she let herself out of the car, straightened her shoulders, ran her hand beneath her hair to free any damp strands from her neck and took a deep breath. Only then did she approach the door.

The chime was a melodic one, five harmonic notes forming their own unique tune. From her sunlit studio at the back of the house, Ruth Landower heard its echo, cast a glance at the wall clock to see that it was nearly twelve-thirty and shook her head in surprise. Lately, when she painted, she lost track of things. Sniffling at the tail end of a summer cold that seemed to have lingered, she lowered the palette to her lap and studied the canvas before her.

Edgar had never understood her work. What a field day he'd have now! Her eye skipped from this latest piece to the three others propped on the floor against the nearby wall. What was she doing? Tears came to her eyes, and she laid the palette on the workbench and stood. Sniffling again, she brushed her forearm against her lower lids, wiped the damp skin against her slim, paint-stained jeans, and propped her hands on her waist, catching in the loose work smock in the process.

Perhaps it was just the season. The girls were out so much, and Richard and Elaine were busy.

Perhaps it was thought of the approaching fall when she'd turn fifty. A milestone indeed.

But, no. Turning a sad gaze to the canvases which expressed her soul, she faced the truth. It wasn't any of these things. . . .

"Ma'am?" A soft voice called to her from the door of her studio.

"Yes, Rosa?"

"There's a young woman, a . . . Rachel Busek, downstairs to see you."

"Rachel Busek?" Ruth's echo was half whispered.

"She's in the front hall. Shall I show her into the living room?" The maid's gaze dropped to her mistress's paint-studded attire in silent suggestion that she might want to change before greeting the singularly attractive young woman below.

Ruth's eyes followed hers. "Uh . . . no . . . no. Don't . . . uh . . ." She wiped suddenly damp palms down the sides of her smock. "I'll go. Thank you, Rosa." Stepping quickly into the open sandals that lay beside her easel and tucking a stray strand of hair back into her loose topknot as she walked, she followed the maid silently, parting company with her on the first floor landing, holding her breath as she approached the top of the stairs.

She'd have to leave. That was all there was to it. Rachel would have to leave. She didn't belong here. This was Landower territory. Rachel Busek would have to leave.

It was the smallest sound, the catch of a breath, that brought Rachel's head up. From where she stood just inside the front door she could only make out a pair of denim-sheathed legs on the stairs. They were slender legs, feminine legs bottomed by sandals. One of the daughters? Then she caught sight of the woman's left hand as it pressed against her ribs. There was a slim gold wedding band. The daughter-in-law? Rachel wanted to put her own hand to her heart to stop its God-awful thudding, but she paused, intrigued. That hand. She looked down at her own, then back. It wasn't the hand of a woman in her twenties. Slender and shapely it was, but it had quite a few years on Rachel's.

Suddenly she knew who stood on the stairs. Driven by a need so overpowering as to move her when she otherwise might be rooted to the floor, she took a step forward, then another and a third until she could see the face of the woman who had haunted her for years.

For an instant both women stared at one another. Neither doubted the other's identity. The resemblance was too strong, the face opposite too close to that each had seen in the mirror day after day after day. With Rachel her most chic and Ruth her most unadorned, the years between them blended together as had the shades of mauve and gray with which Ruth had been working moments before. They might have been sisters, rather than mother and daughter.

Simultaneously that thought wound its way

through both minds. Rachel had never had a sister, much less a mother. Ruth, on the other hand, had another daughter. Two of them.

Rachel stared wide-eyed as the woman before her started down the stairs, moving gracefully and with far greater confidence than Rachel felt, down the first leg of the flight, then turning at the vee to descend the remaining eight steps. She came to a halt directly before Rachel. They were close in height and a mere arm's length away. Neither reached out. Neither moved to shorten that distance.

Then Rachel heard her mother's voice for the first time. It was as soft and gentle as she'd imagined it. Only the words were foreign.

"You shouldn't be here, Rachel."

You shouldn't be here, Rachel. She had said it all. In that instant, despite everything she'd been through, despite the distance she'd come, Rachel understood.

"I know," she whispered. She'd learned what she'd wanted to learn, seen what she'd wanted to see. The expression on Ruth Landower's face was taut, giving credence to her words. Rachel turned and, head bowed, walked slowly back to the door. It was only when her hand was on the knob that she realized that she *hadn't* learned everything. Her father was dead, *her* father. And someone named Landower had made his final weeks unnecessarily tense.

Turning back to the woman who stood stock still in the middle of the hall, Rachel cleared her throat and swallowed hard. Her eyes were remarkably clear, her conviction stronger than ever. She spoke in a quiet voice, but the words bore a subtle force. "For the past few months someone has been trying to sabotage a project on which my father spent the last years of his life. We've discovered that one of our men has received money from your son. Do you know anything about it?"

Before her eyes, the meager bit of color that had been on her mother's face washed completely away. "What?" the older woman whispered in disbelief.

But Rachel knew she'd heard. She also knew that her mother had *not* known about it. "We were stumped for days, totally mystified at what someone named Landower would want with SCT. It's all stopped now. And I assume it will stay stopped, since Dad's gone. I . . . just thought you . . . should know." Turning, she twisted the knob and let herself out. Had she looked back, she might have seen the tears streaming down her mother's face. But she didn't look back. She couldn't. Her life lay ahead of her now.

So she thought. So she was still telling herself the following afternoon while her fingers moved on their own in collaboration with her flute to produce a melody she couldn't begin to identify.

She'd taken it well, she decided. No flood of tears. No ranting or raving. Simple acceptance that, for whatever her reasons, Ruth Drummond had decided that she could neither marry Tom Busek, nor raise his daughter.

But Ruth Drummond had indeed married. She'd had three children of her own. She lived in a lovely house with a husband who was evidently fond enough of her to keep her around for twenty-eight years. And, to her credit, she'd known nothing of her son's involvement with Renko and SCT.

It was this last matter which she and Jim had discussed on the trip back to North Carolina. It was still, in many ways, a mystery. What Richard Landower had against Tom Busek was questionable . . . unless he'd somehow found out about his mother's early relationship with the man. It might be natural for a son to be protective of his mother, to lash out against someone he saw as a threat. But Tom was dead, and, seemingly, so was the entire issue. The directorship of SCT had been taken over by the former executive vice-president, and though Rachel had decided to hold her SCT stock, she planned to be a very silent partner.

Indeed, her life lay ahead of her now. She said it again, then again. Her melody broke. She wavered, unsure as to what note to play next. In an attempt to complete the thought, she went back to the beginning, replaying the tune, faltering once more. Sighing, she leaned back against the window seat and closed her eyes.

⋆ ⋆ ⋆

Far below, a woman walked slowly up the drive. Having had the cab let her off at the street, she'd chosen to approach the house on foot. She wasn't dressed for the walk, and it was warmer than she remembered North Carolina summers to be. But then, she chided herself, she'd only seen one.

The walk was worth it. The wide brim of her hat kept the sun from her face as did her large sunglasses from her eyes. It was a beautiful house, she admitted. Tom had done well. She was pleased. Pleased for him. Pleased for . . . Rachel.

Her heels made the faintest dull tick on the sunbaked pavement, then slowed and ceased when she came to a gradual halt. Bowing her head, she listened.

Rachel was playing. Beautifully, as always. It wasn't the first time she'd heard her. She'd followed her career over the years, had even gone to a matinee performance once in New York. The pride she'd felt then . . . oh, the pride . . . and sorrow and regret and so many other things that she'd vowed never to punish herself so again.

No, she'd never gone to another concert. But she'd followed the comings and goings of Montage, growing melancholy each time the ensemble was in town, helplessly devouring the reviews that were ever positive in their mention of Rachel.

The sound of the flute took an upward turn. Raising her eyes, she sought its source. There, the music was coming from that large open window on the second floor. Actually a set of three windows slightly bowed. She could not see a figure, simply a piece of the sun as it danced along the sparkling silver pipe.

Suddenly the melody broke. She held her breath, waiting as Rachel began the ascending tune once more, reached the same peak, and faltered again. Then there was silence. Even the gleam of the flute disappeared.

Taking a deep breath, Ruth mustered her courage and walked on. Her knees were weak as she mounted the front steps. Her stomach felt as it had when she'd been carrying Rachel. She'd feared so much then—her parents' wrath, Tom's pain, her own future. Now it was her daughter she feared, the daughter she'd deserted and refused to acknowledge for twenty-nine years. Though she couldn't change things, she owed Rachel an explanation.

She rang the bell, then stood back and waited, nervously touching the nape of her neck to assure herself that her sandy hair was safely tucked beneath her hat. It had been blond then . . . as blond as Rachel's. . . .

"Yes?" Mrs. Francis asked.

"I'm looking for Miss Busek. Is she in?"

"I am," came a quiet voice. Mrs. Francis turned in surprise to find Rachel poised on the lowest rung of the winding stairs. Her feet were bare, her hair flowed free. She said a soft "Thank you" to the housekeeper and waited until the kindly woman disappeared from sight.

Only then did she approach her mother.

eleven

For a minute neither woman spoke. The air vibrated across the threshold of the front door, as though two racing hearts had stirred it up. It was Rachel who finally broke the silence, looking down at herself and laughing self-consciously.

"I'm sorry. I must look . . . terrible." She was wearing an old pair of jeans and a shirt of Jim's.

"You don't," Ruth replied, her voice as unsteady as her daughter's. To her, Rachel looked beautiful. Perhaps tired. Maybe even a little fragile, but beautiful.

"Uh . . . would you like to . . . come in?"

"You don't mind?" Ruth had been well aware that Rachel might turn her away just as she'd done the day before.

But Rachel shook her head. "No," she murmured. "I don't mind." Though she had no idea why her mother had come, it somehow seemed inevitable. Her pulse raced in testament to the occasion.

She waited until Ruth had stepped into the hall before closing the front door, then led the way into the living room. It was a large room, decorated by an interior designer, but with a warmth that spoke of Tom Busek's two bits here and there and fifteen years of family living. "Please," she said in a small voice as she gestured toward the sofa, "have a seat." She took her own in a nearby wing-backed chair, one she'd always loved, one in which she'd always felt sheltered. She crossed her knees, then uncrossed them and drew one bare foot up under her. It felt startlingly cold.

Head downcast, Ruth Landower slowly removed her dark glasses, then raised her eyes. One fist was held tight in her lap. "I had to come. After yesterday . . . I couldn't leave things that way."

Rachel nodded, tucking one hand inside the other and resting them on her stomach. She couldn't speak. She didn't know what to say.

Ruth did, though. She'd been choosing her words since Rachel had turned her back and left yesterday. Without preliminaries, she began. "I met Tom in Durham. I was spending the summer at Duke in a special art program." With the flow of memory, she gave a soft smile. "He was struggling to get himself established. There was something big and lovable about him. He was curious and bright and eager to learn everything . . . and so handsome."

A nearly imperceptible headshake snapped her from the trance. "We fell in love and . . . well . . . you were conceived." Her courage waned and she looked away. "I didn't know I was pregnant until I returned home. When I told my parents, they were upset, to say the least. They envisioned me marrying someone within my own circle, rather than someone like Tom, a foreigner, a man with no roots in this country, a man with not much going for him except a brilliant mind and lots of good intentions." Her gaze returned to Rachel. "That was *their* analysis of him. I was young. I couldn't fight it. I told them I loved him, but they assured me that I'd get over it. The only problem was what to do with the baby."

She took a deep and tremulous breath, reliving the agony she'd suffered then. "Tom wasn't one to give up easily." She shook her head and forced a smile. "I have to hand it to him. Within a day after I told him about the baby, he was on our doorstep demanding that I marry him. Needless to say, my father wasn't thrilled with that idea. He was very blunt about why he wouldn't allow it, about why *I* would never agree to it."

"You refused Dad's proposal?" Rachel asked, wondering what had happened to the invincibility of love.

"Yes," Ruth answered, "and I've regretted it ever since." The look of skepticism Rachel sent goaded her on. "I took what I thought to be the only way out at the time. Tom desperately wanted the baby. My father proposed that I come down here where no one knew me, have you, then hand you over to Tom. Under the threat of our giving you up for adoption"—she saw Rachel wince but could do nothing to sweeten the words—"Tom agreed to the plan. He also agreed, on threat of losing you, never to seek me out." Her voice cracked. "He never did."

Rachel sat, numbed and speechless. To know that she'd been conceived in love was some solace for the subsequent bartering that had been done. "You said that you regretted the decision," she said softly. "In what way?"

Ruth grew bolder, her brown eyes expressing a fire that had only come with time and confidence. "In every way. I loved Tom. I wanted you. But I was terrified of my family's rejection, so I went along with the plan. But I was crushed. I've always been crushed in that sense." Her tone softened, her eyes were suddenly hazy. "Tom was my first love. My only love."

"But your husband—"

The eyes cleared. Rachel realized that they were more hazel than her own. "My husband married me for the same reasons I married him. In theory, we were perfectly matched. His family was society. So was mine. He was four years older than me, six inches taller, fifty pounds heavier. He wanted a house on the Island, another in the Caribbean. I wanted a large diamond ring and a maid to make the beds and do the cooking and cleaning. We seemed to be well suited to each other."

"Weren't you?"

Very slowly Ruth shook her head. "We were never in love."

"But you've been married for so long—"

"And we're not unhappy. Please believe me. We like each other. Our lives fit together very nicely. It's just that the house on the Island, the one in the Caribbean, the diamond ring, the maid . . . well, they're . . ."—she frowned, searching for the word—". . . they're finite. They have a price. They crack and tarnish and get old. . . . Love is different. Priceless. Self-renewing. Edgar and I . . . we've never been in love." She sighed, seeming suddenly far older to Rachel. "There's one part of me that craves love. That's always craved love."

"But your children—"

"That's different. The love of a child is something unique and separate," she said softly. "The love of a man . . . ah, that's the essence of life." Her eyes grew misty. "I just wanted you to know that I've always loved Tom. Always missed him." Her voice caught for a minute as her eyes filled with tears. "I felt his death as keenly as I would have had *he* been the man I married so long ago."

The grief Rachel saw was real. Fighting the urge to reach out in offer of comfort, she wrapped her arms around her waist. Then a thought came to her.

"You did know of his death," she murmured. "And you recognized my name instantly."

"I've kept up with you both. It wasn't hard."

"But your family. Didn't they . . ." Her voice trailed off, sabotaged by another thought.

Ruth took a tissue from her bag and blotted the moisture from her lower lids. "No, they didn't know. I managed very successfully to keep it from them. I never made a big thing out of the newspaper articles or the SCT Annual Report. When I bought stock in the company, they thought it was simply a woman trying out her wings in the financial world. My victory was twofold when the stock value doubled, then tripled."

"You bought it when SCT first went public?"

"Yes."

Rachel shook her head in amazement. "But your son, Richard. He had *something* against us."

"Yes," Ruth admitted, her expression pained. "I was careless once, about six months ago. I'd taken an old diary out to read and hadn't had a chance to lock it away again. Edgar and I were going out. I sent Richard to my studio to pick up a painting that I was to bring with me. He saw the diary. After we'd left for the evening, he had himself a good read. I never knew. Not until last night when I confronted him about what you said he'd done."

"You confronted him?"

"Richard was always a willful child." She grimaced. "That may be putting it mildly, particularly since he's a full-grown adult now. Anyway, he easily admitted everything. I'm ashamed to say that he wasn't particularly remorseful. What he'd read in my diary told him that I loved another man. Not knowing the truth of the situation, he felt threatened. He wanted to discredit Tom in any way possible. Stalling the irrigation project seemed to him the least harmful, most effective method." She paused. "I want to apologize on behalf of my son. You have every right to prosecute him—"

"I'd never do that!"

"Why not?"

Taken off guard, Rachel spoke from her heart. "Because it's over, for one thing. For another, it didn't work. And besides, if we went to court, it would all come out. For God's sake, he's my half-brother."

Ruth's tone was low and even. "He doesn't know that."

"You didn't tell him?"

She shook her head. "He only knows that I loved Tom. He doesn't know where or when I met him. He doesn't know about you."

"Does your husband?"

"None of them do. And I can't tell them." She closed her eyes for an instant. Her lips were pressed shut, her jaw taut. It was as if she waged an inner battle . . . and lost. When she opened her eyes, they bore that overwhelming defeat. "I wish I could, Rachel. I wish I had the courage. But I guess I'm not all that much different now than I was way back then."

"You came here," Rachel whispered in gentle rebuttal, a poignant reminder.

"I did," Ruth said, standing abruptly. "And I've had my say." Eyes downcast, she walked past Rachel, then stopped in her tracks and looked back. "I wanted you to know that I loved your father. That giving him up—giving you up—was a decision I've had to grapple with every day of my life. I also wanted you to know that Richard won't be bothering you again." Turning once more, she left the living room, crossed the front hall, and had the door open before Rachel could get herself to move, but when she did it was at a run.

"Wait!—" She came to a halt mere feet from Ruth and reached out, only to rebound from an invisible wall just before her mother's ramrod straight back. It took her a moment to realize that those shoulders had begun to shake ever so slightly. With a small step to the side, she saw the tears sliding down those pale, pale cheeks.

"Wait," Rachel repeated, in a whisper this time. "Don't go."

Ruth pressed the tissue to her upper lip. "I have to. My cab is waiting. I've got to get back to New York tonight."

Rachel's insides knotted as she sought to prolong the meeting. "Will I . . . see you again?" It suddenly occurred to her that this was a woman she might like to get to know.

"I don't know," Ruth whispered, crying silently. "Perhaps . . . next fall . . . when you're in New York. . . ."

Her own eyes suddenly awash with tears, Rachel could restrain herself no longer. Reaching out, she touched her mother's arm, very timidly, very tentatively. When Ruth didn't object, Rachel spoke. "In a way I should be grateful to Richard."

"Grateful?" Ruth sent her a look of skepticism.

"When Dad discovered the trouble with the irrigation project, he hired an investigator to sort things out. His name's Jim Guthrie. I'm going to marry him."

Through tearful eyes, Ruth studied her daughter, wishing she could claim motherly instinct at work. But, sadly, she didn't know Rachel. No, it was simply a woman's intuition that cued her. "You love him, don't you?"

Rachel felt her own eyes brim. Nonetheless, she grinned. "Very much."

"Then . . . I'm happy for you, Rachel," Ruth said, mirroring the grin and the tears. "I wish for you . . . everything I didn't have . . . and then some." Catching her lower lip between her teeth, she simply looked and looked at Rachel, her brows drawn high in an expression of hope. Then she lifted a hand to her daughter's cheek. "Be happy," she managed as her eyes filled again. Before Rachel could catch her this time, she left.

Suddenly and strangely dry-eyed, Rachel watched the slender figure walk, then half run, down the drive and vanish into the waiting cab. The cab drove off. Rachel continued to stand there, her hand on the door, her eyes on the drive, her heart growing lighter by the minute. Then, feeling free at last, she turned and ran up the stairs.

An hour later, wearing a soft-swirling pink sundress and strappy high-heeled sandals, Rachel Busek swung through the door of James P. Guthrie and Associates. Wayne was in the outer office and looked up in surprise. She held up a hand to keep him in his seat, then looked sharply toward Jim's office, from which suddenly emerged a spate of choice epithets. Frowning toward Wayne, she approached Jim's door and sidled up to its jamb with one hand cocked on her hip.

Jim sat behind a cluttered desk, his back to her, one leg propped irreligiously on the window-sill. "I don't give a good God damn about your stoolie son of a bitch! He's lying through his teeth, and you know it!"

Rachel arched a brow toward Wayne, who looked in dire pain. She pursed her lips to keep from grinning, then looked back at Jim.

"What?" He used his foot to kick his seat around and came suddenly forward. "Why that mother—" The oath hung suspended as he caught sight of Rachel. A deep crimson tinge crept upward from his neck. "Hmmm? No," he gritted. "Nothing. Listen, Digger, I'll get back to you. . . . Yeah." His eyes didn't leave Rachel's. "And work on that jerk, will you?" he barked before curtly hanging up the phone. He stared at her a moment longer, then, to her delight, grew sheepish.

"Foul language. One of the occupational hazards."

"It's all right. Nothing I haven't heard before . . . Digger?"

"A nickname."

"Like Jimbo?"

"Where did you hear *that*?"

"My father."

Trying to salvage his dignity, Jim scowled. "So help me, the guy loved that. I think it was the reason he hired me."

"Very . . . American."

"Hmmmmph."

For an instant there was silence. Then Rachel spoke. "Aren't you going to invite me in?" She'd been to his office before, but never on her own initiative.

Without a word, Jim rose from his desk, crossed the room in two long strides, grabbed her by the elbow and gently hauled her over the threshold. Then he shut the door tight. His large hands held her upper arms, lifting her nearly off her feet while he kissed her quite thoroughly. Only when he raised his head again did he speak. "Do come in," he growled, then groaned at the dissatisfaction of a single kiss and remedied the situation with another. "Damn," he muttered breathlessly, "how can you do this to me?" He pressed her close for an instant, elaborating on the message.

"I had to see you," she whispered as breathlessly.

He jacked a dark brow in mockery. "This is a business call?"

"Lord, no. And if you close yourself off behind that desk, I'll scream."

He backed to the desk, but perched on its corner and drew her snugly between his legs.

His thighs were warm and taut, a sensual prison. "How's this?"

She smiled. "Nice."

He looped his wrists loosely at the small of her back. "Now. Tell me. Why did you *have* to see me?"

Her own arms had comfortably settled around his neck. Her fingers found their place in the vibrant hair at his nape. "To tell you I love you."

"What else is new?"

She thought she heard a trace of sarcasm in his voice, and knew he had reason for it. She'd put him through hell. It was time to remedy *that.* "I'd like you to marry me."

He grew suddenly still. "Is that a proposal?" he asked warily.

Her answer was a pert "Yes."

"And you're ready to go through with it?"

Without any hesitation at all. "Yes."

His amber-eyed gaze narrowed, gold shards flashing in challenge. "When?"

"Today? Tomorrow? How soon can we do it?"

She was utterly calm and utterly serious. He stared at her incredulously. "You mean it?"

"Of course I do! It's not every day that a woman proposes to a man!"

"Christ, Rachel, I've been proposing for weeks!" he exclaimed. But he held his excitement carefully at bay. "Was it . . . yesterday?"

"In part . . . In part it was today."

"Today?"

Rachel positively beamed. "I had a visitor a little while ago."

"A visitor? . . . Who?"

"Her."

Jim's face registered his surprise. "Your mother?"

"Uh-huh."

"She flew down from New York?"

"Uh-huh. She wanted to tell me about Dad and her. They were in love." She related the story as Ruth Landower had told it to her. By the time she had finished, her eyes were moist again. "She is a good person, Jim. I'm not sure I would have been quite the stoic she was, but I do respect her. She suffered her share as a result of that decision long ago." Rachel averted her eyes, thinking, then mumbled, "She mentioned New York in the fall. . . ."

"Hmmmm?"

She snapped back. "She said she'd always kept tabs on Dad and me over the years. I have to believe her. When I . . . when I asked if I'd see her again, she said something about next fall in New York. Montage always hit New York in November. She must have known."

Jim nodded. "And . . . will you see her?"

Brushing away a last tear from the corner of her eye, Rachel tipped up her chin. "I don't know. . . . I told her about you."

"You did?" he asked with an endearing, if questioning, smile.

"Yes. I told her I was going to marry you."

"You did?"

"I am. You may not have given me an answer yet, but I promise you I'm not giving up." She'd taken lines from his script, but he wasn't laughing. Rather, he seemed suddenly quiet and very sober.

"And you think you can be a wife . . . and a mother?"

She bit her lower lip, then offered a low-murmured "Yes."

"Why, Rachel? Why the confidence all of a sudden?"

"Because I love you," she cried, on the verge of tears once more. "And because I now know how lasting love is, how crucial to happiness. I want to marry you because I want us to be together for the rest of our lives. I want your children because they'll be made of you and me and our love." A single tear trickled down her cheek, then another. "I don't want anything like what happened to my parents to happen to us. Maybe thinking of my mother's grief made me realize how tenuous happiness can be." She raised her hands to his face, threading her fingers through the hair behind his ears. He was so alive, so vibrant. He gave meaning to her life. "I don't want anything to destroy what we have. I want us to do it right!" Voice breaking, she dissolved into tears. With a sudden softening of his features, Jim drew her close.

"We will, darlin'. We will."

"Then . . . you will . . . marry me?" she

murmured, her choked voice muffled against his shirt.

He lifted her face and kissed away the worst of the tears. "Of course I will. It's my happiness, too. You've only drawn the conclusion now that I drew weeks ago. You know, I've had doubts, too."

Her eyes widened. "You have?"

"Uh-huh. In so many ways I identified with Tom, the raw, uncultured cad courting the polished woman of the world."

"You're no raw, uncultured cad," she chided, then dared a half-smile. "Well, only at times, and I love it then. . . ."

He sucked in a fast breath and squeezed her in punishment. "This is no laughing matter, Rachel Busek. Here, I'm trying to be honest about my insecurities—"

"You've *always* been honest about your insecurities. What I'm trying to tell you is that there's no basis for them. I love you. I love everything you are . . . and everything you aren't. And in that sense I intend to be different from my mother." Her voice softened. "I intend to fight for what we have. It's too good, Jim. Too good to lose."

His mouth moved closer. "Then it's not going to be a case of history repeating itself?"

Hers parted warmly. "Not by a long shot."

He halted a breath away. "And your career? What about that? Can we work it around ourselves?"

Her tongue darted out to taunt a tiny spot on his upper lip before retreating. "I think so."

"Then you won't be in New York in November?"

"Not unless my husband decides he'd like to treat me to a weekend there."

His lips whispered against the far corner of hers. "That might be arranged."

"But what about the flight?"

"No problem," he murmured, pausing only to nibble on her lower lip. "I'll buy one seat and hold you on my lap the whole way. That will distract me plenty." He held her back and was suddenly serious as his eyes worshipped her features one by one. She felt positively treasured. "I'd do anything to be with you. Haven't you realized that yet?" His eyes were so intent with pleading that she could only shake her head in wonder.

"You are something," she whispered at last.

"So are you."

Then he kissed her and Rachel's world exploded with the hopes and dreams of generations.

"It's a variation on a theme," he murmured, when at last he could catch his breath.

". . . What?" She smiled up at him dazedly.

"I said," he intoned carefully, "that it's a variation on a theme."

"What is?"

"Our love. Our story. So much like that of two people deeply in love a long time ago . . . but different. A variation on a theme." When Rachel's smile widened, he went on. "You see, there's this thing in music." He cocked his head to the side, then corrected himself in his most didactic tone. "Well, maybe it's not a thing. We'll call it a theory. . . ."

"We'll do that," Rachel humored him, her heart bursting with joy. It was indeed a variation on a theme. One with a happy ending.